DEADLY ACCUSATIONS

# Deadly Accusations

## Debra Purdy Kong

*Enjoy!*
*Debra Purdy Kong*

TouchWood
Editions

TouchWood Editions
www.touchwoodeditions.com

**Library and Archives Canada Cataloguing in Publication**
Kong, Debra Purdy, 1955–
Deadly accusations / Debra Purdy Kong.

(A Casey Holland mystery)
Also published in electronic formats.
ISBN 978-1-927129-06-7

I. Title. II. Series: Kong, Debra Purdy, 1955– . Casey
Holland mystery.

PS8571.O694D43 2012     C813'.54     C2011-907339-0

Editor: Frances Thorsen
Proofreader: Lenore Hietkamp
Cover image: Bus stop: Marcus Clackson, istockphoto.com
Texture overlay: Dimitris Kritsotakis, stck.xchng
Design: Pete Kohut
Author photo: Jerald Walliser

We gratefully acknowledge the financial support for our publishing activities from the Government of Canada through the Canada Book Fund, Canada Council for the Arts, and the province of British Columbia through the British Columbia Arts Council and the Book Publishing Tax Credit.

MIX
Paper from responsible sources
FSC® C103214

The interior pages of this book have been printed on 100% post-consumer recycled paper, processed chlorine free, and printed with vegetable-based inks.

1  2  3  4  5  16  15  14  13  12

For my sister, Val, who's been there for every chapter in my life.

# ONE

CASEY HOLLAND LEANED BACK AGAINST the wooden chair in her supervisor's office and fought the urge to pop a fat pink bubble while Stan spoke. She knew Stan didn't mind the gum chewing, but blowing bubbles was another matter. Still, the need to release a little hot air was soaring.

When Stan finished talking, she said, "I don't understand why you want two of us on the M10 bus when the kids aren't threatening passengers. Can't Jasmine handle a few twelve-year-olds alone for one shift?"

"She doesn't have your experience."

True. This was only Jasmine's second undercover assignment. Sure, the woman had apparently worked in security before joining Mainland nearly four months ago, but hadn't Stan told the team that Jasmine was hired for camera surveillance and then a few mobile patrol shifts in the security vehicle? How had she landed undercover work so quickly?

"Listen," Stan said, scratching his trim gray beard, "things have been heating up between the two groups lately, and some of the drivers think the situation could become violent fast."

"Is this a race issue, or is there more to the story?"

"All I know is the white kids are feuding with the brown kids, and I don't want a bunch of twelve-year-old twerps brawling on my buses."

Casey smiled. For a guy who didn't own Mainland Public Transport, Stan Cordaseto sure took it personally when something went wrong on one of Mainland's buses. For ten years, she'd seen him work his butt off for staff and passenger safety. He would have been promoted from security manager to vice-president ages ago, if he hadn't been so anti-technology until recently.

Stan's phone rang. "Don't leave yet," he said as he picked it up.

Casey stood and ambled toward the open window. A gust of wind ruffled her loose perm. She didn't like the way it tickled her shoulders. Time for a haircut soon. Maybe she'd try a deeper shade of brown this time, too. Lou might find it kind of sexy. From this second-floor view, she easily spotted his truck in the parking lot below. Beyond the lot, a bus pulled out of the yard. She looked up at the overcast sky and felt the humid, late-September air. Forecasters were predicting a thunderstorm. Vancouver had few storms, so when the thunder rolled in, people paid attention. Some were even willing to get off the golf courses.

When Stan hung up, Casey returned to her chair and said, "It's supposed to rain tonight, and it's been a week since the rockhound's last strike. I guess you'll want me on the M6?"

"Definitely." Stan started tapping a pencil. "The jerk must be getting antsy."

"Yep." The elusive rock-throwing nut apparently loved cracking bus windows on rainy nights.

"The kids board the M10 at five past three and you'll be back here by four. Your shift on the M6 doesn't start till eight, so you'll have plenty of break time." Stan stopped tapping the pencil. "Your face is all scrunched up. What's wrong?"

"Nothing." Except she hated the idea of working with Jasmine Birch. When Jasmine joined Mainland, they'd gotten along fine for a few weeks. Casey had no idea why Jasmine had stopped talking to her.

"Come on," Stan said, "out with it."

"It's just that I don't think Jasmine will want to work with me."

"Why not?"

Casey ran her finger over the pits and rivets scarring his ancient mahogany desk. She'd sat in front of this desk so many times that she could locate every flaw with her eyes closed. "We don't click."

"I don't get it. You're both young, divorced, and working in security."

"Marie's divorced too, and she and Jasmine both have kids."

"So what? You're a parent now as well."

"I'm a legal guardian who's only been at it since the end of May. Maybe I haven't paid enough dues to join their club."

And she wasn't going to tell Stan how Jasmine always showered attention on Lou, when she damn well knew he was attached. If Jasmine had asked around, she would have heard all about the "Lou and Casey story," as coworkers called it.

Stan swept his hand over his brush cut, something he always did when he needed to think. Casey was amazed that he hadn't developed a bald spot over the years.

"Casey, I've got a busload of kids whose feuding is scaring passengers enough to lodge complaints. We can't afford to lose customers, so my team needs to work together, okay?"

"Understood."

"You're too much of a pro to let personal stuff interfere."

Casey focused on the dwarf jade bonsai in the corner of Stan's desk. His wife had bought the miniature tree with the bright green leaves six months ago to help Stan manage stress. Casey could use a little help herself.

"Does the bonsai help keep you calm?" she asked.

"When I'm clipping and trimming, yeah."

After a quick rap on the door, Jasmine stepped inside. She barely glanced at Casey before she turned to Stan. "You wanted to see me?"

He clasped his hands behind his head. "How come you don't like Casey?"

Casey cringed and took a deep breath. She should have seen this one coming. Subtlety wasn't Stan's strong suit. She could almost feel Jasmine's sapphire eyes searing her flesh.

"We're just different people. No biggie."

Casey chomped on the gum.

"Good, then you'll work with her this afternoon. Marie has some sort of dental emergency with one of her kids."

Jasmine examined her shiny blue nails. "No problem."

Casey wanted to tug the liar's long black braid until she told the truth.

"Be on the M10 in fifteen minutes, ladies."

Jasmine left the room. Casey didn't follow.

"Okay, I sensed the strain," Stan said, "but you'll do your job, right?"

"The only gripe you'll hear from me is about that tie." She headed for the door. "Yellow and black polka dots don't go with the red and blue shirt, Stan. I'm just sayin'."

"As did my wife." He snorted. "At least I'm not a fashion slave."

Casey smiled as she left the department and jogged downstairs, catching up with Jasmine.

"So, Little Miss Perfect's been whining about me," Jasmine remarked.

"Miss Perfect? You're joking, right?" Casey followed her down the steps. "Stan told me to ride with you and I said you'd probably want to work alone. He wanted to know why."

"Just stay out of my way, super-cop." Jasmine gave Casey the finger and hurried down the remaining steps.

"Un-friggin'-believable."

At the bottom of the staircase, Casey tossed her gum in the garbage, crossed the corridor, and exited the glass double doors. On the other side of staff parking, Jasmine was sharing a laugh with Roberto.

If anyone could improve a girl's mood, it was Mainland's coolest mechanic, Roberto de Luca. His well-defined muscles, brilliant smile, and green eyes brightened the day for most of the female staff. Roberto was the only man Casey knew who made denim overalls and the silver strands in his dark hair look hot.

"Hi ya, Casey," Roberto said as she approached. "How's the Tercel running?"

"Great." To Casey's amusement, irritation spread across Jasmine's face. "Thanks again for the new spark plugs. What do I owe you this time?"

"One lasagne, extra cheese."

"You got it." Their bartering had worked well over the past five years. All Roberto ever asked in payment was a home-cooked meal and the occasional relationship advice.

"So, what are you up to today?" he asked.

"Filling in for Marie on the M10."

"I'm surprised. Lou's driving that one today."

"Stan's made an exception, I guess." Or maybe he hadn't realized. Stan believed that office romances distracted staff from their tasks, so he rarely scheduled her to work with Lou.

Roberto turned to Jasmine. "Want to go dancing tonight?"

"I wish I could, but I've made plans." She clasped his hand. "Why don't you come for dinner tomorrow? Jeremy would love to see you."

"Sounds good."

While Jasmine beamed, Casey sighed. Roberto owned three address books filled with women's numbers. He could do far better than a bitchy woman with a two-year-old. On the other hand, Roberto was shallow enough to only see Jasmine's slim build, waist-length hair, and a heart-shaped face guys seemed to think was cute.

"Hi." Lou joined the group and kissed Casey's cheek.

She loved the way his eyes filled with warmth when he looked at her. She swept back strands of thick brown hair from his forehead. "You and I are riding together."

"Really? Cool."

"Hi, Lou," Jasmine said. "Our fourth shift together this week. I'm a lucky girl."

"You sure are." Casey put her arm around him and grinned at Jasmine's souring expression. The sweetie-pie act wouldn't get her anywhere with Lou.

"See ya, babe." Jasmine wrapped her arms around Roberto and planted a lingering kiss on him.

Lou chuckled as he and Casey headed for the M10. "I hope Stan's not watching."

"I hope he is. That was completely unprofessional."

Jasmine followed them onto the bus and sauntered to the back. Casey chose a seat in the middle. Unzipping her jacket, she checked her pockets to make sure her ID and handcuffs were within easy reach. Thankfully, she didn't need the cuffs often. Most kids were pretty scared when she caught them committing some petty crime, but adults with drug, anger, or mental issues were another story. After five years in security, she had to admit that she still loved this job. The only boring part was waiting for the police to show up. Petty offences were a low priority and she'd clocked many hours waiting to transfer offenders into police custody.

Casey opened a window to get rid of the sweat and garbage smells. Since management started cutbacks two months ago, Mainland's fleet wasn't as clean as she would have liked. Fifteen minutes later, five sullen white kids—two of them female—and all wearing a ball cap on backward, slumped into seats near the front of the bus. A group of South Asian preteens, including one girl, all sporting black leather jackets, boarded next and strutted past Casey. The last boy in their group gaped at Casey's chest. She glared at the twit until he got the message and joined his friends in seats behind the center exit.

With voices raised, the jackets started yakking about the girl with long, red hair at the front. The girl, sitting sideways in her seat, scowled at the boys. Two older passengers in front of Casey exchanged wary glances.

Lou eased the bus forward and glanced in the rearview mirror. One of the boys up front, a cutie with freckles and blond curls poking out from beneath his cap, stared past Casey's shoulder. Casey followed his gaze to the South Asian girl who suppressed a smile at the boy's goofy stare.

"Stop looking at my sister, freak!" a boy shouted at the freckled cutie.

"Shut up." The sister punched her brother's bicep.

"Why are you assholes looking at me?" the redheaded girl yelled at a couple of the South Asian kids. "Mind your own damn business!"

Casey stood and saw Jasmine just sitting there, staring at the kids. Why wasn't she stepping up to control the situation?

The boy who'd leered at Casey's chest shouted, "When are you going to grow boobs like her?" He pointed to Casey.

Ignoring the laughter, Casey removed her ID card from her pocket. "All right, settle dow—"

"Who wants to look like that fat cow?" the girl yelled.

Fat cow? Casey moved closer to the redhead. A few extra pounds around the middle hardly qualified for cow status. Somewhere behind her, a woman laughed. Probably Jasmine.

"I said settle down." Casey flashed her ID at the girl.

"You should scrape the fat off your big ass and put it some place useful, ho-bag!" one of the jackets shouted at the redhead.

The redhead's face turned crimson. "You're dead!"

"Enough!" Casey's voice rose. "Everyone calm down."

The words were barely out before an apple flew past Casey and struck the freckled cutie's shoulder. The jackets whooped and high-fived one another. The ball caps began scrambling through their backpacks.

"Keep the food in your packs," Casey ordered, "or you walk home."

Passengers mumbled and shook their heads. The exit bell rang

Jasmine stood and said, "Do as you're told."

A banana flew past Casey and nearly hit a passenger. Lou stopped the bus.

Jasmine marched up to the jackets. "Put that pear down!"

Casey glanced at the ball caps when something thunked the side of her head. "Ow!" She looked down to find a partially eaten pear rolling along the floor.

"Oops," one of the jackets said. "Sorry, lady."

"How stupid are you?" Jasmine said, shoving her ID in the kid's face.

Casey gaped at her colleague. Jasmine knew better than to insult passengers.

"Leave my brother alone!" His sister swatted Jasmine's arm.

"Don't tell me what to do, little girl."

Why was she making things worse? As Lou stopped the bus, Casey watched Jasmine grip the girl's shoulder. "You're out of here," Jasmine said.

The girl punched Jasmine's stomach. Jasmine recoiled and then slapped the girl's face.

Casey gasped and rushed toward them. "Jasmine!" What the hell was she doing?

The jackets swarmed Jasmine, who screamed, "Get out or I'll charge you with assault!"

"Good lord," a middle-aged woman muttered as she hurried to the front exit.

"You kids in the black jackets will have to go." Casey kept her voice firm but calm while Jasmine stood there, hands on hips, glowering at the group who were either too smart or too inexperienced to retaliate. Lou joined Casey as the jackets exited the bus while muttering obscenities.

"You're in so much trouble!" the girl yelled at Jasmine from the threshold. "My parents will have you fired, bitch!"

"Tough talk for someone in a training bra," Jasmine shot back.

Casey shook her head. Stan would be furious.

"Can you get this bus moving?" a passenger yelled at Lou. "Some of us have appointments."

Lou hurried back to his seat. "Sorry for the delay, folks."

Before he could pull away from the curb, the ball caps opened the windows and shouted more obscenities at the jackets.

Casey approached the group. "Stop that right now, or you're all out of here at the next stop."

The freckled cutie, who hadn't taken part in the verbal abuse, turned his back on Casey while his friends complied. Casey walked the length of the bus, apologizing to passengers for the altercation. Jasmine slumped back in her seat and looked at Casey with disgust.

Casey kept her voice low as she leaned close to her. "Where in the operations manual does it say you can slap anyone?"

"She punched me first, and if you didn't see it, then you need glasses," Jasmine replied. "You are thirty, after all."

"I have perfect vision and am absolutely clear about what I saw," Casey whispered. "You didn't try to control things until it was too late, and then you completely lost it. This all goes in my report."

"Whatever, super-cop."

Tempted to do some slapping of her own, Casey marched back to her seat. Lightning sliced through the clouds and muggy air. Thunder cracked, but she was too angry to pay much attention to the approaching storm. Minutes later, Lou pulled into Mainland's yard. Jasmine wasted no time stepping off the bus. Casey and Lou followed.

Jasmine was several paces ahead when Casey said to Lou, "Did you see the slap?"

"Uh-huh."

Jasmine spun around. "I didn't need your help! I didn't even want you here, but there you were butting in and acting like you know everything. It's pathetic."

"What's pathetic is your behavior." Casey's heartbeat quickened. "You were completely unprofessional."

"And you've never made mistakes because you're just so perfect." Her eyes blazed.

"What's wrong, Jasmine?" Lou asked. "I've never seen you lose it like that."

"I've never had to work with *her* before." Jasmine charged toward the administration building.

"What is her bloody problem?" Casey asked.

"Who knows? You've got a bit of pear stuck in your hair." Lou removed the scrap of food and flicked it on the ground.

"Thanks." She stroked his freckled cheek. "I need a hot shower."

"Seeing as how Stan will probably hear from the parents of a girl in a training bra, maybe you should write your report first."

"True." Raindrops started to sprinkle her face. "How loud do you think he'll yell after he's read it?"

# TWO

CASEY STARED AT HER COMPUTER screen and wished to god that Jasmine would get off the damn phone. Her desk was so close that words like "Miss Perfect," "meddling," and "self-righteous" were especially distracting, not to mention galling. Where in hell had Jasmine come up with the "Miss Perfect" notion? Nearly everyone at Mainland knew about Casey's failed marriage. Some knew about her estranged relationship with her mother, and how things were still unresolved when Mother died last spring. Sure, there'd been some success at work, but she'd also made mistakes. Who hadn't?

"I'll be okay," Jasmine said. "No, it's not just that. I'll tell you about the other stuff later; too many big ears around here."

Casey felt rather than saw Jasmine's stare. She hadn't wanted her desk to face the one Jasmine and Marie shared, but the security department was cramped. Over the summer, Stan restructured the security department, making Casey second-in-command and ensuring she had her own desk. Marie still complained now and then about having to share hers.

Casey started to reread the last paragraph of her report when a familiar voice said, "Who called you an ass?"

She looked up to find Summer standing behind her chair, reading a Post-it note fastened to the top of her screen. "Oh, hi." She checked her watch.

"It says, 'Don't forget time sheets, ASS,'" Summer said.

"Remember Stan's assistant, Amy? The tiny lady with the white hair you met last month?"

"Yeah, she was nice."

"Her full name is Amy Sarah Sparrow. I think she uses her initials on purpose."

"Oh." Summer smiled and looked at the cluttered desk beside Casey's. "Where is she?"

"Delivering documents for Stan. Shouldn't you be at swim practice?"

Summer's gaze drifted to the accounting and human resources areas at the other end of the room. "I quit the team."

"What?" Six months ago, this child was determined to make the national team one day. "Why?"

Summer glanced at Jasmine, who'd finally ended her call. "I've got too much homework, and my grades are bad."

"What grades? School started only two and a half weeks ago."

Summer sat on the edge of Casey's desk. "I had a math quiz today and couldn't answer half the questions. Grade seven's way too hard."

Casey folded her arms. "Did you study?"

She looked away. "With Tiffany and Ashley, yeah."

That explained it. Those two girls had been hanging around the house ever since Summer met them at the rec center in August. All the girls did was listen to rap music and gossip about boys. Apparently, no one else's mom was cool enough to hang with. Casey sensed that the girls didn't think of her as a real parent.

She still remembered the tears in Rhonda's eyes as she practically begged her to become Summer's legal guardian. Part of Casey had wanted to say no, but Rhonda had been Casey's surrogate mom and later, her close friend. She'd helped Casey through tough times, so turning Rhonda down wasn't an option, especially when Rhonda's emotional state had been so fragile.

"Don't tell Grandma about the test, okay? She still wants me to change schools and move in with her."

"Don't worry, I won't say a word." Winifred's frequent remarks about how and where Summer should be raised bothered Casey. "You know she can't make you move unless I allow it, right?"

Summer bit her lower lip. "Are you sure?"

"Totally." Casey squeezed her hand. "I'll help you with math, but I want you to rethink quitting the team, okay?"

"What for?"

"You've always loved competing." Aware that Jasmine was staring at her computer screen but not typing, Casey murmured, "You have a room filled with medals and ribbons proving how good you are."

"That's for babies."

Where did this come from? Summer had always been proud of her accomplishments. Still, the poor kid had changed a lot since Rhonda's sentencing four months ago. The naïve little girl who used to tell Casey everything had lost most of her sweet-natured innocence and, sadly, her willingness to confide. Neither of them had talked about Rhonda since her last tearful, phone call on Summer's birthday in early August. Her incarceration was still too painful to think about, let alone discuss.

"Can my friends come over?" Summer asked.

"Sorry, no. I have another shift this evening, and it's a school night. Anyway, it sounds like you have lots of math to review."

"But Tiffany and Ashley help me."

"Not this time." She'd been hearing too many protests lately. "I'll ask Mrs. Nally from next door to stay with you."

"I don't need a babysitter."

"Hi," Lou said, entering the room, his eyes widening when he saw Summer. "How's it going?"

"Craptacular." She stomped to the row of palms and dracaena separating security from the other departments.

As Lou's smile faded, Casey could almost guess what he was thinking. He'd had misgivings about her becoming Summer's guardian; said that parenting a teen who'd be missing her mom would be tough for a busy single woman with no experience. Lou didn't know what it felt like to have a mother leave home. The shame and anger Casey had once felt over Mother's adultery had gradually transformed into sadness and emptiness. At least she'd had Dad and Rhonda. No one even knew who Summer's father was.

"Who's your young friend, Lou?" Jasmine's voice was all honey and charm.

"Summer."

"Hey, Summer," Jasmine called out. "I hear you hate math. Me too."

Summer strolled to Jasmine's desk and started complaining about her teacher.

"Stan wants to see me," Lou whispered to Casey.

"I figured he would."

"Lou, come here a sec." Jasmine waved him over.

Seeing his hesitation, Casey said, "Go ahead, I need to finish my report."

Once he moved to Jasmine's desk, the woman started whispering. Casey bit the inside of her mouth to keep from saying something petty about the obvious attempt to exclude her. The sooner she finished this report, the better. She resumed typing, careful to stick to the facts and not add her opinion about Jasmine's behavior on the M10. The facts were damning enough.

Stan stepped out of his office, scowling. "Jasmine, I want you in my office right now. Have you finished your report?"

"Almost."

Yeah, sure, Casey thought.

"What about you, Casey?" he asked.

"It's printing."

"Give me five minutes, then bring it in." Stan looked at Lou. "I'll talk to you after Casey has her say." He started to follow Jasmine into his office, and then stopped. "What the hell happened out there?" He raised his hand. "Wait, don't answer; just bring your report and a damn good explanation."

Stan spotted Summer. "Hey, kiddo, how's it going?"

"Okay."

"That's a hell of a lot better than me." He stepped inside and slammed the door.

Summer started to smile. "Are you guys in trouble?"

"Maybe," Casey replied. "Why don't you start your homework while I meet with Stan."

"Okay, but I hate the way Mrs. Nally treats me like a baby. Can't Lou stay with me?"

Casey had asked Lou to stay with Summer twice before while she worked the rock-throwing assignment. Taking advantage of him wouldn't be right.

As if reading her thoughts, Lou said, "I don't mind."

"Thanks." She winked at him. "Come for dinner."

"Can we order a pizza?" Summer asked.

"We've had pizza three times in eight days. I'll cook something nutritious."

"Watch out." Lou smirked at Summer. "She could be on a health kick again."

Summer groaned. "The last time she did that some gross green glob stuck to my plate."

"That was a month ago. Let's get over it and move on, shall we?" They still looked uncertain. "We'll have spaghetti. A little tomato sauce, some peppers, mushrooms, onions, and fresh herbs."

"Pizza would be easier," Summer said.

"It's not been an easy day. I thought I'd keep the theme going."

"Days don't have themes. School dances do, which reminds me." Summer shuffled her feet. "I, like, need to talk to you about Friday night."

Oh geez, this kid was growing up way too fast.

# THREE

CASEY SHIVERED ON THE CHILLY M6 bus. Although the thunderstorm had rumbled out of Vancouver and headed east into the Fraser Valley, the air was nippy and occasional wind gusts were trying to sweep pedestrians off the sidewalk.

She'd asked Wesley to switch on the heater, but he'd said, "I ain't turning my bus into a frigging sauna."

Small wonder that staff called him Rude Wesley. Since the guy was built like a refrigerator and covered in hair, he obviously didn't feel the cold that normal people did.

While Wesley stopped for passengers, Casey thought about Stan's reprimand this afternoon. He'd told her and Jasmine about the irate phone call from the father of the girl Jasmine had slapped.

After reading Casey's report, he'd started in on Jasmine. "You should have stepped in the second the shouting started, and there should have been better communication between team members."

Casey cringed all over again. Stan was right. Her anger with Jasmine had sabotaged any desire to form a plan.

"If you ever slap a passenger again, you're fired," Stan had gone on. "You'll be let go anyway if the parents press charges. Regardless, you're now on a week's suspension without pay."

Casey was still baffled by Jasmine's lack of response. The woman was either a master at hiding her feelings when she wanted, or she really didn't care. Casey's punishment was to keep riding with the warring students until Jasmine's suspension ended. Stan's message was clear. Stay on the assignment and get the job done. It'd be a challenge juggling two work assignments and her criminology course over the next few days, unless she caught the rockhound tonight.

Across the aisle and two seats ahead of her, three young women yakked without pausing for breath. In the greenish hue of the bus's fluorescent lights, their hair color looked like varying degrees of orange. Near the front, a forty-something woman in scrubs and a long sweater had her eyes closed. Behind Casey, a male passenger hacked and coughed. For ten o'clock on a Tuesday night, this was as crowded as the M6 would get, which was just as well. If the rockhound struck, the fewer passengers the better.

The rockhound had chosen to break windows between nine and eleven, perhaps because there were fewer pedestrians at this time of night to identify him, or get in his way. He'd chosen to strike along the stretch of Columbia Street with the most traffic lights, where the M6 would have to make frequent stops.

Although the glass manufacturer had assured MPT management that fist-sized rocks wouldn't shatter a window, Wesley was required to warn people about the potential for danger, should they prefer to ride the TransLink buses also servicing this route. Since those buses didn't show up as often, MPT's ridership numbers hadn't diminished, but Casey had heard that vice president David Eisler was worried they would. Staying competitive was hard enough. Management was always saying that Mainland had to be a safer, better service provider than TransLink's larger fleet. Repeated vandalism was bad for business, and if a passenger got hurt, a lawsuit or negative publicity would mean layoffs and more cutbacks.

"I'm doubling your shifts on the M6 until this rock nut is caught," Stan had told her this afternoon. "Stop this jerk, Casey."

Since Columbia Street ran through the City of New Westminster, Stan had contacted the New West Police, who'd agreed to step up their patrol of this area. Their station was only two blocks from the rockhound's turf, though Casey hadn't noticed any police presence tonight.

She scanned the sidewalk on her right, wishing the M6 cruised past the gorgeous, stately heritage homes built decades ago at the top of the hill. She loved looking at those places, but the M6 only served New West's busier, commercial routes. In five minutes, they'd reach the hot zone: a stretch of Columbia Street populated by stores, restaurants, and bars.

Columbia ran parallel to the Fraser River. Between the river and Columbia, Front Street was hidden from view except at intersections. At this time of night, the antique and pawn shops would be closed and there'd be little traffic around. Next to the street, rail tracks, bushes, and trains provided plenty of hiding spots for anyone needing a quick escape.

By all accounts, the rockhound was a lone male of average height and weight. Witnesses had described him as wearing a hoodie or a raincoat. He'd also been spotted wearing a ball cap or a black tuque on different nights. Some said he wore a moustache while others said he was clean-shaven. Some thought he was young; others insisted he was old. Until Casey saw this guy pitching a rock, she wasn't sure how she'd identify him.

Her cell phone rang.

"Casey, this is Winifred. I just called Summer and it sounds like she's having a party, for heaven's sake. I heard horrible music blaring in the background. Do you have any idea how late it is?"

Casey slumped in her seat. The last person she wanted to talk to, aside from Jasmine, was Summer's grandmother. "Summer likes to listen to music when she's finished homework."

The M6 cruised under the Pattullo Bridge. Casey glanced at the Fraser River.

"Who's supervising her?"

"Lou."

They travelled under the Fraser River Rail Bridge and adjacent SkyTrain tracks. Casey sat forward. They were in the hot zone. "Winifred, I have to go—"

"A twelve-year-old shouldn't stay up this late."

The bus rolled past Blackwood Street on Casey's right. Fourth Street was half a block ahead. Casey spotted three guys strolling across the Fourth and Columbia intersection. As the M6 cruised past them, she took note of their jeans and dark jackets. Two of them had their hands in their pockets and none were wearing hats. She couldn't see their faces clearly.

"Are you listening to me?" Winifred demanded.

One of the orange-haired girls pulled the cord.

"Sorry, I can't talk right now."

Wesley eased to the stop.

"I still think it's best if Summer moved in with me."

Damn it, she'd brought this up at least twice a month since Rhonda's incarceration. When would the woman let it go? "She wants to stay with—"

A loud thunk and cracking glass brought Casey to her feet. The girls yelped while the woman in scrubs sat upright and looked around. Casey spotted someone turn the corner at Fourth and disappear. She shoved the phone in her pocket and, glancing at the window, charged toward the exit. "Anyone see who did it?"

The coughing guy shook his head and sneezed.

"He took off up Fourth," another man answered. "I didn't see his face."

Outside, two of the three guys who'd been strolling down the sidewalk stopped in front of the damaged window. The third guy was gone.

"MPT security." She flashed her ID. "Can you two wait here? I'll be right back."

Casey sprinted to the corner, turned left onto Fourth, and scanned the road's steep upgrade. Part way up the hill, a man darted across the street and into a lane. Casey sprinted after him, but it wasn't long before her heart was trying to beat its way out of her chest. Drizzling rain sprinkled her face and she blinked droplets from her eyes.

When she reached the narrow alley, she stopped to catch her breath and study the dumpsters and parked vehicles. There was no movement anywhere. Bending over, she propped her hands on her thighs and took deep breaths. It had been a long time since she'd chased a suspect uphill. Obviously, yoga routines and the occasional spin on her stationary bike weren't enough. She straightened up and scanned the alley. Nothing. She trudged back down the hill.

The M6 was waiting, not that Wesley had a choice. Drivers weren't supposed to leave during pursuits until they heard from the security staff.

He stood on the sidewalk, tossing a good-sized rock up and down. "About bloody time."

"Where are the guys I told to wait?"

"They said they didn't see a thing, so I let them go."

"The suspect was walking right beside them."

Wesley shrugged and headed into the bus. "Passengers didn't see nothing either."

"Don't we need to talk to the police?"

"I already called and told them what I just told you." He sat down. "Girls shouldn't be handling this stuff. Where are the guys?"

"Doing other things." Casey crossed her arms. "I know my job, Wes, so leave the questions to me next time."

"Hey, I got to stick to the schedule."

Casey shoved her hands in her pockets, felt her phone, and realized she'd forgotten about Winifred. She picked it up. The line was dead, so she called Summer. Wesley lurched the bus forward, forcing Casey into the seat behind him.

Summer answered on the second ring. Casey could almost feel the rap music vibrating through the phone as Summer said, "Grandma doesn't want me to have any fun. She treats me like a baby and it's not fair!"

Casey rubbed her temple. She wanted to say that whining about it made her sound like a baby, but the thought of another argument today held no appeal. "It's nearly ten-thirty. You should be getting ready for bed."

"Why can't I stay up? My friends do."

"I don't care." Casey's voice rose. "I want you to—"

"Oh fine!"

She hung up before Casey could ask to speak to Lou.

"I heard about your cat fight," Wesley said.

She stood to see him better. "Excuse me?"

"You and Jasmine." He kept his gaze on the road. "You need to control your temper there, girl."

Jasmine must have told him her version of events. "She was the one who slapped a child, Wes, or didn't she tell you that bit?" Casey waited for a reply, but none came. "There were witnesses and a complaint about her, which was why Stan suspended her for a week."

"Well, don't go blabbing it around. It ain't professional."

She didn't know whether to laugh or yell, but she'd had enough of people telling her what she'd done wrong today. "Do you think it was professional for her to call me names, throw herself at Roberto, and slap a child?"

His red bushy brows fused together. "What do you mean, throw herself at him?"

How convenient for Wesley to ignore the rest. When she told him about the kiss this morning, Wesley said, "It's no big deal. Jasmine isn't hooked up with anybody, so she can do what she wants."

Casey watched him. "I didn't know you were a fan of hers."

"She's a friend."

Really? So, what did those two have in common? Jasmine liked dancing. Wesley was training for the pro wrestling biz. They had rudeness in common, and Casey understood Wesley's attraction to Jasmine. What did she like about him?

"Why are you looking like someone just dangled a worm in your face?" Wesley asked.

She didn't know she was.

The exit bell rang. Casey turned and saw both guys at the back preparing to leave.

"There's nothing wrong with Jasmine hanging with more than one guy," Wesley added. "The only sleazy thing is the married jerks who hit on her."

"Are you talking about guys from work?"

Wesley grunted and shook his head. "Ask your gossipy friends."

Maybe she would. Casey walked up to the damaged window. Stan would be ticked. She studied the crack. If she hadn't been talking to Winifred, she might have seen the freak in action. She sat down to call home again. Lou answered right away.

"Is Summer getting ready for bed?" she asked.

"Slowly. She's being a pain."

"Sorry, Lou."

"Don't worry about it."

Casey did worry. They couldn't go out as much as they used to, or take off for romantic weekends.

"How'd it go tonight?" he asked.

"Awful. I was trying to get off the phone with Winifred when the rockhound struck. I couldn't catch him," she mumbled, glancing up and down the bus. "Wesley thinks I have a temper problem because of the Jasmine thing."

"Yeah well, she's the only woman in the world he likes. They've gone out a few times."

"He told you?"

"Jasmine did."

"I didn't realize she discussed her personal life with you."

"Once in a while."

"It's pretty clear she likes you." Casey paused. "Has she asked you out?"

"No."

"She comes by on bowling nights a lot, but you're the only team member she makes a point of talking to. And she always involves Marie in those chats, probably so I won't get suspicious."

"You've got it wrong, and I've never heard you this insecure before."

"What did I get wrong?"

"It's not important."

"Come on, Lou."

"Look, the chats aren't about Jasmine trying to hook up with me."

"Meaning she's been trying to get you and Marie together?"

"It won't happen, so don't worry about it."

Casey fumed. Marie had lusted after Lou for a long time, and used to flirt with him outrageously. She'd thought Marie had given up, but maybe Jasmine had decided to play matchmaker so Marie wouldn't be so obvious. Worse than their conspiracy, though, was the depressing realization that Lou had kept this from her.

"Why didn't you tell me?"

"I didn't want to make things worse between you and them."

Casey leaned back in her seat, suddenly exhausted.

"Will you be home soon?" he asked.

"Yes."

"Good. Don't let the rockhound thing get to you. You'll catch him, I know it."

That was Lou. Always optimistic and supportive; trying to make the best of things. Sometimes, deep in her heart, she wondered if she deserved him.

# FOUR

**ON THE SECOND FLOOR, CASEY** rushed into the security department and glanced at the wall clock. Twelve-thirty, damn. She'd lost track of time researching comparative police systems for her essay, and should have had her report on last night's fiasco finished by now. Stan would be demanding it any second. She also had to record this morning's uneventful shift with the kids on the M10 bus.

Casey spotted a yellow Post-it note stuck to her computer screen. "Time sheet needed by 2:00 PM. No excuses! ASS." Casey sighed. She was supposed to have done her time sheet yesterday, but after Stan's lecture and Summer's unexpected visit, Casey hadn't felt like hanging around to record two weeks' worth of shifts on a spreadsheet.

She booted up her computer and, collecting her thoughts, began to type. She'd barely finished the first paragraph when Stan's door opened. "Casey, can you come in a minute?"

Something in his tone made her turn around. The parts of his face not covered by hair were flushed. Worse, Stan couldn't quite meet her eyes.

"What's wrong?"

He glanced around the room. "No one else here?"

"It's lunch time." When he didn't say anything, Casey said, "I should have my report about last night finished soon."

"It can wait." He unloosened the knot in his mint-green tie. "Come inside."

Oh, this was bad. She'd never heard Stan say that reports could wait.

In his office, Casey took the chair nearest the open window. Stan fiddled with the pens and pencils in the cup, and then zeroed in on his bonsai. When his lips started quivering and he wrung his hands together, she started to worry.

"Marie called a few minutes ago." Stan tried to meet her gaze and failed. "I don't know how to say this." He paused, and then opened his mouth, but nothing came out.

The room started to feel hot. The only sound Casey heard was distant traffic. "What is it?"

Stan rested his elbows on the desk. "Someone shot Jasmine . . . She didn't make it."

"What?" A prickly sensation ran down her back. "When?"

"A little over an hour ago."

"It can't be." Casey's mind went blank. "Are you sure?"

Stan nodded. "It happened in the parking lot at her church." He cleared his voice. "She was waiting to pick up her son from preschool."

"For real?" Casey gripped the arms of her chair. "I don't understand this."

"The police found Jasmine's Mainland ID in her purse and contacted me just after Marie called." He cleared his voice again. "I told the corporal she has no family; that's when he told me what happened."

"Who on god's earth would want to kill her?"

"I heard there were problems with the ex. She was trying to get a restraining order."

Unable to think of anything to say about Jasmine that wouldn't sound phony and hypocritical, Casey slipped into an investigative role. "Were there any witnesses?"

"Apparently, someone heard one shot and saw a van peel out of the lot."

Casey's mind raced. "The guy was either close or knew what he was doing. Did the police say if this looked like a targeted hit?"

"They wouldn't say much of anything."

The wood chair felt painfully hard beneath her. "Jasmine's son wasn't in the car, was he?"

"No, she was killed at eleven-ten. Jeremy's class finished at eleven-thirty."

Casey remembered Jeremy from Mainland's company picnic last month: a chubby-cheeked boy with large brown eyes and Jasmine's black hair. While Jasmine was flirting with Roberto that day, her son had approached Casey and showed her his toy truck.

"I don't know why she arrived so early to fetch him." Stan's eyes glistened. "Jasmine lived only two blocks from the parish she belonged to. If she'd gone later . . ."

A bus entered the yard. In need of fresh air, Casey walked to the window and watched employees either returning from lunch or beginning and ending shifts. No one looked upset.

"I take it employees don't know?"

"Just you and Marie. I called David Eisler, who's probably telling supervisors right now. Eisler intends to have each supervisor inform his own team."

David Eisler was the last person Casey would look to for guidance in a crisis, since his disrespect for employees was almost legendary. With the president on vacation in Europe, they were stuck with the egotistical VP. She glanced at the sky. After yesterday's thunderstorm and rain, the sunshine was back, the sky free of cloud. A diesel engine near the building roared to life. Normally, she liked the smell of diesel. Right now, it made her queasy. She turned to Stan.

"How did Marie find out so fast?"

"The preschool phoned and asked her to pick up Jeremy. The poor woman's devastated."

No doubt. Marie and Jasmine had hit it off from day one.

"Jasmine was a sweet kid." Stan booted up the PC he'd finally agreed to use as part of his restructuring program. "She made great peanut butter cookies."

Which she'd offered to everyone but her. Casey blushed at the petty thought.

"Corporal Lundy from the Coquitlam detachment's coming here this afternoon to go through her locker." Stan handed Casey a slip of paper. "That's her combination. Show him where it is."

"Coquitlam RCMP?"

"That's where it happened, where she lived."

Friends had told Casey that Coquitlam was one of the safest and fastest growing suburban communities in the Lower Mainland. "Is the corporal part of IHIT?" Casey had never met anyone from the RCMP's Integrated Homicide Investigative Team. Under the circumstances, she wasn't sure she wanted to.

"I didn't ask. Employees who worked directly with Jasmine will be contacted by phone," Stan added. "Since you worked with Jasmine yesterday, Lundy might question you right away."

What should she say if the corporal asked what kind of person Jasmine had been? Sooner or later, he'd hear about their altercation on the M10; probably ask questions she wouldn't feel great about answering.

"Eisler's called a mandatory meeting for everyone at four-thirty," Stan said. "Marie's exempt because she's looking after Jasmine's son and won't be in for a couple days."

"Jeremy won't be with the father?"

"I hear he's an alcoholic who had some visiting rights, but who knows?" Stan clicked the mouse. "Uh, I've got a lot to do, so . . ." He stared at the monitor.

"Sure." She headed for the door. "I'll finish my reports."

"Let supervisors tell their people, okay? It wouldn't seem right coming from staff."

"No problem."

Casey stepped outside and leaned against the wall. Her legs were too shaky to make it back to her chair. She took a deep breath, inhaling through her nose and out the same way, just like her yoga tape had taught. This time, there was no calmness. Lunch hour was nearly over. The accounting people would be traipsing in here any moment.

Shuffling back to her desk, Casey wondered if she should call Marie. After Lou's revelation last night, Marie was her least favorite person, right now. Still, she should at least offer condolences. Casey made the call and heard Marie's trembling voice.

"Stan just told me what happened, and I'm sorry, Marie. I know you and Jasmine were close." Casey listened to some nose blowing. "He said the preschool called you?"

"I was doing laundry," she mumbled. "The phone rang and a woman said something had happened to Jeremy's mother, and could I pick Jeremy up? It was so surreal."

An accounting employee strolled into the room. Casey turned away. "Why would they call you?"

"I'm the emergency contact person on Jeremy's registration form." She blew her nose again. "He'll miss her so much. Jasmine was a wonderful mother."

A wonderful mom and a church-going woman who baked cookies?

This wasn't the Jasmine that Casey had known. "Stan said that someone saw a van leave the scene."

"Another parent showed up early. It was so awful. Her head . . ." Marie's voice cracked. "Destroyed."

Casey inhaled sharply. "She was shot in the head?"

"Yeah." She sniffed. "There was blood running down the door and bits of . . ." Marie choked back a sob.

"Oh no, you saw her? Did you have to identify the body?"

"No, the tarp on the car wasn't fastened down, and the wind lifted it."

"Oh, Marie."

"What am I supposed to say when Jeremy wakes up for his nap and asks for her? He's only two, for shit's sake."

She wished she knew the answer. "If there's anything I can do, let me know."

"Could you take some of Jasmine's pets? She has—had—a lot. Wanted to be a vet."

"Actually, Summer's dog has the run of the house and he doesn't play well with others. What about the SPCA?"

"They're swamped. Can't you keep the smaller ones a few days until I find them homes? They'll be in cages."

"They aren't lizards or snakes, by any chance?"

"Gerbils, hamsters, and guinea pigs. I'll take her cat and dog."

Casey propped her elbows on the desk. "I don't have any experience with rodents."

"All you do is feed and water them, which her landlord's doing until we get them. I'll let you know when." She hung up. No thank you, or goodbye, or thanks for phoning.

Stan stepped out of his office, his face still flushed and grim. "I'd like everyone's attention," he called out. "Could you all come down here a minute?" He turned to Casey. "You can go, if you want."

She couldn't bear to hear it again, to see their faces. Casey grabbed her things, hurried out of the room, and didn't stop until she reached her Tercel.

As she opened the door, Roberto stepped out of his Corvette two stalls from her, and grinned. "Where are you off to, sweetie?"

"The library. Have to research something for school."

"Is Jasmine around?"

Oh, hell. "No." She scrambled to change topics. "Your coveralls look too clean for the middle of the day. Are you just starting?"

"Yeah, I had a bloody root canal." He glanced around the depot. "The place looks deserted. Where is everyone?"

"Working, I guess. Lunch is over."

Roberto watched her. "You look totally stressed. What's up?"

"It's a bad day."

"Why, what happened?"

Casey stifled a groan. "Your supervisor will tell you."

"Has there been an accident?" His eyes narrowed. "Did someone get hurt?"

"Yes." She slipped behind the wheel.

"Casey, you're freaking me out. What's going on?"

"Sorry, I don't mean to." She started the engine.

"Casey?"

"I've been told not to say anything, Roberto. The news is supposed to come from supervisors. I'm really sorry."

She felt guilty for leaving him looking worried and confused, and she was ashamed for not having the guts to tell a friend the truth.

→    →    →

CASEY RETURNED TO Mainland two hours later, frustrated by the wasted trip. All she could think about was Jasmine's death, the contradictions in her personality, and her son. It was hard to understand someone who could slap a child and mouth off to a colleague one day, yet bake cookies for Mainland staff on another. And why had Jasmine gone out of her way to help Marie hook up with Lou without bothering to find out what he wanted?

Stepping onto the bus, she saw Lou's sullen face. "You've heard?"

He nodded. Despite last night's lovemaking, there'd been uneasiness between them when Lou left for work this morning. She wasn't sure if the problem was Summer's behavior or her jealousy over Jasmine's scheme to bring Lou and Marie together. She'd been too tired and demoralized over yesterday's events to talk it over. Small wonder that superficial conversation had filled the blank spaces where heartfelt words should have gone.

Lou eased the M10 out of the depot.

"Marie asked me to take some of Jasmine's pets," she said.

His silence was no surprise. Lou rarely spoke when he was upset, and seeing as how he'd gotten along with Jasmine, her death obviously hit him hard. Casey placed her hand on his shoulder. He reached up and squeezed her fingers.

"Are you okay?" she asked.

"Stunned."

"How did the drivers take the news?"

"Most are in shock. Some act like they don't care."

He pulled up to the first stop, where four people prepared to board. Casey held onto the pole behind his chair and waited for Lou to merge back into traffic before she said, "The police will want to talk to Roberto and Wesley, and anyone else she was seeing. Do you know if she went out with other guys?"

"Just Marie's brother, Noel."

"Really?" Typical of Marie not to mention it. "Wesley said something kind of disturbing last night. Apparently, some married guys had hit on Jasmine. Do you know if any of them were from work?"

"Only one that I heard of."

"Who?"

He didn't respond right away. "Eisler."

"Our snobbish VP who's barely left his office in two years? I've never even seen him acknowledge Jasmine."

"He wouldn't in front of people. Jasmine said he called her a few times. She was afraid he'd fire her for rejecting him."

So, she'd confided in Lou? Jealousy flitted through Casey until she realized how childish it was.

"I don't know if it stopped," he added, "but Marie said that Eisler's wife started phoning him at work more than usual, and making surprise visits to his office."

"How does Marie know this?"

"She's friendly with Eisler's admin assistant."

How many private conversations had Marie and Lou shared? Casey looked out the window as Lou pulled up to the warring kids' stop.

"The tweens look more miserable than usual," Lou said.

Casey removed her ID from her pocket, shoved thoughts of Jasmine aside, and prepared to do her job.

# FIVE

**CASEY SQUIRMED IN HER CHAIR** at the back of the lunchroom as red-eyed colleagues shuffled in. Some women dabbed their eyes and hugged one another. A few guys looked pale and scarcely made eye contact with anybody. Grief was a solo act for a lot of men. Most of the guys she knew didn't seek hugs during tough times, they sought solitude. A handful of Mainland's employees showed no emotion at all. Was it an act, or apathy?

Roberto trudged into the room, shoulders slouched, face bewildered. He slumped into a chair near the front. Casey clasped her hands on the tabletop as two women from accounting and human resources approached.

"It's so sad, Casey," one said to her.

"Yes."

"Terrible," the other added. "I didn't really know her, but she seemed nice."

Casey's shame deepened. She couldn't think of a kind thing to say about Jasmine; didn't share their level of grief.

While the women moved on, Lou arrived and took the seat she'd saved for him "You okay?" he asked. "Your face is all red."

"I hate watching them go through this."

"The heat in here doesn't help. Place feels like a sauna." Lou took off his uniform jacket, unclipped the matching forest green tie, and undid the top two buttons on his shirt. "It smells like rotting compost, too."

The late afternoon sun blazed through the long row of windows. Casey looked at the rush-hour traffic on the highway. She used to love zipping out of Vancouver, through the suburbs, and into the rural Fraser Valley. Years of development had transformed stretches of it into another clogged thoroughfare leading to more developed urban sprawl.

Wesley Axelson stomped into the room and glowered at everyone as he headed toward the back.

"Looks like Wesley got hurt again," Lou murmured.

Casey saw the wrapped knee beneath Wes's baggy gym shorts. In his bid to become a pro wrestler, Wesley had injured body parts so many times that he was often wearing some type of bandage.

"He's not in uniform," she said. "Is this his day off?"

"He switched with someone a couple of days ago."

Wesley leaned against the back wall near Casey and crossed his arms.

"Who's the tall guy following Eisler?" Lou asked.

Casey turned and observed the solemn, thirty-something man scanning employees' faces. "RCMP, I think. Stan said a Corporal Lundy wants to look at Jasmine's locker. I'm supposed to open it for him."

"Good thing you were in class when she was shot."

"Why, because she and I argued yesterday?"

Lou squeezed her hand. "We'll all need alibis, sweetheart."

"Maybe some more than others." Casey watched Eisler tug on his shirt collar. His perpetual tan glowed with perspiration and it looked like strands of hair had escaped from his perfect, light brown layers. "Eisler sure seems nervous."

"He should. I wasn't the only one who knew he was hot for Jasmine," Lou mumbled.

Once Stan and the rest of management arrived, the VP made a lacklustre speech about Jasmine's "warm sparkling personality" and "tremendous contribution" to Mainland. By the end of it, Casey was disheartened. It wasn't that Eisler had lied about her. After all, lots of coworkers had liked Jasmine and she'd volunteered on Mainland's social committee. She'd also worked shifts no one else wanted. Why hadn't she let Casey see that warm sparkling side? What had she done to earn Jasmine's wrath?

As soon as the corporal was introduced, Roberto said, "Have you arrested anyone yet? Is there even a suspect?"

Casey could only see the back of Roberto's head, but the anger in his voice was clear. She heard Wesley snort and saw him roll his eyes.

"I'm afraid we don't have much to report at this time," the corporal answered.

"At this stage, the authorities need to gather information, not give it," Eisler said. "And I must ask that none of you speak to the media. If you're approached, refer them to me."

"Won't that make it look like we're hiding something?" a driver asked.

Eisler's gaze bore into the driver. "It will look like you don't know anything about Jasmine's death, which I assume is true."

Pensive glances darted around the room.

"Have you checked out her ex, Elliott Birch?" Roberto asked. "He was stalking her and that's a fact."

Casey glanced at Lou who stared straight ahead. She hadn't heard about any stalking.

"You should discuss that privately with the corporal," Eisler answered.

"Should we be worried?" a dispatcher asked. "I mean, the killer isn't targeting Mainland staff, is he?"

"At this time, ma'am," Lundy replied, "we have no reason to believe employees are at risk."

"Officers will be contacting those of you who'd worked with Jasmine recently," Eisler stated. "Make yourselves available. That's all for now."

Wesley swore under his breath and stomped to the exit. Others shuffled out while murmuring to one another. Casey spotted Stan chatting with Lundy while Eisler rushed out of the room.

"I'd better get this locker thing over with," she told Lou.

A minute later, she'd introduced herself to Corporal Lundy and he was following her down the hall.

"Did you know Mrs. Birch well?" he asked.

"Not really. We didn't socialize or work many shifts together."

"Your supervisor told me about an altercation she had with a student?"

"Yes, the girl was on the bus today. All of the kids were quiet." She watched Lundy jot something on a notepad. "You do know the kids are only twelve years old, right? They're not gangbangers, just cliques with attitude."

He peered at her. "I understand you and Mrs. Birch also argued yesterday."

She knew this was coming. "I was mad that she'd slapped the girl, yes."

"I meant before your shift," Lundy said, "in the stairwell yesterday morning?"

Casey stopped walking. Damn, someone must have overheard her with Jasmine.

"For reasons I don't understand, Jasmine didn't like me much. She made it clear she didn't want to work with me and that's why we argued." She resumed walking. "A colleague said Jasmine was sitting in her car when she was shot in the head. I also heard that a van was seen driving off. Is that true?"

"Which colleague told you this?"

"Marie Crenshaw. She described the crime scene, Corporal, and it sounds like Jasmine was shot at close range, which makes me wonder if she recognized the driver and didn't think he'd be a threat." His stare irritated her. "Yesterday was warm. Jasmine usually drove with the window down and music blaring. If music was on and her eyes closed, she might not have heard or seen anything until it was too late."

"Do you know people who have access to guns?" Lundy asked.

"I can't think of anyone." Oh, crap. Wesley had a gun rack in his truck but she'd never seen a gun in the rack, or even heard him mention one. "Do you know if she was killed with a shotgun or a handgun?"

"That information's not yet available to the public."

And she was the public; no more, no less. Casey pictured Jasmine slouched in the driver's seat, her head against the door, music playing. She imagined the van drawing nearer, the driver raising a gun. Jasmine might have turned her head and spotted the weapon just as . . . Casey's stomach churned.

"What time did you finish your shift this morning?" Lundy asked.

"Ten o'clock. I then had a ten-thirty class at the Burnaby Mountain campus, but I was a half hour late because I forgot my textbook and binder, and had to drive home." Casey stopped at the women's locker room.

"Can anyone verify when you returned home?"

"I'm not sure."

"Then you don't live alone?"

"Yes and no. I rent the top floor apartment in a large house on Napier Street in East Van. The owner's a good friend who's away for a while, so I'm acting as landlord to two other tenants. I'm also legal guardian to my landlord's daughter, who would have been at school. The tenants each have a room on the second floor at the back of the house, and I don't know if they were home."

"Do you share a common entrance?"

"The tenants usually enter through the front door. I park at the back and go in through the kitchen. The house is on a corner lot, so the tenants park either in front or on the side street. I honestly didn't notice if their cars were around or not."

"What are the tenants' names and phone numbers?"

"I don't have their numbers handy." After she gave him their names, Lundy said, "You were in class at the time of the murder then?"

"Yes, I got there at eleven." She watched him jot down the time. "The prof glared at me when I came in."

"What kind of car do you drive?"

"A red Tercel. Why?" He didn't answer. "How can I help you, Corporal, if you don't meet me halfway?" She knew she sounded impatient, but didn't care. "I promise confidentiality."

He seemed to be thinking it over. "A silver compact was also seen leaving about the time of the shooting, and that is confidential." He peered at her. "We don't know the make and model. Do you know anyone who drives this type of vehicle?"

"Tons of people."

"Including employees?"

"Sure." She entered the locker room. Lundy didn't follow but just stood there, fiddling with his pen and notebook. Casey smiled. "All clear, come on in."

He stepped inside and took a furtive glance around. She saw his nostrils twitch, possibly from the clashing smells of perspiration, perfume, and cologne.

"Do you know anything about Jasmine Birch's activities last night?" he asked.

"I heard her tell someone she had plans for the evening."

"Plans with whom?"

"I don't know."

"Who was she talking to?"

Casey shrugged. She hated the idea of involving Roberto.

"This isn't the time to start withholding information, Miss Holland."

"I work with these people, Corporal. Many of them are friends."

"I appreciate that, but, as we've established, this conversation is confidential."

"I'm the only one who heard them talk, and if you mention this, he'll know I told you."

"Miss Holland." His voice was stern.

"Jasmine was talking to Roberto de Luca."

He started scribbling. "Was the big guy with the reddish beard at the back of the lunchroom Wesley Axelson?"

She had a feeling he already knew the answer. "Yes." The corporal would find out why nearly everyone referred to him as Rude Wesley.

"Were Mrs. Birch and Mr. Axelson a couple?"

Geez, who'd told him this stuff? "I heard they dated casually, but neither of them confided in me." Casey removed a slip of paper from her pocket. "You should talk to people who knew her better, like Marie. She and Jasmine were good friends."

Casey read Jasmine's locker combination on the slip of paper. She turned the knob slowly, anxious to get it right the first time. Normally, she didn't feel this uncomfortable around cops. She'd never had to supply an alibi or rat out coworkers, though. Casey opened the locker and found it crammed with clothes, towels, toiletries, and paperbacks. Lundy removed several dog and cat magazines.

"Pet owner?" Lundy asked.

"So I've heard."

Two photographs fell out of a magazine. Casey picked them up. One was a head shot of Jasmine with her eyes closed and jaw slack, as if asleep. A rumpled, sky-blue comforter with yellow roses covered her chest. In the second photo, a jubilant Jeremy was splashing in the bathtub. Why would Jasmine keep the pictures here?

Lundy took the photos from her. "Thanks for your help, Miss Holland. That's all I need for now."

A driver entered the room.

"Oh Casey, it's so horrible!" The woman threw her arms around her.

"Yeah, it is."

"Jasmine was only twenty-four, and who'll look after her little boy?"

"I don't know."

While the driver wept, Casey found herself thinking about Jeremy; how he must be asking for his mother right about now. A lump appeared in her throat.

# SIX

"LOOK, CASEY, I'M SORRY YOU'RE run off your feet," Marie said as she slid her SUV's side door open, "but it's not my fault we're short-staffed."

Good lord, all she said was that this had been one of the busiest, most stressful weeks she'd had in ages. Casey buttoned her sweater. An autumn chill had already invaded the Lower Mainland this late September morning. Marie's attitude wasn't making her feel any warmer.

"I can't cope with those brats on the M10 this afternoon." Marie handed her a pet carrier. "Jasmine's only been gone twenty-four hours."

If anger was part of the grieving process, Marie was well into it. Casey looked at the three-story apartment building in front of them. The old wood and stucco exterior needed cleaning. Sliding glass doors opened onto balconies just large enough to fit a chair and a hibachi. Still, Jasmine had chosen a good location. Whiting Way was quiet and the mall, SkyTrain, and buses were within walking distance.

Casey counted five balconies on the left side of the building's entrance and five on the right. "Which apartment was Jasmine's?"

"It's the ground floor, corner suite to your left." Marie handed Casey a second pet carrier.

"How many animals did she have?"

"I've never counted them."

That many? Casey hoped the critters came with a how-to manual. "I can only take a few."

"They're not that much work. The guinea pigs are loving balls of fur that coo when they're happy. Didn't you have pets as a kid?"

"No, which is why they'll be better off with someone more experienced. I'd feel terrible if one died."

"Help me find them caring families, then." Marie started toward the building. "Hurry up, I've got tons to do."

Casey struggled with the temptation to give Marie's ass a kick. Obviously, the woman didn't care about the homework, mountains of chores, and rock-throwing assignment Casey was juggling. She'd ordered her to be here at ten-thirty and then had the gall to show up fifteen minutes late. Marie pressed the manager's intercom button. Seconds later, Casey heard a man's voice.

When a buzzer sounded, Marie opened the glass door and waited for Casey. "Come on, let's move."

"I'm carrying two frigging cages, Marie." She edged past her. "What are you carrying?"

"A heavy heart, which is more than I can say for some people."

So that was it. What was she supposed to do, fake grief? They turned right and walked to the end of the corridor. The landlord's suite was also at the front of the building. A man answered Marie's knock and gave her a quick hug. Casey's eyes widened. They knew each other?

"I already miss her," he said, voice cracking. His moist, brown eyes turned to Casey. "Hello, I'm the building manager, Paval Gallenski."

"Casey Holland."

Thinning hair and a web of tiny creases around his eyes placed him in his forties. His nose was too large for his face, brows too sparse.

"Excuse the mess." Paval opened the door wider. "It's rent day and tenants are keeping me from getting anything done."

Stepping inside, Casey saw two toddlers sitting on a navy carpet, playing with a large collection of plastic toys. The red sofa and chair were covered with diaper bags, more toys, and picture books. A playpen filled a corner of the room. Posters of animals, flowers, and butterflies covered most of the walls. It was like living inside a toddler's play school.

"This is cheerful." Casey put down the cages.

"Thanks. My wife and I run a daycare for tenants."

A laundry basket filled with stuffed animals sat next to the playpen. Considering all the dirty diapers he probably dealt with, Casey could only smell orange-scented air freshener. A cocker spaniel emerged from the dining area on the other side of the sofa. The pooch wagged its tail and scampered toward Marie.

"Belle!" She scratched the dog's head. "How are you doing, girl?"

"The poor thing misses Jasmine." Paval turned to Marie. "How is Jeremy?"

"I wish I knew." She straightened up. "His dad barged into my house last night and took him. I smelled booze on his breath and tried to stop the jerk, but he threatened me." Marie tucked thick red hair behind her ears. "I called the cops and Child Protection Services, but no one seems eager to do much because Birch has no criminal record and he didn't touch me."

Casey hadn't heard any of this. "Is Jeremy in danger?"

"Good question. Jasmine said Birch was always good with him, but when he drinks he's out of control. The jerk beat Jasmine; that's why she left."

"I had no idea," Casey murmured.

"I can't say I'm surprised," Paval remarked. "I've seen him standing outside her apartment shouting obscenities."

"The bastard was seeking joint custody." Marie removed a tissue from her pocket. "Birch was so pissed with Jasmine for not allowing him more time with Jeremy that I really think he could have . . ." Her voice trailed away.

The toddlers, a girl and a boy, started fighting over a toy phone. When the little girl lost the battle, Paval picked her up and murmured soothing words.

"How's Noel coping?" Paval asked Marie.

"Barely." She stroked Belle once again. "The cops came to his house. I gather it didn't go well."

Lou mentioned that Marie's brother had gone out with Jasmine. If the police were paying more attention to Noel than they were to Jasmine's ex, Casey figured there had to be a reason. So, why was the manager asking personal questions?

"I take it you two know each other?" Casey looked from him to Marie.

"I was over here a lot," Marie replied.

"As was Noel," Paval added. "Getting to know the regular visitors makes it easier to figure out who should and shouldn't be in the building." He placed the little girl on the sofa and gave her a teddy bear as he glanced at Marie. "Do they really think he'd use his own van in a shooting?"

"They shouldn't, given that Noel reported it stolen the night before." Marie frowned. "Birch was stalking Jasmine, so he probably knew what

Noel drives. He could have rented one to practise driving. Anyway, I heard that the cops have a description of the driver: dark jacket, royal blue ball cap, and sunglasses."

Which fit half a million guys in the Lower Mainland, Casey thought, and why would someone have to practise driving a van?

A thirty-something woman in a lime bathrobe and matching slippers shuffled down the hallway toward them. When she reached the living room, she squinted at everyone through smudged eyeliner, then yawned without bothering to cover her mouth. Judging from the size of her abdomen, she looked about seven months pregnant.

"Good morning, sweetheart." Paval turned to Casey. "This is my wife, Ursula."

"Hi," Casey said, noticing that Marie kept her gaze on the dog.

"Mmm." The woman headed for the kitchen.

"Ursula's a waitress," Paval said, "and working late shifts this week. She'll come alive after a mug of java."

Casey was amazed the woman could sleep with all these kids around. She watched the little girl wriggle off the sofa.

Paval removed a key from one of three dozen hooks near the door. "The police are finished with Jasmine's apartment." He handed the key to Marie. "Thanks for taking the animals. Birch and that awful half sister wouldn't have helped."

"Half sister?" Casey asked.

"Gabrielle O'Reilly," Paval answered. "She and Jasmine had the same birth mother, who lives in Parksville. Anyway, Gabrielle came to our door Sunday afternoon, looking for Jasmine. I had Jeremy with me, so I showed him to her. She barely looked at the boy. It was the coldest thing I ever saw."

"Where does this half sister live?" Casey asked.

"Also in Parksville."

"It's a three- to four-hour trip from Parksville to here, and ferries aren't cheap," Casey said. "The lady must have a good reason for coming to see Jasmine."

"Bull," Marie blurted. "She said she was Hannah's *real* daughter, and that Jasmine had better stay out of Hannah's life, if she knew what was good for her. Jasmine told her to go to hell."

"There's no way Jasmine would have backed down," Paval remarked. "After her adopted parents died, she started looking for her birth mother, and found her in July. She was so excited, I think she told everyone she met that day. It's too bad they never got a chance to meet face to face." Paval shook his head. "The poor woman had a stroke one week after Jasmine made contact with her."

For a landlord, the guy sure knew a lot about Jasmine's personal life. Had they been friends, or was he into gossip?

"I heard that Jasmine had been stressed lately," Casey said, turning to Marie. "Was Gabrielle the reason?"

"I don't know. She called me from work Tuesday and told me about that horrible shift you two had. She said she'd tell me something else later." Tears filled Marie's eyes. "That was the last time we talked."

Casey remembered that call. She was tempted to ask who Jasmine had plans with that night when Ursula reappeared, carrying an oversized coffee mug, a cigarette, and an ashtray.

She stared at Marie. "You're Jasmine's friend."

"Uh-huh."

Casey noticed Marie's tightening jaw, the way her lips pursed when something, or someone, displeased her.

"This is Casey," Paval said to Ursula. "She works with Marie and Jasmine."

Ursula plunked onto the sofa, put her things down, and then tied her blond streaks back into a ponytail. "Working with Jasmine couldn't have been easy."

"Ursula," Paval murmured.

"What? All I'm saying is that she could be quite the snob and smart mouth, which really put some people off."

Had Ursula experienced Jasmine's vicious side? Casey noticed the way Marie glared at Ursula, who was too busy lighting her cigarette to notice.

"Uh, darling?" Paval said, glancing at the smoke. "Remember what the doctor said."

"Just one this morning, one this afternoon, and one tonight, okay?" Ursula replied. "I'm trying, Pav."

"I know it's hard." He looked like he wanted to say more, but turned to Casey instead. "We're expecting a baby in four months."

"Congratulations," Casey said.

When the toddlers began fighting over a stuffed koala bear, Casey headed for the door, hoping Marie would take the hint and leave.

"If you need to hear something nice about Jasmine," Ursula said, "she was a good dancer. Always had willing partners at the Silver Groove."

"What's the Silver Groove?" Casey asked.

"A funky new retro club that plays disco," she replied. "Dancing's the only kind of exercise I like." She watched Paval referee the feuding toddlers. "Paval's favorite is housework and babysitting." The doorbell rang. "And chatting with losers."

Paval winked at his wife as he went to answer it.

"Jasmine collected business cards from her one-night stands," Ursula continued. "I saw them when we were feeding her animals. Probably repeat customers."

"Jasmine's dead, for god's sake," Marie said. "Show some respect."

"Who are you to tell me how to act in my own home?" Ursula took a long drag on her cigarette.

Paval shut the door. "Idiot." He waved a check at Ursula. "It's only half. Says he'll pay the rest next week."

"Kick him out if he doesn't."

"Do you personally know any of these alleged one-night stands?" Marie asked Ursula. "One of them could be a killer."

"Or not." Above Ursula's head, the smoke ring looked like a dissolving halo.

"We should get going." Casey picked up the cages. "Marie has a ton of things to do."

Marie opened the door and stepped into the hallway. Belle followed. Paval grabbed the leash hanging on the back of the door and attached it to the spaniel's collar.

"Nice to meet you, Ursula," Casey said.

"Back at ya."

Paval handed the leash to Marie. "Could you bring the key back when you're done?"

"Sure." Midway down the hall, Marie said, "I can just imagine what that hag told the cops about Jasmine."

How well had Marie, or anyone else, really known Jasmine? She'd gone out with Roberto, Wesley, and Marie's brother, so why not pick up guys in bars? The prostitution angle was possible, she supposed. Mainland didn't pay well, Jasmine had a child to support, and she would have needed money for veterinary school.

Marie inserted the key in the lock, hesitated a moment, and then opened the door.

Belle bounded inside and raced down the hall, as if searching for Jasmine. Casey put down the cages. Her nose twitched from the stench of over-ripe litter box. The living room was crowded with plaid furniture, six wire-meshed cages, and two rows of bookshelves stuffed with toys and CDs. The dingy beige walls were bare and the red shag looked in need of a good cleaning.

"Aren't there bylaws about the number of pets tenants can have?" Casey asked.

"Paval bent the rules for Jasmine." Marie sat next to a cat watching them. "Hey there, Muffin."

A furry creature darted past Casey, making her jump. "What was that?"

"Fagan. He's a ferret who gets into absolutely everything."

"I'm surprised Jasmine could save for veterinary school after feeding this bunch."

"She was good with money; bought her clothes from thrift stores." Marie stood up. "Her ex works for Canada Post, but only paid child support when he felt like it."

Casey ran her hand over a footstool embroidered with sunflowers. "This is gorgeous."

"Jasmine made it. She was terrific at needlework."

Casey shook her head. She really hadn't known the woman at all. Marie headed down the hall and entered the first room on the left. Casey followed. When she saw the sky-blue comforter with yellow roses, a chill swept over her. The photo of Jasmine asleep had been taken in this room.

Marie sat on the bed, tears sliding down her face as the cat leapt up beside her. Casey took another tentative step into the room. Oh geez, more cages. Two hamsters in each. She turned and saw sparkling, beaded clothes in the open closet. A red feather boa dangled from a hanger. The top shelf displayed yellow, blue, and pink wigs on Styrofoam heads.

"I take it Jasmine liked to dress up for the Silver Groove?"

"She once said she felt like a different person when she was on the dance floor . . . Freer and happier." Marie wiped her eyes. "She wanted to express that difference in her appearance. She wasn't a whore, let's get that straight."

"I never suggested she was," Casey shot back. "I didn't even know her that well."

"Jasmine had lots of different feelings and needs. Mostly, she just wanted a family to love, which Hannah would have given her."

Yet Jasmine apparently left her son with the landlord on her many dates and nights at the Silver Groove. She hadn't gone to Parksville to see her ailing mother. Had her desire for family been as strong as her desire to become someone else on the dance floor?

Marie reached for a book on the night table. "This is Noel's. I gave it to him for Christmas. He must have lent it to her."

Did she assume Noel hadn't slept here because Jasmine had been seeing other guys?

Muffin meowed and rubbed against Marie. "My brother loves to read." She patted the cat. "He's the funniest, sweetest man I know. A lot like Lou."

"Definitely a winner then."

"Noel will be at the funeral. Are you going?"

Casey hadn't thought about it. Maybe a proper goodbye would offer some peace to their tumultuous relationship. "If Stan gives me the time off." She watched the cat lick its paw. "Does your brother own a camera?"

"Everyone owns a camera. Why?"

"Corporal Lundy and I found a photo of Jasmine sleeping in that bed. I recognize the comforter."

"Where did you find it?"

"Lundy wanted to look in her locker. Stan asked me to open it for him."

Marie's red-rimmed eyes narrowed. "So, you decided to hang around and snoop?"

"It fell out of a magazine when I opened her locker. If she was intimate with someone, the cops will want to know."

Marie shook her head. "It's all so sordid."

"Especially when it could involve people at work, like David Eisler."

"I see the bloody grapevine's flourishing even after she's gone." Marie got to her feet.

"She died violently, Marie, and people aren't likely to forget that. Eisler's fists were clenched through the whole staff meeting, as if he was fighting to keep his emotions in check. I can't help wondering if he felt more than an attraction for her."

"Did the corporal make you his assistant?"

Casey's patience dissolved like cotton candy in water. "Remind me, why am I here? Oh yeah, that's right; to help you."

Marie swept thick hair back from her freckled face. "Sorry, but I'm still upset. I hardly slept last night."

"I understand that, but I didn't kill her, Marie. Jasmine wouldn't let me know her when she was alive, and I did try. What's wrong with wanting to understand how things were for her now?"

"It doesn't matter." Marie turned away.

"Yes, it does. It bothers me that the longer I knew Jasmine the more she hated me. I'd like to know why."

Marie picked up the cat. "Get over it, Casey."

"What do you think I'm trying to do?"

"There's a goldfish in Jeremy's room." She headed for the hallway. "Could you take it too?"

Casey had worked with Marie long enough to know when a discussion was over. "I think I can manage one goldfish and a few hamsters."

At least it was better than taking home Fagan the ferret.

# SEVEN

CASEY MANAGED TO KEEP HER food-laden paper plate steady while she nudged her way through Marie's crowded living room. She didn't really want to be here, but commiserating with grieving colleagues seemed like the right thing to do.

"It was a beautiful service, don't you think?" Paval Gallenski said.

Casey glanced at the landlord's moist eyes, and then focused her plate. "Yes, it was."

"What happened to your fingers?"

She wiggled three bandaged fingers. "Jasmine's pets." They didn't like her any better than Jasmine had. "Who knew guinea pigs could draw blood?"

Casey had been fostering the animals for a week and Marie still hadn't found them homes. She'd been so edgy lately that Casey had left the issue alone. She wished Lou was with her, but not everyone had been able to take time off work for the funeral. Two other supervisors besides Stan had attended, but Stan was the only one who'd come to Marie's house. David Eisler hadn't made an appearance at all.

"Why is that horrible ex-husband of Jasmine's here," Paval asked, "and who's looking after poor Jeremy?"

Casey followed Paval's gaze to the short, sulky guy dripping artichoke dip onto his shirt. Elliott Birch's shiny black hair was slicked back and his thick triangles of sideburn were decades out of date.

"Marie looked furious to see him at the church," Paval said.

"I noticed." Just before the service began, Birch had plunked beside Marie in the front pew. The disgust on Marie's face had made his identity easy to figure out.

"She shouldn't have let that asshole in her home," Paval said.

"She didn't. He slipped in with a group of people while Marie was talking to our supervisor." Casey watched Birch shovel food into his mouth. "Apart from the free food, why would he come at all?"

"The psycho likes to stalk and taunt. Whenever I saw him by Jasmine's balcony, I called the cops, but he always took off before they got there." Anger darkened Paval's face. "Maybe he's playing games with Marie because she didn't want to give Jeremy back."

"I take it you were good friends with Jasmine?"

"I am with most of the parents in our building. We've only had one tenant leave since we took over a year ago. When you offer people respect and friendship, they stay loyal. Jasmine was a great gal."

Casey focused on her plate so Paval wouldn't see her guilt. She hadn't shed many tears at the service, and she felt as out of place now as she had last week in the lunchroom. The peace and closure she'd hoped for hadn't happened.

"Do you know how the investigation's coming along?" Paval asked.

"No, the police have asked staff so many questions that no one wants to talk about it anymore."

"Birch should be their main suspect."

Better him than Mainland staff, Casey thought. After Roberto and Wesley were interviewed twice, employees started wondering if those who'd been closest to Jasmine were under suspicion. People had begun taking sides. In eight days, the laid-back, chatty work environment she'd enjoyed was now filled with suspicion and silence. Friendly expressions had grown furtive; greetings were reduced to half-hearted murmurs. She glared at Birch as he checked out the women while stuffing his face with cocktail sausages.

"Some people think Birch paid a coworker with his height and build to do his mail route the day Jasmine was shot," Paval said.

Casey had heard this as well, and didn't buy it. "Wouldn't someone at work or on his route have noticed the difference?"

"Maybe Birch bought their silence. What if he stole Noel's van the night before, hid it somewhere on his route, and then used it to kill Jasmine the next morning?"

"How would he know she'd arrive early to pick up Jeremy?"

"He could have been stalking her again; waiting for an opportunity."

"What the hell are you doing here?" Marie charged toward Birch.

"Trying to figure out which one of you killed my wife."

Casey and Paval exchanged pensive glances. Conversations stopped.

"As far as I'm concerned, you did, you abusive freak," Marie said.

Casey cringed. Why couldn't she just ask him to leave and be done with it?

"I've got witnesses who'll prove I didn't shoot her," Birch said. "If I had something to hide, I wouldn't be here."

"Get out!" Marie shouted.

Birch threw his half-filled plate onto the hardwood floor and started for the door.

"I know you did it," she called out.

"Marie, stop," a deep, unfamiliar voice called from behind a group of people.

Marie moved closer to Birch. Casey held her breath. The woman was far too emotional to think clearly. Casey put her plate on the table and headed for Marie. Stan and Roberto got there first. Each man reached for her arms.

"He's not worth it," Roberto said to Marie.

"Jasmine told me your delivery route's only a five-minute drive from her parish." Marie glowered at Birch. "You knew when and where she took Jeremy to preschool."

"Keep this up and you'll regret it, bitch." He flung the door open.

"You were stalking Jasmine!" She turned to her guests. "Jasmine saw him outside Noel's house one night."

Birch charged outside, and Marie slammed the door. "I know he shot her, I just don't know how he pulled it off."

A few people nodded, but Casey noticed that most of them looked uncomfortable. When would Marie learn to think before she opened her mouth? Declaring war on this guy wasn't smart.

"Marie?" Stan said. "Let's talk a sec."

Casey spotted Wesley Axelson near the staircase opposite the front door. She'd worked with Wesley twice on the rockhound assignment since Jasmine's death, but he'd barely spoken to her. His glum, hairy face stared at the floor. She'd never seen him look so sad.

Casey worked her way toward him. "How are you doing, Wes?" When he didn't look up she said, "You wouldn't be interested in owning one of Jasmine's pets, would you? I'm trying to find homes for her gerbils, hamsters, and guinea pigs."

"I'll think about it."

"Thanks." This was a surprise. He didn't seem like the pet type. "Hearing the priest talk about Jasmine made me realize how little I knew her. I did know that she liked to dance. Did you guys go to clubs?"

"Wrestling matches. She liked wrestling." He looked up. "She had her future all worked out. Was mature for her age, ya know?"

"Well, she had a lot of responsibilities." Given what happened the day they worked together, "mature" was the last word Casey would have used to describe her.

"Somebody has to pay." Wesley's eyes zeroed in on someone behind her.

Casey turned and saw Roberto. Wesley's scowl was burrowing into Roberto's back, but why? Surely he didn't believe Roberto had something to do with Jasmine's death, or was it the way he was flirting with Mainland's newest receptionist? With his hair trimmed, Roberto looked far more distinguished in his black suit than he did in grimy coveralls.

Wesley moved away from Casey, past three of Mainland's female drivers talking to the gorgeous, wheelchair-bound guy with the large blue eyes and dark blond hair hanging just below his jaw line. Even before he'd removed his suit jacket and revealed bulging biceps beneath his shirt, the women had been circling him. Casey first noticed him in the church parking lot when Marie assisted the man out of her SUV. Based on the way he and Marie communicated, and had held hands in the church, she figured he was Marie's brother. She now understood Marie's remark at Paval's the other day, about the killer probably renting a van to practise driving. Vans designed for paraplegics would have hand controls. Most thieves couldn't just jump in and take off. Noel turned and caught Casey watching him. She grinned, feeling like an idiot for staring.

"My brother's pretty cute, eh?" Marie said as she approached. "I'll introduce you."

Although her face was still flushed from her confrontation with Birch, Marie's tone was friendly enough. Still, there was an edge about her, as if one wrong word could set her off.

"Casey, this is my brother, Noel Merryweather."

"It's good to finally meet." He shook her hand. "I've heard a lot of nice things about you."

"Really?" Taken aback, she turned to Marie.

The doorbell rang. "I'll leave you two to chat." Marie hurried off.

"Marie says you're one of Mainland's best security officers."

"She does?"

Noel started to say something until his gaze drifted past her and his mouth clamped shut. Casey turned and spotted a man at Marie's door. Casey recognized him from the Integrated Homicide Investigative Team. A couple of days ago, he'd asked her about Jasmine's relationship with various colleagues. It was an awkward conversation. As the officer moved farther into the room, Casey saw Corporal Lundy follow him inside.

"What brings you two here?" Marie asked.

"We'd like to speak with Mr. Merryweather," the officer replied.

"Forget it, this day's about Jasmine."

"I'm sorry, but we wouldn't have come if it wasn't important."

"Give me a bloody break."

"It's just a few questions, ma'am." The officer gave her a cold stare.

Casey doubted anyone could make them leave until they'd done what they came to do. As the officers headed toward Noel, guests cleared a path for them.

Lundy nodded when he noticed Casey. "Miss Holland."

"Corporal."

In a firm, quiet tone, Lundy said, "Mr. Merryweather, may we have a private word?"

Noel attempted a smile. "Let's talk out back."

"No!" Marie rushed to his side. "You don't have to do this now."

Noel clasped her hand. "It's okay." He turned to Casey, "I hope I'll see you again."

"Me too." Lord, they weren't going to take him in for questioning at a funeral reception, were they?

Roberto opened the door for Noel and two German shepherds charged out of the kitchen, followed by Jasmine's cocker spaniel, Belle.

The crowded room erupted with barks and surprised exclamations as guests struggled to keep their cups and paper plates upright.

Roberto tried to grab one of the shepherds. "When's the last time you fed them, Marie?"

Marie's face was filled with anguish as she watched the officers follow Noel into the kitchen. It took a couple of minutes for people to corral the excited shepherds. Casey tried to rescue Belle who was under the table and turning in circles. Huge brown eyes looked up at Casey as if pleading for help. Once she'd coaxed the dog out, she headed for the kitchen. If the cops didn't like the intrusion, too bad.

No one was in the kitchen, but Casey heard voices outside. Paval and the German shepherds entered the room, followed by Marie. Marie rushed to the back door and peered out the window while Paval left the room.

When Marie turned to around her freckled cheeks were scarlet. "Can't those idiots see he's being framed?"

Casey didn't know what to say. "Aside from the van, what else do they have on your brother?"

Tears filled Marie's eyes as she shrugged. When she sat down, the shepherds padded up to her. One of them whimpered while the other nuzzled her hand. Belle curled up under the kitchen table.

"Marie, does Noel own a gun?"

"No, he hates firearms. He does live less than ten minutes from Jasmine's place."

Casey approached the window overlooking the yard. The officers were accompanying Noel to a police van.

"All the evidence is circumstantial." Marie smacked the table. "They have to see that!"

Casey turned around. "What do you mean by all?"

Marie hesitated. "They found Jasmine's blood on the driver's door of his van."

Not good. "Where did they find the van?"

"At a park near Noel's house." She wiped away her tears with her hands.

"I gather he has no alibi for the morning of the murder?"

"If he did, the cops wouldn't bloody be here, would they?"

Since Marie was upset, Casey overlooked the surliness. She wanted to ask what Noel was doing at the time of the murder, but the question wouldn't be appreciated.

Paval poked his head into the room. "Sorry to intrude, Marie, but I thought you should know that people are starting to leave."

"Thanks."

Casey followed her into the living room, where subdued colleagues hugged Marie and murmured goodbye. Casey couldn't help feeling sorry for her. She couldn't make Marie feel better, but she could at least help clean up. Casey started with the food Birch had dumped on the floor.

"You don't have to do that," Marie said after the last person had left.

"I don't mind. Housework helps with stress; so does yoga, but I figured you'd rather see me clearing plates than doing strange poses. Besides, I want to hear how you plan to prove Birch's guilt."

Marie picked up coffee cups. "I'll figure something out."

Casey wiped food off the floor with serviettes. "What if he really is innocent?"

"I'll check out the names on those business cards Jasmine collected. It's possible that one of her dance partners was some psycho who got the wrong idea about her. I should look into Eisler's activities as well." She headed for the kitchen. "I can't believe Roberto or Wesley would kill her."

"Me neither." Casey followed her. "Still, people are capable of anything, if provoked enough."

"Jasmine wouldn't provoke anyone to the point of murder, unless they were psychos to begin with."

Was she kidding? The day before Jasmine died, she'd provoked twelve-year-olds into wanting to beat her up.

"Jasmine might not have been killed by her ex, or by a man at all," Casey said. "Maybe the killer was the jealous girlfriend of someone Jasmine was seeing."

Marie began loading the dishwasher. "I wonder if Birch owns a handgun."

Casey sighed and shook her head.

# EIGHT

**"SEE, CASEY, ALL IT TAKES** is a little patience." Lou sat on the cushioned window seat in her living room and stroked the guinea pig in his arms. "They're real friendly when you give them a chance."

Since the most recent bite on her finger still stung, Casey had her doubts. "There might not be many more chances. Marie's dropping by any minute, so maybe she's found homes for them."

"You said she sounded upset on the phone."

"Yeah, but that's normal for her these days."

With any luck, the visit would be short. Summer was at her weekly Sunday brunch with her grandmother, and Lou, having stayed the night, would be leaving soon. All the activity and extra shifts since Jasmine's death had put Casey seriously behind on homework. She glanced at the library books and research notes on the kitchen table.

The intercom rang. Seconds later she was telling Marie she'd be right down.

"I should go too." Lou returned the guinea pig to its cage, then zipped up his hoodie.

This was one of those times when Casey didn't mind having to go downstairs to let visitors in. She hated the idea of Marie finding her way up here and invading her refuge. On her way down, Casey heard Summer's golden retriever bark from what sounded like the kitchen. When she and Lou reached the ground floor, Cheyenne jogged down the hall toward them, wagging her tail. Rhonda had promised Summer a dog for her birthday a few weeks back. During a trip to the SPCA, Summer fell in love with a four-year-old golden retriever. She'd made a good choice, though living with a dog still took some adjusting.

Casey opened the door and stared at Marie's nervous, blotchy face. "What's wrong?"

"Everything." Her voice trembled. "Someone fired a bullet through my son's bedroom window."

"Oh, no!" How could someone do that to a twelve-year-old? "Is he all right?"

"Yeah, Kyle wasn't hit, but he's still shaken." Marie stepped into the foyer. One look at Lou and her mouth fell open. "I didn't know you'd be here."

"I usually am," he replied. "Where did the bullet land?"

"In the wall above his head." She wrung her hands together. "It happened at three this morning. The breaking glass woke Kyle, and he was still dazed when he came to my room. He wasn't even sure what had happened."

"The poor kid," Casey said.

Cheyenne, who'd been sitting quietly, lifted a paw to Marie who gently shook it.

"He was telling me about the glass on the floor when a bullet hit my window." Her eyes glistened. "I pulled Kyle onto the floor and waited. God, he could have been . . ." She knelt down and started to stroke Cheyenne, but lost her balance and landed on her butt.

Casey and Lou helped Marie to her feet.

"Sorry. Still shaky, I guess."

They ushered her to the sofa in Rhonda's living room. Casey sat beside her, grateful that Lou did the same. She wasn't sure she wanted to deal with Marie alone.

"At least the girls weren't targeted. Their room's across the hall. Kyle's window is next to mine." Marie grasped Lou's hand. "Before I could call the cops, the phone rang, and a whispered voice told me to stop investigating Jasmine's murder or the bullets would hit my kids next." She slumped against his shoulder.

"I take it the cops haven't found the shooter?" Casey asked, watching Lou free himself from Marie's grasp.

"No." She straightened up. "The kids are at staying my mom's until the shooter's caught. I think it was Birch. The asshole must have found out that I've been checking into his alibi."

Cheyenne settled on the floor by Casey's feet. In a way, she was glad Marie was investigating on her brother's behalf. The cops' interest in Noel was troubling; using his own vehicle to murder someone mid-morning and abandoning it near his house was too stupid to believe. On the other hand, angry people did stupid things. Had Noel been angry with Jasmine about something?

"I talked to a couple of retired folks on Birch's mail route," Marie said. "They saw him at ten in the morning on the twenty-eighth, but so far I haven't found anyone who saw him at ten past eleven, when Jasmine was shot."

"I wonder if the bullets in your house came from the gun that killed Jasmine," Casey said.

"They couldn't have." Marie wrung her hands together. "They found a handgun under a bush near Noel's place the day after the murder. No word yet on whether it's the murder weapon."

Casey glanced at Lou. Marie hadn't told her this at the reception on Wednesday.

"Birch is trying to destroy my brother's life because Noel caught him stalking her a couple of times and told him to get lost."

"You think Birch took a break from delivering the mail to shoot his ex-wife?" Casey asked. "Then planted the gun and abandoned the van he stole the previous night?"

"Absolutely. He could have hidden Noel's van by the church and dumped it near his own car after the shooting. Traffic wouldn't have been heavy at that time of day, and he could have thrown a jacket over his uniform. The whole thing probably took less than twenty minutes."

Lou crossed his arms. "It would have required a hell of a lot of luck, what with traffic and potential witnesses."

"Maybe someone did see something, only we haven't found that person yet, which is why I'm here." Marie turned to Casey. "I need your help clearing my brother's name."

"He hasn't been charged with anything, though."

"I know that, but they've questioned him twice now. I have a horrible feeling that it's only a matter of time."

Casey frowned. "How do you know?"

Marie gave her an impatient look. "You're not the only one who knows people in the police department. Anyway, we really need your help."

Alarm ricocheted through her. A loud knock on the door offered a quick escape. Casey left the room, opened the door, and saw David Eisler jiggling car keys in his hand. What the hell was Mainland's VP doing here? How did he even know where she lived?

"I apologize for not calling first, but I was in the area." His Adam's apple bounced up and down. "There's something I wanted to ask you."

He couldn't do it at work? "Come in." She led him into the living room, where Marie was leaning close to Lou and murmuring something undecipherable. "We have a guest."

As Eisler entered the room, Marie and Lou's expressions froze. Surprise and displeasure flickered across Eisler's face. Cheyenne wagged her tail and sniffed Eisler's pant leg. Eisler looked at the dog with disdain and edged away.

Casey said, "Have a seat."

"Thanks." He nodded to Lou and Marie and sat without letting his back touch the chair. "I apologize for not attending Jasmine's funeral." His tan developed a reddish hue. "I heard it was a nice service."

"It was," Marie said, scrutinizing him.

Eisler lowered his head. Casey caught Lou's puzzled face and returned a haven't-got-a-clue expression.

"I'm looking after some of Jasmine's pets," Casey said. "Would you like to adopt a hamster, gerbil, or guinea pig?"

"My wife's not an animal person." He glanced at Cheyenne who had again settled down. "She's at a tennis tournament near here, so I thought I'd pop by to ask you where Jasmine is buried." He paused. "I'd like to send a wreath."

"She's in Parksville, where her mother lives," Marie answered, and gave him the name of the cemetery.

"Thanks." Eisler cleared his throat. "I was shocked to hear about your brother's arrest."

"He's not been arrested, just questioned," she answered, glancing at Casey.

"Yes, well, I understand that Jasmine associated with volatile people," Eisler remarked. "Apparently, one of them is a Mainland driver."

"Are you talking about Wesley Axelson?" Marie asked.

"I can't say, but since you've mentioned his name, I have seen the gun rack in his truck. Presumably, he has access to firearms."

Casey noticed Lou's disapproving frown. He and Wesley weren't buddies, but they'd worked together a long time and Wesley's integrity had never been questioned.

"Jasmine was shot with a handgun," Lou said. "You don't need a gun rack for that."

"Wes and Jasmine were good friends," Marie said. "There were no problems between them." She looked at Casey. "After last night's scare, I have to stop searching for proof that Birch did it, which is why I need your help."

"What scare?" Eisler asked.

As Marie filled him in, Casey wondered if blabbing everything was a smart move. Marie might be targeting Elliott Birch, but Casey's suspicions were broader.

"Noel's taken some friends' advice and hired a lawyer, but it's really expensive. Neither of us can afford a private investigator. Now that his van is crime scene evidence, he doesn't have a vehicle and can only afford to rent one for a week." Marie turned to Casey. "After that he'll be pretty much housebound, so I was wondering if you'd talk to the people I couldn't get to on Birch's mail route."

"You shouldn't ask her to get involved," Eisler said as he rose. "MPT staff have no business investigating the murder of a colleague." Eisler headed for the hallway. "Thanks for your time, Miss Holland."

Casey followed him out of the room. The guy had a point. On the other hand, what if he'd killed Jasmine and didn't want the truth coming out?

At the front door Eisler said, "Don't let Marie bully you. She's not thinking rationally."

"I know." That wasn't the problem: it was the guilt she'd feel for turning her down.

Eisler lowered his voice. "What if her brother really is guilty? Think about it. The police aren't fools."

"I realize that, and thanks for coming by."

When Casey returned to the living room, Marie was running her hand over the sofa cushion. "You could help and watch out for Casey at the same time. No one would have to know about your involvement, Lou. It'd be our secret."

Lou stood and gave Casey a hug. She didn't know why, except maybe to prove something to Marie.

"Eisler sure looked ticked to see us," Marie said to her. "If you'd been alone, I bet he would have asked you not to say anything about his visit. The jerk wouldn't want staff knowing he'd been thinking about Jasmine."

"Maybe."

"So, will you at least talk to Noel?" Marie got to her feet. "Then you can decide if you want to help."

"Why me?" She watched the way Marie's mouth twisted, as if reluctant to let the words out.

"Everyone knows you're a good investigator. You have the highest arrest rate, and you're resourceful and thorough." Her lips began twitching as if about to go into a spasm. "Look, I know we've had our differences, but my brother's future and my kids' safety are at stake, so will you please help us?"

"I don't know. I'm working double shifts, I'm behind at school, and Summer needs me at home more. Things aren't going great for her."

"I could take some of your shifts. Could you at least chat with Noel and make a decision then?" Marie pleaded. "That's not too much to ask, is it?"

Casey didn't appreciate the petulant tone. "I'll think about it."

"Well, if your commitments are more important than an innocent man's entire future, I can't fight that kind of selfishness."

"She's not selfish." Lou slid his arm around Casey's waist. "She's covered for you at work this past week, and is taking care of Jasmine's pets like you asked. She's also looking after this huge house and parenting a cranky teen who misses her mom. Worse, you could be putting a bull's eye on her and Summer."

"I'm sorry." The words caught in her throat. "I don't know what else to do."

Casey took a deep calming breath. If she turned Marie down, the woman would be hell to work with. Security functioned better with strong co-operation and communication among team members. Besides, she was curious to hear Noel's take on who killed Jasmine. Casey rubbed her temple. Deep inside her skull, a headache had begun to form.

"Look, I'll talk to your brother and then decide what to do."

"Thank you." Marie removed a slip of paper from her purse. "This is Noel's cell phone number." She handed the paper to Casey. "One more thing. I'm really worried about Jeremy. Could you drive by Birch's place and see if he's okay? He lives in Coquitlam, not far from Jasmine's apartment."

"How do you know?"

"I drove Jasmine out to his trailer one day because he wouldn't bring Jeremy back when he was supposed to. The trailer park's easy to find."

Pushy broad. "How am I supposed to do that without being recognized by Birch? He saw me at your house."

"Like I said, you're smart and resourceful." Marie handed her another slip of paper. "Here's Birch's address and mail route. I checked off the addresses I've already been to."

The front door opened and slammed shut. Summer stomped past the living room entrance. Cheyenne galloped into the hallway to greet her.

"Summer?" Casey called.

"I have to go." Marie started to leave. "I'll give Noel your phone number." She hurried out of the house, as if afraid Casey would change her mind.

Casey stepped into the hallway and found Summer slumped against the wall just before the kitchen entrance.

"What is it, Summer?"

"Grandma's bugging me to live with her again. She thinks my friends are a bad influence just because Tiffany and Ashley got caught smoking." Summer rubbed Cheyenne's head. "The principal practically forced me to say I saw them doing it."

Casey said, "Were you smoking too?"

"If I was, you would have gotten a phone call on Friday."

"There's no need for the snarky tone. So tell me, have you tried cigarettes before?"

Summer avoided eye contact. "No."

She never had been a good liar. "The truth, please." Casey rubbed her throbbing temple. "I promise not to scream in shock."

"I tried it once, but it nearly made me puke."

"How did your grandmother find out about the incident?"

"She lit a cigarette in the car and I asked her why she smoked, and she said it relaxes her." Summer scratched Cheyenne's ears. "I told her Tiffany said the same thing, and then Grandma started asking questions and she, like, totally freaked."

Casey rubbed her forehead. "Why didn't you tell me your friends smoked?"

"They didn't want me to."

Wonderful. She should have remembered that twelve-year-old girls with absentee mothers made secrets and acting out inevitable. Hadn't her own rebelliousness escalated after Dad kicked Mother out of the house? "You know you don't have to listen to your friends, right?"

"Yeah." Summer peered at her. "Are you sure I won't have to move in with Grandma?"

"You're staying with me, kiddo. We're a team."

Casey hugged her, well aware that Winifred's wants weren't as troubling as the impact of devious peers. Summer's old friends wouldn't have asked her to keep secrets, but clearly these girls did.

"Never do what anyone—especially friends—tell you to if it makes you uncomfortable, okay?"

"'Kay."

Casey thought of Marie. They weren't even friends and Marie was pushing her into an uncomfortable—maybe even dangerous—situation. "So," she said, stepping back, "how's the math homework coming?"

"Not good." Summer shrugged. "Can you help me?"

"I have to work on an essay, so how about we work together?"

Cheyenne started whimpering at the door.

"I'll take Cheyenne out first."

"All right, I'll meet you upstairs."

After they left, Casey leaned against the wall and closed her eyes. The headache could become a migraine. She didn't get them often; only when under major stress or after too much chocolate and wine. She'd take something for it now. There was too much to do to end up in bed for the rest of the day. On the upside, a chat with the gorgeous Noel Merryweather would be a welcome break from homework and endless chores.

Casey opened her eyes and stood up straight. Had she agreed to meet the guy because she was attracted to him? Was she that shallow?

"I should be off," Lou said, approaching her. "Is everything okay? Your cheeks are a bit flushed."

Oh, good lord; she'd been thinking about another man while her boyfriend was here. How tacky was that? "I'm all right. Summer had an argument with Winifred, but she's fine now. We're going to do homework together."

Lou kissed her. "Sounds like you've got everything under control."

She didn't know how to tell him that sounds could be deceiving, so she returned his kiss and said nothing.

# NINE

**THE MOMENT CASEY PARKED IN** the driveway of Noel Merryweather's single-story, sandstone home, the street became hidden behind a tall, evergreen hedge. The greenery stretched along the front of his property and down both sides. Privacy was a double-edged sword. No one knew your business, even when you needed them to. A wheelchair-bound person living alone, even one with Noel's upper body strength, could be vulnerable to danger. Judging by the intercom and the sign stating that this house was protected by a security system, Noel thought so too. The system hadn't kept him out of trouble, though.

Casey checked her makeup in the mirror, and then adjusted the pale blue chiffon scarf around her neck. She felt a little guilty for dressing up to see him, if one could call a scarf and a pair of silver earrings dressing up. At least she hadn't gone all out. Her navy pants and jacket were old.

She had to admit that part of her looked forward to this visit. Not in a swooning, Jello-legs way, but in a sexist, eye-candy way. If Noel wasn't a murder suspect, he'd qualify as one of life's guilty pleasures. She'd met great-looking, charismatic guys before and had even been attracted to some of them. Never in a million years, though, would she let herself fall for a man she didn't trust. Besides, she had a man, and Lou was the best.

Casey stepped out of her car and strolled along the cement walkway past a neatly trimmed lawn. She'd reached the ramp leading to the door when it opened and Noel appeared. Oh lord, he must have been watching her. Had he seen her check her makeup?

Her cheeks grew warm. "Hi."

Thanks to the black T-shirt hugging his biceps, Noel looked even more appealing than he had at the funeral. Today, his hair was tied back in a ponytail. A white husky stood next to his wheelchair.

"Thanks for being on time." He moved his chair back from the door. "Not many people even try these days."

"It's a thing with me." As the husky ambled up to her, Casey reached out her hand so the dog could sniff her. "Who's this?"

"This is Sam. Come on, buddy, let's give her some room."

As they backed up, Casey stepped over the threshold, shutting the door behind her.

"I really appreciate you coming by." He rolled toward the back of the house. "Marie said you're busy these days."

"No problem." Especially when she was with the poster boy for charming, ruggedly handsome studs. "You wouldn't be interested in owning one of Jasmine's pets, would you? The gerbils and hamsters are pretty cute, and the guinea pigs seem to have personalities."

"I'm not sure how Sam would take to them, but I'll think about it."

In the living room, floor-to-ceiling windows provided a wide view of a small lake and surrounding parkland.

"Wow," Casey said. "Who knew you'd find waterfront property thirty minutes east of Vancouver?"

"Como Lake's man-made. I always wanted to live near water and this place was more affordable than Vancouver waterfront."

Still, a property this size wouldn't be cheap. A pair of swans floated near tall reeds. Ample green space separated Noel's windows from a walking trail around the lake.

"Can I get you some coffee?"

"I've had my quota for the day, but you go ahead."

She didn't want to trigger another migraine. Yesterday's pain hadn't been severe, but one migraine usually made her vulnerable to more if diet and stress weren't monitored.

"I'm pretty wired myself," Noel said. "Make yourself at home."

Casey sat on a black leather sofa against the wall while Noel stayed on the other side of a rectangular, smoked-glass coffee table. She noticed the notepad on the table. Someone had drawn a cute goggle-wearing dolphin leaping out of the water. A mug and nearly empty coffee pot stood beside the notepad. Noel was angling his chair, presumably so he could see her and the lake. Sam lay down beside him. When Noel stared at her, her cheeks heated up again.

"I'm sorry," he said, glancing at Sam, "but you have the most gorgeous violet eyes I've ever seen."

"Thanks." His eyes were pretty great, too.

"Would you like to hear about my relationship with Jasmine first, or my alibi?"

"Let's start with your relationship."

"Jasmine and I were great friends more than anything."

"You knew each other well?"

"I guess that depends on what you mean by well." He paused. "I knew she was adopted and that her family situation was tough."

"In what way?"

He paused. "I'm not sure her family problems are relevant. Then again, how will you know unless I tell you?" Noel looked down. "Jasmine was molested by her grandfather when she was six. Jasmine's mother literally caught her father-in-law with his pants down in Jasmine's bedroom."

Casey took a quick intake of breath. "Oh, god."

"The father was afraid of scandal, so they sent the old man to live with a relative whose kids had grown and moved out."

"Unbelievable."

"Jasmine only talked about it once. We were watching the news and a story came on about the same type of thing. She got upset and, well . . ."

"Did she get any counseling?"

"No, and that's the other sick part. Some of the relatives decided Jasmine made it up. Said she wasn't real family and began questioning her gene pool. The rift in the family never healed and after her parents died, the relatives disowned her."

"That's friggin' awful."

"Yeah well, the twenty-first century hasn't banished ignorance." Noel looked out the window.

The bitterness in his voice made Casey wonder if he was referring to more than Jasmine's abuse. How many times had his disability forced him to confront ignorance?

"Jasmine must have built up a lot of anger."

"She tried not to let it get to her, but sometimes . . . Anyway, here's something relevant." Noel shifted in his chair. "The night before Jasmine's murder, she and I had a fight."

"Oh."

Given the nastiness between Jasmine and herself the day before she died, plus Jasmine's altercation with the girl on the M10, a fight with Noel would have been Jasmine's third confrontation in one day. She remembered Lou telling Jasmine that he'd never seen her lose it like that.

"Earlier that day, I heard Jasmine say she had plans for the evening," she said. "Were they with you?"

"Yeah, I brought over burgers and fries. After Jasmine put Jeremy to bed, we started talking." Noel began stroking Sam. "It turned into arguing."

"Sorry if this is too personal, but I have to ask, what was the argument about?"

Noel stopped stroking the dog and clasped his hands in his lap. "I told Jasmine that I thought she was compromising her values to get what she wanted, and what she wanted was money for veterinary school."

"How was she compromising her values?" Based on Ursula Gallenski's theory about Jasmine's business card collection, she thought she knew. Still, she wanted to hear his response.

"Jasmine liked to go to clubs, meet people. She swore she only had dinner with men, nothing more. Said the free meals helped her save money."

So, the man had asked his girlfriend if she was a whore? "Jasmine went ballistic, huh?"

Noel's mouth twisted the same way Marie's always did when a topic made her uneasy.

"Yep. But why accept free meals from strangers when she had to pay her landlord for babysitting? She wasn't gaining much and could have spent more time with Jeremy."

"Maybe she wanted nights off from parenting." Seeing the slight frown on Noel's face, Casey added, "I've been legal guardian to a friend's daughter for four months and I really miss my freedom. I mean, the job never ends. The best you can hope for is a break now and then."

Noel rubbed his chin. "Jeremy's a sweet-natured kid who smiles far more than he cries. Jasmine just liked to go out a lot."

"I'm sorry if this sounds cold, but do you think Jasmine told the truth about these celibate dates?"

"I don't know." He watched an elderly couple meander along a trail next to the lake. "I stayed the night after one dinner together. She never asked me for money."

That was more information than she had a right to know. "Have you ever taken pictures photos of Jasmine and Jeremy?"

"No, why?"

"Two snapshots were found in her locker. One was of Jasmine in her own bed, apparently asleep. The other was of Jeremy in a bathtub." Given the way Noel's jaw tightened, he didn't like this. Was he was thinking Jasmine had slept with her dates after all? "My next question's also personal."

"Go ahead."

"Did the thought of Jasmine sleeping with other guys make you jealous?"

"Yeah, it did."

"Even though you were just good friends?"

It took him a few moments to answer. "I had strong feelings for her."

The longer Casey watched him, the tougher he was to read. She usually interpreted body language well, yet Noel's signals were muddled. Sorrow was there, yet something else. Regret? Guilt?

"Did anyone hear you two argue that night?"

"Probably not. We kept our voices low so Jeremy could sleep."

"Marie said your van was stolen the night before the murder."

He nodded. "I heard the engine start about three in the morning. The van was long gone by the time the cops showed up." He shifted in his seat and glanced at his dog. "I knew I was digging a deep hole by telling them about the argument, but the truth seemed important. Naïve, huh?"

"The truth *is* important." Casey spotted a couple of trophies on a shelf across the room. The engravings were too small to read from here. "Did you notice anything unusual about Jasmine's mood a couple of days before her death?"

"She'd been grumpy most of the week. In hindsight, I should have picked a better time to confront her, but I'd been stewing about it for weeks and finally worked up some courage."

"Do you think Elliott Birch killed Jasmine?"

"Good question. All I know is that Birch threatened to hurt Jasmine if he didn't get more time with Jeremy. She was trying to obtain a restraining order because the jerk kept showing up outside her building."

Interesting that he didn't mention the part where he'd told Birch to get lost. "Marie wants me to check out Birch's place to make sure Jeremy's okay."

Surprise and worry flashed across his face. "She's probably hoping you'll find a murder confession taped to Birch's door."

"I'll settle for a quick peek through the window."

"Don't. Listen, Birch used to hit Jasmine. He's violent."

Alarm made her sit forward. "Violent enough to hurt Jeremy?"

"I don't think so. But if he got wasted, he could forget about Jeremy, and who knows what would happen."

"I've done surveillance work at dozens of bus stops. What if I used binoculars and took a quick peek at night?"

"Why would you do that when you're so busy?"

"Two reasons. A colleague's asked for help, and I'm worried about that little boy, too. I know how it feels to suddenly have an absentee mother, and I was much older than Jeremy when my mother left. A child feels the loss, regardless of age." Casey turned to the window and watched three Canada geese nibble the grass in front of the trail. She thought of Summer.

"Sam brought Jasmine and me together, you know," he said. "In early July, he got out and was hit by a car. After his surgery, Marie said she had a friend who wanted to be a vet. Jasmine helped me take care of him."

A woman walked a chubby basset hound along the trail. The hound started after the geese, but the woman reined him in.

"We have a golden retriever at home," Casey said.

"Marie mentioned that."

"Did she?" What else had Marie had told him about her? "Noel, please don't take this the wrong way, but you don't seem overly upset that someone's trying to frame you."

"I'm angry and scared; just don't show it much."

"You're sure different than your sister." She liked his smile. "Were you here when Jasmine died?"

"Yeah, I work at home; started my own company about six months ago, but it's been tough." The smile faded. "I design flyers, brochures and other promo stuff for people." He nodded toward the notepad on the table. "I'm working on a logo for a company that wants to sell snorkelling and scuba lessons to kids."

"That explains the goggles on the happy dolphin."

"It's all wrong. I'm supposed to target older kids. Off my game, I guess."

Casey watched him. "Marie hasn't told me much about you."

"I'm probably a depressing topic right now."

He seemed so resigned. Maybe she could help a bit; talk to people on Birch's mail route. At least Marie couldn't accuse her of selfishness or apathy then. What if new information led her back to Noel?

"Maybe I can find out if Birch really does have an alibi," she said.

"Casey, really; I'd steer clear of him."

"I plan to." The question was how?

# TEN

**"HERE IT IS—PULL OVER."** Casey leaned forward as far as her seat-belt would allow and read "Cedarbrook Estates" on the sign. She stroked Cheyenne who sat between her and Lou. "Lofty name for a trailer park."

Lou parked on the shoulder of winding, two-lane Dewdney Trunk Road. This was a quiet, residential area of Coquitlam. Casey scanned the tree-covered slope to her right. At the top of the slope, houses were built back from the road and overlooked the trailer park. A haphazard assortment of evergreens and bushes grew in front of the park. Through the foliage, Casey counted a dozen single-wides backed up against the fence.

"Interesting that Jasmine lived only a short distance away," Lou said.

Casey turned to him. "You knew where she lived?"

"Marie's car broke down a few weeks ago and she needed a ride there."

Irritation and jealousy was irrational. After all, Lou wasn't interested in Marie. Still, he hadn't told her, probably because he thought she'd overreact . . . Maybe she would have. Casey slung her arm over Cheyenne and got her face licked. The dog seemed to love this excursion. Cheyenne didn't go for car rides often, but tonight Casey needed her presence.

"We should have come earlier," Lou said. "The lights are off in some trailers."

"Summer was giving me grief." Casey fiddled with the binocular strap.

"Which is her own fault for not starting on homework when you asked."

Easier said than done. Summer had wanted to come along too, but Casey knew she had too much homework, so she'd called Mrs. Nally, who agreed to babysit. As Summer's whining escalated into a rant, Casey threatened to ground her for the rest of the week if she didn't get the work done. She hated resorting to threats, but Summer had been procrastinating all week. Besides, this excursion could be dangerous.

Casey focused the binoculars on the mobile homes. "I can't see any numbers on the trailers. They must be on the other end of the units." She handed Cheyenne's leash to Lou. "Let's walk the dog, dear."

"If Birch isn't home, you're not going to wait for him, are you? I have an early shift tomorrow."

"I'll just take a quick peek to make sure Jeremy's okay, then leave."

"That won't really tell you anything."

"Maybe I can find out if he has a bed to sleep in and isn't crying. At least I'll have tried to do everything Marie asked, which should get her off my back."

"Then let's get moving." He opened the door.

Casey understood Lou's irritability. He was tired and had tried to talk her out of this, but when he realized it wasn't working, he'd volunteered to come along.

After her talk with Noel yesterday, Casey interviewed three retirees on Birch's mail route. Each person had spotted him shortly after 11:00 AM, right around the time Jasmine was shot. Two seniors had even greeted him, and both were adamant this was the same man who delivered their mail every day. The information had been a little depressing, yet she still wasn't convinced of Noel's guilt.

Casey stepped out of the pickup, raised the hood on her jacket, and put on a pair of glasses. It wasn't much of a disguise, but it was dark outside and no one would see her clearly. As long as she didn't get close to Birch, she'd be safe. She tucked the binoculars under her arm and patted the dog.

"Okay, Cheyenne, act like you belong here, honey." With any luck, no one would pay attention to a couple walking their dog.

The entrance was wide enough for one vehicle to pass through. Evergreens flanked each side of the entrance. An asphalt lane divided the trailer park into two rows, with twelve units on each side. Casey shivered in the cool October air. Thankfully, it wouldn't take long to find Birch's place.

"What number is his trailer?" Lou murmured.

"Nineteen. Marie said he drives an old brown Dodge Dart."

Floodlights on either side of the entrance provided more light than Casey wanted. She pulled her hood farther down, then taking Lou's arm, strolled down the middle of the lane. Even in mobile home parks, trailers were not created equal. Two were double-wides. Some had tiny porches on the side. One enterprising soul had installed fancy pane windows with shutters and flower boxes. The place was quiet; no loud music anywhere.

Casey said, "Judging from the numbers, Birch's place must be near the end on the left side."

"Then let's stick to the right."

"There it is," she whispered. "Single-wide three from the end."

Light came from a small window on the side nearest them. Open blinds covered the larger window overlooking the lane.

"There's his car." Lou nodded toward the Dart in the carport next to the side door.

"I don't see anyone . . . Whoa." Casey stopped. "Who's that?"

A woman in a white T-shirt strolled past the large window at the end of the trailer. Casey could see her profile and dark braided hair, and then the woman moved out of view.

"She wasn't wearing anything under her shirt," Lou whispered.

"You noticed the double D-cup, huh?"

"Hard not to."

True. Strolling past the trailer, she glanced at the windows. All were too high to see if Jeremy was up and about. They reached the end of the lane and turned around. A gust of wind rustled Casey's open jacket. Leaves fluttered in the trees behind them. Buttoning up, she looked at the ravine on the other side of the fence.

"Let's see if I can spot Birch or his guest." She focused the binoculars on the smaller side window. "She's back in view and Birch is with her. Oh, he's kissing her."

Cheyenne gave a loud bark and took off down the lane.

"She's after a raccoon!" Lou started running.

Casey raced after him. "I thought you had her leash."

"I did, loosely."

Afraid of attracting attention by yelling the dog's name, Casey kept quiet. Cheyenne disappeared between two single-wides. They caught up with her whimpering in front of the chain-link fence bordering the ravine. Casey grabbed her leash. Movement on the other side of the fence made Cheyenne bark. Crap. Everyone in the park would know they were here.

Casey knelt beside her. "Hush, Cheyenne."

"The raccoon must have escaped through that hole." Lou pointed to a small opening at the base of the fence.

Casey glanced at various trailer windows and froze. "We're being watched."

Across the lane, a man stood in front of his window. Fighting the urge to dash for Lou's pickup, Casey strolled toward the exit. If they were lucky, Cheyenne's behavior wouldn't prompt anyone to confront them. She looked down the lane and saw a face peer out of Birch's window. Oh no, had he spotted them running past his place?

After they clambered into the truck, Casey said, "I wonder if the girl's just a hot date or his girlfriend."

"Does it matter?"

"It could. What if Birch had an accomplice shoot Jasmine? Someone who'd do anything for him."

"You really think that Noel is innocent?"

Casey stroked Cheyenne's head. "He seems sincere, and the evidence against him is a tad too convenient."

"Aside from sincere, what else does he seem?"

Casey hesitated. Why was he asking? "Quiet, polite, intelligent. The complete opposite of Marie." Lou's downcast expression surprised her. Was he a bit jealous, or did he think she was being naïve?

"Marie once told me he lost the use of his legs in a motorcycle crash," Lou said. "It seems he had a passion for Harleys and speed."

More candid conversations with Marie. How many other personal things had she shared with him? "Did she ever mention if Noel can get around with crutches or other support?"

"No." Lou headed east toward Vancouver.

"Marie will go ballistic when I tell her that two strangers gave Birch a solid alibi."

"You've dealt with her emotions before."

"That doesn't mean I'm looking forward to it."

→    →    →

**"NO FRIGGIN' WAY!"** Marie shouted over the phone. "Birch can't be innocent!"

While Marie railed, Lou put his arm around Casey. He'd told her he wanted to hear Marie's response to tonight's events. Casey had a hunch he also wanted to make sure she didn't become further involved.

"Are you sure you didn't recognize the woman with Birch?" Marie asked.

"Yes."

Marie sighed loudly into the receiver. "I'll call Child Protection Services and tell them about the woman. Maybe she's involved in Jasmine's death. Meanwhile, could you check out the half sister's alibi?"

"I don't think—"

"Since Gabrielle O'Reilly was in Coquitlam two days before the murder, and she and Jasmine argued, her activities should be investigated. God knows I can't count on the police to do it," Marie said. "Maybe Gabrielle brought the pistol from home and stalked Jasmine until she saw her chance. That would explain how she learned about Noel and his van."

"I can't do this anymore, Marie, I'm sorry."

"But you've put my brother in deeper shit than he was before, so can't you please help him out a little more?"

Casey did feel guilty about that. "What if Gabrielle has an alibi and I make things worse?"

Lou wandered toward the guinea pig cages.

The line was silent a few seconds. "It makes me sick to say this, but then we'd have to look at coworkers' alibis."

"No way, Roberto's a friend."

Lou turned to her.

"David Eisler isn't anyone's friend," Marie said.

"Do you have a reason for suspecting Eisler?" She watched Lou's eyes widen.

"After I had lunch with Jan today, yeah."

Casey had shared a few coffee breaks with Eisler's administrative assistant. She knew that Jan loathed her boss.

"The day Jasmine died," Marie said, "Eisler didn't come to work until noon, and Jan didn't know where he'd been. Apparently, he's been disappearing a lot lately."

"That doesn't make him a killer."

"It doesn't rule him out either. When he showed up at your place, something was obviously bothering his conscience."

"Then tell your brother's lawyer about it."

"We need more than one person working on Noel's behalf. He might have to sell his house to pay legal fees as it is. We really need your help, Casey."

"Let me think it over."

"Fine, but while you do, also think about what's happening to the life of an innocent man." She hung up.

Casey retreated to the window seat.

"What does she want you to do?" Lou picked up Ralphie the guinea pig.

"Check out Gabrielle O'Reilly's and David Eisler's alibis. It seems that Eisler's pulled a few disappearing acts from work lately."

As Lou stroked Ralphie, the critter began cooing. "Are you going to do it?"

"If I do, it won't be for Marie or Noel, but for Jasmine." She paused. "Noel told me some things about her past and, well, she deserves whatever justice we can get for her."

"What kind of things?"

Casey took a deep breath, and then told him about Jasmine's sexual abuse and the estrangement from her adopted family.

Lou kept stroking the guinea pig. "I had no idea."

"Maybe Noel's the only one who knew. Anyway, if I can help find her killer then maybe I should."

"What if Marie's only interested in making sure that people look at everyone except her brother? If you prove that Gabrielle and Eisler aren't killers, who will she tell you to go after next? Wesley and Roberto?"

"What's so wrong with establishing their innocence?"

Lou rolled his eyes and put his hands on his hips. "Casey, you've worked with Roberto and Wesley a long time. If you start checking into their alibis, you'll create bad blood."

"Shouldn't the search for truth count for something?"

"Sure, but it's not your job to find it."

"The police think they have their man, and Noel can't afford to hire a PI. Will it really matter if I ask a couple more discreet questions?"

Lou's eyes narrowed. "It will if that question freaks out a murderer. What if someone fires a bullet through Summer's window?" Lou placed Ralphie in Casey's lap.

"You're right."

"Can I stay the night?" he asked. "I'm too beat to drive."

"You don't need a reason, and thanks for coming with me tonight."

He headed for the bedroom. "I'd do anything for you, you know that."

She did know and was grateful. As Lou left the room, Ralphie nestled in her lap. Casey touched his fur and began to pat him. His soft cooing made her smile. Ralphie had never cooed for her before.

"Maybe things will work out, huh, Ralphie? Maybe I can prove Noel's and Roberto's and Wesley's innocence, and then things can get back to normal. What do ya think?"

A warm wet puddle seeped into her jeans.

# ELEVEN

THE MOMENT CASEY SPOTTED THE warring groups of kids exchanging dagger stares, she knew this would be a bad shift. The freckled boy who'd been stealing glances at the pretty, leather-jacket girl over recent shifts was now sporting a crimson face and staring at the ground. The object of his affection stood behind her brother, preventing Casey from seeing her face. What had happened?

As usual, the jackets ambled toward the M10 bus in front of their rivals. The brother, whom she'd learned was called Mo, maneuvered his sister to the head of the pack. The girl's large sullen eyes met Casey's and then looked away. Behind them, the ball-capped bunch jogged up the steps and sought their usual seats at the front.

As Casey headed for a spot midway between the groups, she scanned the passengers' uneasy expressions. Marie perched on the edge of her seat, near the jackets, and watched every move they made. The tension swirling around these kids was so strong that one could almost feel an electrical charge.

A couple of elderly passengers bristled in their seats across from Casey. The lady in the aisle seat gripped her cane with both hands and murmured to her friend. The women shook their heads at the group in front. From his driver's seat, Lou turned and gave Casey a wary glance. She returned a don't-like-this-either look. She noticed that he didn't look at Marie. Neither of them had spoken to her this morning, nor had Marie asked for Casey's decision about helping Noel, which was just as well. She still hadn't made up her mind.

As the freckled boy rummaged through his backpack, he glanced at the pretty girl.

Mo sprang into the aisle. "Scott, you freak! How many times do I gotta tell you get your ugly eyes off her!"

Casey and Marie both stood.

"Sit down right now," Marie said to Mo.

Scott moved down the aisle as his hands curled into fists. "She's the one who asked for my notes."

"Liar!" Mo charged forward until Casey blocked his path.

"Both of you, sit down. Now!"

The boys glowered at each other.

"Hello?" Casey waved at Mo. "Are you listening? If you don't do as I ask, you walk home, understand?"

Mo's friends started to rise.

"I said sit down!" Marie ordered.

The sister remained seated, her pensive eyes focused on the boys. As Scott and Mo stepped closer to each other, Lou slowed the bus. Standing sideways in the aisle, Casey held out her arms until her fingertips touched their chests.

"The driver's pulling over; last chance, guys." If they were listening, they didn't show it. "Did you hear—" Casey found herself sandwiched between the grappling boys. Someone tugged on her jacket. Spittle landed on her cheek. "Stop it!" She squirmed to free her arms.

Scott was a little shorter than her, Mo half a head taller. The bus lurched to a stop, knocking the boys off balance and enabling Casey to wedge her elbows against their chests.

"Enough!" Marie yelled. "You two are out of here."

"All right, kids," Lou called out. "Back off."

The boys kept scowling at each other. Neither of them moved. Marie reached Mo just as Scott shoved past Casey and drove his fist into Mo's stomach. Mo lost his balance and grabbed Casey's arm. She tried to break free but couldn't and went down with him. The back of her head thudded against the floor.

"Casey!"

She heard Lou's voice, but her eyes were shut tight as waves of pain ricocheted around her head. Mo's leg jostled under her right thigh and then slid free. The back of her head felt like it was on fire. She opened her eyes, but wavering black dots made it hard to focus on the faces hovering above her.

"Casey?" Lou asked. "Are you okay, hon?"

"I think so." She closed her eyes again, hoping the dots would go away. Her head pounded so hard she could only hear snippets of chatter.

"Sorry, lady." Mo's voice. "I didn't do it on purpose."

"Move back!" Lou reached for Casey's arm. "Let's get you up."

Hands slid under her back. Pain shot across her skull as they helped her sit up.

"Where are you hurt?" Lou asked. "It's your head, isn't it?"

"Yeah."

Casey squinted while hands clasped her back and shoulders. Nausea rippled through her as she was lifted off the floor and into a seat. Perspiration dampened her upper lip.

Lou's warm hands touched her cheeks. "I'll call for an ambulance."

"Don't, I just need aspirin and a cold pack."

"You might have a concussion."

"Sorry about what happened." Scott looked panic-stricken as he appeared in front of her. "I didn't mean for you to get hurt."

Before she could respond, Lou turned on the kid. "She asked you to stop and you didn't!" He removed a notepad from his shirt pocket. "I want your name and phone number."

After Scott mumbled the information, he and his friends left the bus.

A minute later, Marie reappeared. "The other bunch is leaving too. I've got their names and numbers."

Lou turned to Casey, his eyes filled with worry and what she thought might be fear. "You look so pale."

"I'm fine." She tried a smile, but it made her feel worse. "I blew it again."

"You took action from the get-go, and of course you couldn't manhandle a bunch of kids, especially after what Jasmine did."

Casey started to shake her head, but it hurt too much. "I'm off my game. Can't even catch the stupid rockhound."

"Lou, it looks like the fight's continuing outside," Marie said. "It'd be safer if we call the police rather than intervene."

"Then do it," he said as he studied Casey. "Let me check your head."

His fingertips began a gentle probe until she gasped with pain. "You're already swelling. I'll get a pack from the first aid kit."

Casey took slow, deep breaths to calm her churning stomach. Around her, passengers muttered things she couldn't quite decipher.

As Lou returned, he hit the pack, then shook it. "Here, it's already getting cold." He handed the pack to Casey. "I don't have any painkillers, but I'll see if Marie does." He squeezed her hands. "Are you sure you don't want to go to the hospital?"

"Absolutely." Carefully, she held the pack against the part that hurt the most.

"Okay, call if you need me."

Marie joined them. "Are you all right, Casey?"

"I will be."

"I've got Advil." Marie dropped a couple of pills in her hand, then gave her the bottled water she always carried.

"Thanks." After she took the pills, she closed her eyes once again. Gradually, conversations faded as she blocked out everything and tried to relax.

She had no idea how much time had passed when Marie shouted, "Look at that!"

Casey sat up slowly as they turned into Mainland's yard. She didn't notice anything unusual until the bus was facing the garage at the back of the depot. Someone had spray painted "Remember Jasmine" in large red letters across the top of the building.

Lou helped her off the bus. When they reached her Tercel, he stopped to examine the back of her head. "You're growing one hell of a goose egg. Are you sure you don't need a doctor?"

"The Advil's helping." She had no intention of waiting in an emergency room for god knows how long. "I should go in and write my report. Stan will want it asap."

"You can do it from home. Didn't you just buy a laptop so you could send reports from anywhere?"

"Good point. I just need a few more minutes before I get behind the wheel."

"I'll get you another cold pack, and then I should drive you home."

She didn't want to leave her car here. As Lou hurried toward the admin building, Casey leaned against the Tercel and gazed at the sign. Given everything she'd learned about Jasmine this week, how could she not remember her?

She surveyed the silver compact parked next to her. Didn't Eisler's assistant, Jan, drive one? Or was it the new girl? Shit, why was she even thinking this way? The vehicle spotted at the murder scene probably didn't belong to Mainland staff at all.

"Do you like the sign?"

Casey turned to find Roberto strolling up to her, his lunch pail and apple in hand. A grease streak ran down his right pant leg. "Well, it's big. Who made it?"

"That's a mystery." Roberto's amused expression faded as he stepped closer to her. "You look hung over."

"I got caught between two kids fighting. Fell and hit my head."

"Marie must have had a shitty time too." He glanced over his shoulder at the admin building. "I passed her a minute ago and said hi, but she wouldn't even look at me. I wonder if she heard about the pool." He bit into his apple.

"What pool?"

Roberto chewed a few moments. "After Marie started telling people about the VP being hot for Jasmine and that he didn't have an alibi, some of the guys started a murder pool."

"Tacky, Roberto."

"They're just trying to help the morale around here. Anyway, Birch is the heavy favorite despite his so-called alibi, though my money's on Eisler."

"Why?"

Roberto's expression became grim. "The night before Jasmine died, she called me around midnight. Said that Eisler had phoned her earlier, while Noel was there. The jerk wanted to meet her for a drink, but she turned him down."

"Have you told the police?"

"I will when I need to." He took another bite of apple.

"What does that mean?"

"Nothing much." Roberto shrugged and kept chewing.

"Hey, would you like to take one of Jasmine's hamsters or guinea pigs off my hands? I can't keep them."

"No, you know me; I'm rarely home."

The smell of diesel fumes from an incoming bus made her feel nauseous. Nearby, three clerical staff stopped walking to look up at the sign.

One of them turned to Roberto and said, "Nice work."

"It wasn't me," he replied.

Casey wasn't surprised that none of the women spoke to her. Word had gotten around that she was helping Marie find the killer, and staff had started avoiding her. Not everyone wanted their alibis investigated by a colleague. A handful of curious employees kept asking Casey what she knew. Those were the people she'd started to avoid. Still, the truth had to come out. Secrets and lies had a way of piling so high that, sooner or later, they'd topple. The larger the stack, the more harmful the crash. Her parents' deceptions had taught her that.

"Who else is on the suspect list in your pool?" Casey asked.

"Jasmine's half sister, Gabrielle. Marie told us some nasty things about her."

The big mouth had been busy. "Did Jasmine say anything about Gabrielle's visit the Sunday before she died?"

"I didn't even know her half sister was in town until Marie told me a couple of days ago."

"Did you notice any irritability in Jasmine before her death?"

"Jasmine was her usual sweet self." Roberto watched the clerks head for their cars.

Sweet self? Hadn't he heard about her and Jasmine's nasty exchange on the stairwell the day before she died? On the other hand, Jasmine had been friendly with Roberto the same morning.

"Roberto, did you ever take any photos of Jasmine?"

He smirked. "Why, do you want one for your album?"

"Funny; I saw a picture of her recently and was wondering who the photographer was."

"Maybe it was professionally done."

"No, she looked asleep in her bed."

Roberto's eyebrows shot up. "Freaky." He took another bite of his apple. "We never talked about her love life. Just went dancing and out for beers." He glanced at Casey. "You know me. Never serious, always moving on."

Casey knew about Roberto's commitment phobia, and how it often clashed with his inability to be alone. Therapists could build careers on Roberto's relationship issues. She wouldn't be surprised if he'd slept with Jasmine.

Behind them a familiar voice said, "Miss Holland, why are you inter-rogating my staff?"

Casey and Roberto turned to find David Eisler standing by the hood of her car. His arms were crossed and his pinched mouth formed a thin line on his perma-tan face. How long had the jerk been eavesdropping?

"We're just chatting," Roberto said.

Casey knew Roberto didn't like the VP. Eisler probably didn't like him either.

"Are you aware that Miss Holland's helping Mrs. Crenshaw look for a suspect to replace her brother?"

"Not at Mainland," Casey replied.

Lou joined them, his expression wary as he looked at Eisler and Roberto.

"I don't want you asking employees about Jasmine." Eisler glared. "Understand?"

Was he afraid of the truth? "Yes." Casey bit back her anger as she accepted the fresh pack from Lou.

"Roberto, I want that sign gone today, is that clear?"

"I didn't do it."

"I don't care. You work in the garage, so get rid of it." He charged inside the building.

"What flew up his ass?" Roberto asked, turning to Lou. "How's it going?"

"It's going."

Casey wondered why he was staring at Roberto's apple. Why was Lou avoiding eye contact with him? These two were buddies.

"Do you guys think Noel's innocent?" Roberto asked.

"Don't know," Lou answered.

Roberto moved closer to Casey. "You aren't really digging for dirt on the guys Jasmine was seeing, are you?"

"No."

"Then why were you asking me about photos and Jasmine's mood and stuff?"

"Just curious. You know what I'm like."

"Don't start playing games, okay?" Roberto's voice was quiet.

"I'm not." Casey placed the cold pack on her bump. "You came up to me, remember?"

"Maybe that was a mistake." He started to leave, but stopped. "If you want to play detective, then check out Eisler's alibi. Remember when I got back from the root canal that morning and you wouldn't tell me what was going on?"

"Yeah." She still felt bad about that.

"Well, I saw him barrelling into this lot just after you took off, acting all nervous and scoping the place out like he was worried about being seen. He sure didn't look happy when he saw me watching him." Roberto tossed his apple on the ground. "Makes you wonder, don't it?"

Roberto marched to his Corvette. In the decade she'd known Roberto, he'd never been angry with her, and she felt bad for making a friend feel like a suspect. Casey sighed as she watched him peel out of the yard.

"He has no right to judge you or David," Lou said, "especially when he just lied."

"What?"

"He couldn't have had a root canal that morning." Lou looked at the discarded apple. "I saw him eating an apple right after he got to work. Just thought about it when I saw him toss that one."

"As soon as he got out of his car, he asked me where Jasmine was." She lowered the cold pack. "Think I should tell someone?"

"I guess." He turned to the sign. "I find it hard to believe Robert would . . ." He shook his head.

Casey placed her hand on his shoulder. "I'll phone Lundy, though he might want to talk to you."

"Whatever."

She knew Lou hated the thought of ratting on a friend as much as she did. Yet this wasn't about swiping office supplies, or using Mainland's computers for personal reasons. This was murder.

# TWELVE

**RELIEF SWEPT THROUGH CASEY. SHE** was moments away from a hot bath and her comfy bed. When she turned off Violet Street and saw the familiar green Subaru parked behind her home, relief vanished. What the hell was Summer's grandmother doing here on a Wednesday? Winifred always came by on Sundays. Anxiety propelled Casey out of her car and up the steps. When she flung open the back door, the smell of frying liver and onions made her gag.

"Finally home, are you?" Winifred removed two dinner plates from the cupboard.

"It was a tough shift." If Winifred was cooking, things couldn't be that serious. "What brings you here? Is Summer okay?"

"No, my granddaughter is not getting proper care."

Casey tossed her purse and cold pack on the kitchen table. "Where is she?"

"In her room, presumably doing homework like I told her to." Winifred picked up a wooden spoon and began stirring the food.

Summer hated doing homework before supper. "What's happened?"

Winifred smacked the spoon on the stove, and then turned around. "Her principal called. It seems that Summer left the grounds at lunchtime without permission and didn't return."

"He should have called me."

"Apparently, your cell phone wasn't on."

Oh, hell. She'd shut it off before she boarded the M10. The ride was short and the job had required her full attention. Besides, Summer was supposed to have been in school. She turned the phone back on.

"What did Summer say about it?"

"That she'd been in a park with those delinquents she calls friends, and I could smell the smoke on her."

Casey stared at the tall, scowling woman. "Summer's friends smoke, but she doesn't. We talked about it last Sunday."

Winifred gave her a sarcastic smile. "You assumed she was telling the truth?"

Casey had counted on it. The thought of Summer resorting to more lies and deeper acts of rebellion was too unsettling to think about.

A pouting Summer shuffled into the kitchen, Cheyenne trailing after her. Casey gaped at the dirty jeans drooping below Summer's hips and the pink tank top exposing her midriff. She hadn't gone to school looking like that. In fact, Casey hadn't seen those clothes before.

Winifred said, "The principal told me that you've been late for school a number of times, Summer, and have been using foul language in class." She removed a pack of cigarettes and a silver lighter from her sweater pocket. "What do you have to say for yourself?"

"Everyone swears," Summer replied. "It's no big deal."

Casey hoped she didn't look as shocked as she felt.

"Is that supposed to justify your behavior?" Winifred lit the cigarette.

Cheyenne padded up to the stove, raised her snout, and sniffed the air.

Winifred glared at the retriever. "Must that dog be in the kitchen?"

Casey clapped her hands. "Come, Cheyenne."

Wagging her tail, the dog approached her.

"You look awful," Summer said to Casey. "Bad day?"

"You could say that." Casey sat as she briefly described what had happened on the bus.

When she was finished, Summer slumped into the chair opposite her and said, "People need to fight sometimes."

"Speaking of your job," Winifred said as she switched off a burner and placed her cigarette in a saucer, "I heard that one of your colleagues was killed."

"Yes."

Winifred didn't approve of her career choice, nor did she like Mainland Public Transport's "lousy service and painfully hard seats." Whenever the company received bad press, she always brought it up. Since Winifred used public transit only as a last resort, Casey didn't care what she thought.

"Summer shouldn't be exposed to violence." Winifred poured boiling water out of a pot. "Hasn't she had enough—"

"No one should be exposed to violence," Casey interrupted. "But it happens."

"Summer needs stronger supervision." Winifred shook potatoes onto two dinner plates. "So, I've moved into Rhonda's room."

Casey and Summer exchanged horrified glances. If Rhonda had wanted her mother living in the same house with Summer, she would have asked her.

"You can't do that!" Summer sat upright.

"Moving in is unnecessary," Casey said, trying to stay calm.

"You're both wrong." Winifred dumped broccoli next to the potatoes. "Look, Casey, you're not here when she comes home from school, and now you're working nights, too. No wonder this child is running wild."

"I'm not!" Summer shouted.

"The extra shifts are temporary." As Casey's anger rose, her head pounded harder. "Lou or Mrs. Nally are always with her if I'm working late."

"A man," Winifred muttered. "You let a man stay with her. That has to stop."

"Winifred, I really don't think—"

"I help pay the taxes on this drafty old house, so I'm entitled to stay here now and then. I've already moved my things in and that's that."

The old bat had a point. When both of the second floor studio suites were rented out, the income covered Rhonda's mortgage and living expenses. When Rhonda had trouble keeping tenants, as she often did, Winifred helped out. This year, she'd paid the property taxes. Casey had hoped to pay for everything herself, but she'd shelled out big bucks to have the plumbing fixed, which had nearly cleaned out her savings.

When Mother died four months ago, she didn't leave a will, just a boatload of debt which would take time to sort out, according to the lawyer Casey had retained. Her deceased father's West Vancouver home—which she'd only learned about last spring—apparently came with its own set of problems, including two joint owners (one recently deceased) with legal and financial problems. She was still furious with Dad's former business partner for misleading her about this.

"You want to spy on me!" Summer jumped up. "Make me live your way, but I won't! I'm not old and boring like you."

"You've become much ruder since Casey took over," Winifred said.

Summer started to say something, but Casey raised her hand. "Summer, no."

"You need stronger guidance," Winifred added, scooping liver and onions onto a plate, "especially when it comes to appropriate clothing."

Casey wanted to pull every gray curl out of the woman's skull. "I can help her with the clothes, Winifred, but the serious mistakes are happening at school, not here."

"Behavior at school reflects behavior at home, or doesn't university teach you that?"

Casey's patience wilted. "I'm her legal guardian. She'll live by my rules, not yours."

Winifred dropped Casey's handbag and pack onto a chair. She plunked the plate in front of Summer.

Casey tried to ignore the brown chunks and chopped bits of limp, translucent onion. As a kid, she'd been forced to eat this stuff whenever her own grandmother had decided she needed an iron-enriched meal. She'd sit at the table, long after everyone had finished, until those cold, slimy chunks finally wobbled down her throat.

"I'm not eating that shit!" Summer yelled.

"Summer!" both women replied.

Tears dripped from her chin as she turned to Casey. "I'm not living with her!" Summer swept the plate onto the floor and tore out of the room.

Before anyone could react, Cheyenne was gobbling up the liver.

"Stop that disgusting beast!" Winifred ordered.

Casey reached for Cheyenne's collar. "Come on, Cheyenne. Onions will make you sick. Let's get you some real food."

"I might as well wash this filthy floor. Don't you give that child chores?"

"She's been busy with school."

Summer had neglected too many chores since Rhonda left. Letting her get away with it was a mistake, but Summer had been so devastated by Rhonda's departure that Casey had been afraid to argue over it. Ensuring that she finished her homework was enough of a challenge.

"I gather you're also too busy to keep this place clean?" Winifred asked.

"I take care of my own apartment and vacuum the rest of the house.

I also keep this kitchen tidy. Summer looks after her room and we do the rest when we can."

"Her bedroom is a pigsty. That child is deteriorating into an irresponsible and unstable delinquent. If we don't intervene, she'll become as violent as her mother. Rhonda's actions have nearly destroyed her!"

Leave it to Winifred blame her own daughter. For as long as Casey could remember, Winifred had criticized Rhonda for every flaw, mistake, and mishap.

Winifred took a drag on her cigarette.

"If you're staying, you can't smoke inside," Casey said. "This house is my responsibility and everyone has to follow the rules. If our two tenants see you smoking, what will keep them from doing the same?" She picked up her purse and cold pack. "And wouldn't it be less hypocritical if you didn't smoke in the first place?"

Casey marched out of the room, wondering how in hell she'd calm down a troubled twelve-year-old sinking into more misery and rebellion. Summer probably felt that every adult close to her had either betrayed her or let her down. The awful part was she wouldn't be wrong. She hadn't spent nearly enough time with this child lately.

She hadn't really wanted the rock-throwing assignment, but Stan had insisted. The guys in security—most of them part-timers—weren't available, and Marie was a single parent who wouldn't work nights unless absolutely necessary. What choices had she or Summer been given over Rhonda's absence? What options did they have now?

As much as Casey hated the idea of sharing a house with Winifred, the woman was Summer's family. If grandmother and granddaughter spent more time together, maybe they'd find a way to bond or at least understand each other better. Besides, help with housework would be welcome.

Casey had nearly reached her apartment when her cell phone rang. She stopped and rummaged through her purse.

"Hello?" No response. "Hello?"

"Stop investigating the murder."

The raspy, hostile whisper took her breath away. "Who is this?"

"If you don't, then Summer dies."

Fear slithered up her spine and tickled the hairs on the back of her neck. "I'm not investigating! I just asked a couple questions for a friend, and I'm done."

"You've been warned." The line went dead.

Casey plunked onto the carpeted step. She stared at the screen's "Call One" message. She tried star sixty-nine to find the number and heard "We cannot complete your call as dialed." She looked up the call log. No numbers displayed. This is what she got for buying the cheap package. Her cell phone wasn't listed in any directory that she knew of, nor had she added it to her business card. The only people who knew this, or about Summer, were friends and coworkers.

Casey thought she'd be sick.

# THIRTEEN

**CASEY DROVE WEST ON BROADWAY** and, for the fourth time this morning, glanced in her rearview mirror to make sure she wasn't being tailed. Despite her curiosity and questions about Noel's guilt, investigating Jasmine's murder any further would be a horrible risk.

However, Wesley Axelson called her landline last night and said he wanted to talk about the murder, in person. Wesley had never phoned her before. He even apologized for calling. In the eight years she'd known Wes, he'd never asked her for a favor, let alone apologized for anything. Still, she told him she wasn't investigating for Marie anymore. Before she could tell him why, he said, "But this is real important, and you're one of the few people at Mainland who can keep her mouth shut. See, the cops showed up at my place with a warrant. When Marie finds out, she'll think I'm the killer, which I ain't."

At that point, Casey's curiosity had taken over and she'd agreed to see him. She just wished she'd insisted on a better meeting place than a gym filled with pro-wrestling wannabes. Again, she glanced in the rearview mirror. Since yesterday's anonymous threat, she'd been fighting paranoia. She'd contacted the cell phone provider to see if they could trace the call. After several transfers and what felt like a long wait, she learned that the call came from a pay phone in Coquitlam. Noel lived in Coquitlam. So did Elliot Birch.

Every time Casey thought of the threat to Summer, the bump on the back of her head throbbed like some sort of warning beacon. She hated being forced to look over her shoulder. She hated that an anonymous coward was trying to control her through fear, which was turning into anger, and her anger inevitably propelled her into action.

After Wesley's call, Casey phoned Marie to tell her about the threat and to insist Marie tell coworkers that neither of them were investigating Jasmine's murder anymore. Casey would do the same when she got to work.

"I'm sorry about the threat," Marie had said. "Why is the freak targeting our kids?" And then she said what had also been on Casey's mind. "I wonder if someone from Mainland really did kill Jasmine. David doesn't like kids, you know. He and Wesley wouldn't have anything to do with mine at the company picnic last summer. I've also heard Roberto brag that he never plans to have any."

Casey had heard this, too. She still found it hard to believe that any of them could shoot Jasmine and threaten children's lives. For the first time in a long while, Casey didn't look forward to going to work. Mercifully, Stan had told her she wouldn't be needed on the M10 bus until further notice. After yesterday's ruckus, Scott and Mo were temporarily banned from MPT buses, and Stan felt that Marie could handle things alone.

The words "Barley's Gym" were printed in large bold letters across the second floor windows of the building to Casey's right. She eased into a parking spot at the front of the long, two-story structure. Shutting off the engine, she studied the gray stucco exterior. The main floor had no windows on this side of the building. The double black doors reminded her of an entrance to a cave, one occupied by grunting, sweaty men.

Casey rotated her shoulders to loosen stiff muscles. While struggling out of bed this morning, she'd realized her head wasn't the only body part that had smacked the bus floor. She stepped out of the car and, scanning the area, headed for the entrance.

She'd barely opened the door when the smell of sweat and old gym socks made her gag. Good lord, when was the last time fresh air circulated in here? How many billions of bacteria were thriving on benches, mats, equipment, and doorknobs? She tried not to breathe too deeply. Ten strides away, a match was taking place in one of two rings. Between the rings were punching bags and a weight training area. Straight ahead, a hallway led to an exit at the back of the building.

A dozen guys sporting layers of hulk-like muscles stood around the ring watching the match. A guy with biceps as thick as her thigh hit the ground hard, groaned, and rolled onto his back. Wesley. He jumped up and growled at his opponent like an angry bear. Wesley lifted the guy, turned him upside down, and rammed his head into the mat. Some guys cheered while others yelled obscenities. The referee ended the match. Spittle and sweat flew from the loser as he swore at Wesley and stumbled around the ring.

"There's a girl in here," some genius said.

Ten gigantic heads turned to her.

"Gotta beat the groupies back with a stick," a short, stocky guy added.

"Casey!" Wesley called and climbed out of the ring. Grabbing a towel, he wiped his dripping face as he trudged toward her.

Casey sat on a bench near the door. Wesley sat beside her and rubbed his head with the towel.

"If you want to shower first, go ahead," she said. "I can wait outside."

"Nah." He watched two combatants enter the ring to their left. "I heard Birch's alibi is real. Is that true?"

A wrestler sporting two dozen corn braids strutted past Casey and winked at her. Ignoring the gesture, she turned to Wesley. "It is, and Marie still believes her brother's innocent."

"I was here the morning Jasmine died; got witnesses to prove it." Wesley's flushed face peered at Casey. "It was my gun that shot her."

Casey sat up straight. "Say again?"

"The Glock they found near Merryweather's house was mine. That's what the cops were looking for." He glanced at the match. "I keep the guns in boxes on the top shelf in a closet. There's so much shit up there that I didn't know they were missing until the cops came."

"How many guns are we talking about, Wes?"

"Two Glocks, a twenty-seven and a thirty-five, and a Winchester seventy hunting rifle."

Sweat dripped from the ends of his hair. Casey shifted away from him. "Are they registered?"

"Just the rifle."

"I take it your prints weren't on the murder weapon?"

"They should have been." He gave his face another wipe. "The pistol was wiped."

"Were there any signs of forced entry to your place before the murder?"

"I didn't see nothin', but that don't mean much. I always keep the windows open; sometimes forget to close them when I go out."

Had David Eisler put the police onto him? "What did the cops say to you?"

"Nothing much. I don't know why they haven't busted me."

Casey stared at the concrete floor. Thick mats were placed around the rings and under the exercise equipment, but otherwise the floor was bare.

"Who knows that you keep firearms in your apartment?"

"A few people at work, including Marie. The broad butted in while I was talking to a couple of guys about the Glocks a few weeks back." Sweat trickled down his chest and arms. "That busybody has to know everyone's business."

No kidding. "Who were you talking to at work?"

"Joel and Savio. We go huntin' now and then."

Both of them were sixty-something mechanics on the verge of retiring. As far as Casey knew, they were devoted family men. "So you didn't talk to Roberto de Luca?"

He scowled. "No."

An ugly thought occurred to her. What if Wesley was guilty? What if he'd resented Jasmine for dating other men and had concocted this story to divert suspicion? A wrestler crashed to the ground. "Wes, do you have issues with Roberto?" She watched his brows form a long, damp line. "I saw the way you looked at him at Marie's place, so what's up?"

"I heard the asshole lied about his alibi, and you should know that Jasmine was way more serious about him than he was about her."

A wrestler somersaulted over the ropes and hit the mat hard. Casey's goose egg throbbed. "How serious?"

"She loved the douche bag." Wesley's overheated face darkened. "Hung out with me to make de Luca jealous 'cause she knew he don't like me."

"Were you okay with this?"

"She was straight up about it. I respected that."

The guy with the braids swaggered past Casey again, but she didn't make eye contact.

"Every time de Luca asked her out she got her hopes up," he went on. "The jerk knew it and did it anyway." Wesley spat on the floor.

Oh, gross. "You should be telling the police this, not me."

"I did. They don't give a crap." Wesley peered at her with an unsettling intensity. "But you do or you wouldn't be helping Crenshaw."

"I told you last night, I'm out of it now."

And was he telling the truth? Wesley claimed he was here the morning

Jasmine was shot. Maybe he was. This bunch didn't look like they'd go out of their way to lie for him. On the other hand, they wouldn't want bad publicity for their gym either. Clearly, Wesley had cared for Jasmine, maybe even loved her. If she'd rejected him, would he have gone over the edge? Casey shifted a little farther from the guy.

"I keep hearing that you're good at finding out stuff," he said. "Don't you want to know the truth?"

"Yes, but—"

"The cops asked if I hung out with Noel or knew where he lived. I think they're starting to wonder if he and I were in on it." Wesley wiped his face. "De Luca could have framed us. He knows where we live; knew Jasmine's routine too."

"I don't see why Roberto would kill her. The guy never had problems breaking up with women, and why would he wipe your prints off the gun?"

"He probably wasn't wearing gloves." Wesley glanced at the action in the ring. "What if de Luca dumped her, so she threatened to cry rape or something?"

"Would Jasmine stoop that low?"

Wesley shrugged. "Chicks in love." He shook his head. "They get screwed up."

True. Casey thought of what Rhonda had done for love, and for love gone wrong.

"All she'd have to do is accuse him. Eisler hates de Luca so he'd fire his ass," Wesley stated.

"Did you know that Eisler was interested in Jasmine?"

"Hell, yeah. Jasmine told me the freak had been phoning her. Maybe the cops should ask that candy-ass shithead where he was when she was shot."

"They probably have." Wesley seemed eager to point the finger everywhere but at himself.

"You could find out where he and de Luca were that morning."

"I'm sorry, Wes, but no. When you called last night, I didn't get the chance to tell you about the phone threat."

When she finished filling him in, Wesley draped the towel over his shoulders. "What'll you do about your girl?"

"I'm arranging for protection." She'd told Summer there'd been a threat to hurt her, not to kill her. Although Summer had tried to act cool, Casey could tell that the news shook her up.

"She's got no dad?"

"No." Wesley didn't need to know the sordid cliché about the drug-addicted mother whose father could have been one of several johns.

"If she needs protection, a couple guys here have done bodyguard work and wouldn't mind the extra bucks."

Did he actually care about Summer's safety, or was this just an act? "Thanks, I'll keep that in mind." She watched one wrestler pin another down, prompting more shouts and obscenities.

"Jasmine had a real mom who's been sick, and a half sister, Gabrielle, who showed up at her place two days before she was shot," Wesley remarked.

Casey turned and saw sweat fall from the tip of his nose. "Jasmine told you that?"

"Yep, she came over Sunday night with her boy." He wiped the back of his neck. "The half sister told her to stay away from the family. So, if the sister stayed in town and followed Jasmine around, she would have seen her friends and known where some of us live."

"How would Gabrielle know about the guns in your closet? Did you show them to Jasmine that night?"

"Why would I? Someone at work could have tipped off the broad."

Unlikely. Two more guys strutted past Casey. She kept her focus on Wesley. "Did you notice a change in Jasmine's mood that night?"

"She was griping about family shit and how her apartment sucked."

"Really? I thought Jasmine had it made there. She could keep as many pets as she wanted and had a babysitter close by."

"She wanted to be near her mom."

"Gabrielle wouldn't have liked that."

"Jasmine wouldn't give a crap."

"True."

The combatants in the ring threw themselves at each other with a ferocity that made Casey cringe.

"What if Noel really can walk?" Wesley asked. "What if he could reach the top shelf in my closet?"

"I've wondered about that as well." Casey slung her purse strap over her shoulder. "Noel and Jasmine were just friends, though, weren't they? Like you and Jasmine."

"No, not like me and Jasmine," he shot back. "Noel asked her to marry him. She showed me the ring Sunday night. Wanted to know what I thought."

Whoa. Neither Noel nor Marie had thought to mention this. "What did you think?"

"That it was a bad idea. She didn't love him. She planned to give it back."

Noel had told Casey he and Jasmine argued Monday night. What else had the guy kept from her? "Why did Jasmine even take the ring?"

"She said she'd been too shocked to say anything." He rubbed his hair. "I think she wanted to use it to make de Luca jealous."

"Did she show Roberto the ring?"

"Don't know, ask him."

Two spectators began yelling and shoving each other. A third man tried to break them up. Casey moved to the door.

"Could you still help?" Wesley followed her. "I wouldn't blab it around like that mouthpiece you work with."

No, she couldn't, but to tell him on his own turf without appearing to think it over wouldn't be smart.

"I'll let you know. Have you ever taken photographs of Jasmine?" She should probably let it go, but that picture of a sleeping Jasmine still bothered her.

"Casey, in all the years we've worked at MPT, have you ever seen me with a camera or even talk about stupid photography?"

"It's just that I saw snapshots of Jasmine and Jeremy in her locker. The one of Jasmine was taken in her bedroom, and she looked like she was asleep."

Wesley scowled. "Ask de Luca about it."

She already had. Why wasn't anyone admitting they'd snapped a picture of Jasmine at a vulnerable moment? Maybe Noel hadn't been honest about that either.

# FOURTEEN

**RELUCTANT TO ATTRACT ATTENTION, CASEY** slipped into Mainland's admin building and hurried upstairs to the security department. Between this morning's disturbing chat with Wesley and yesterday's phone threat, she felt as vulnerable on Mainland property as she did anywhere else, and increasingly suspicious of coworkers. Roberto had lied about his alibi, Wesley owned the weapon that killed Jasmine, and Marie was desperate to exonerate her brother. Then there was the VP's puzzling behavior.

First, a solemn David Eisler had come to her home asking about Jasmine's gravesite, but later he didn't want her name mentioned at work. Worse, he'd been harassing Jasmine. No wonder Mainland Public Transport felt more like a landmine-filled war zone than the safe, cheerful place she'd enjoyed and respected.

As for Noel, she understood why he'd kept his proposal to Jasmine a secret, but she sure as hell didn't like it. Did Corporal Lundy know about it? Did Marie?

And what else had Roberto lied about? She was so disappointed in him. She knew he craved female company, but to string Jasmine along so he wouldn't be alone was disgusting. His New Westminster apartment was only a fifteen-minute drive from Jasmine's place in Coquitlam. Had Jasmine threatened to make his life a living hell if he didn't commit to her?

Casey entered the long rectangular room. Mercifully, it looked like everyone had left for lunch. She removed a Post-it note stuck to her computer screen. "Timesheets by 2:00 PM today! No excuses! ASS." Amy Sarah Sparrow had struck again.

"Good, you're here." Marie entered the room, carrying a coffee and muffin.

"Just to do my timesheet."

"Is Summer okay? How's your head?"

"She's fine; my head is sore."

"Maybe you should call Noel to let him know you've quit the team."

Team? Is that what she called it? "Why can't you tell him?"

"I thought you'd want to tell him yourself. Noel said you and he hit it off."

Meaning what? That they were best buds now? "You can tell him." She removed a notepad from her purse and flipped to the page of recorded hours.

"Look, I know you're afraid for Summer but, as a courtesy, you really should call him."

"Courtesy, huh?" Casey stood. "Why didn't you or Noel tell me he'd proposed to Jasmine? That would have been courteous, Marie."

Marie frowned. "What are you talking about?"

"Jasmine showed someone the engagement ring from your brother, and told the friend she was giving it back."

Two cherry patches spread over Marie's cheeks. Behind her, a couple of clerks strolled into the room. They nodded to Casey and wandered past them.

"Noel said that he and Jasmine fought the night before she died," Casey added, lowering her voice. "He skipped the part about proposing to her."

"That's because it didn't happen. Who told you this crap?"

"Talk to Noel. As I said, I'm not investigating Jasmine's murder anymore." Casey sat and turned to her computer screen.

"It can't be," Marie murmured. "Noel and I have always been close. He never mentioned being in love, and Jasmine was my best friend. She told me everything."

"Obviously not." Casey opened the template. "Since Jasmine turned him down, maybe you were the last person she wanted to discuss this with." Casey looked up. "Did Jasmine ever say anything about moving to Parksville?"

"No, why?"

"No reason." She turned back to the screen. Wesley seemed to know more about Jasmine's life than Marie did. Maybe the friendship between the two women was more one-sided than Marie wanted people to think.

"Did Roberto tell you all this garbage?"

"I have to get this done, Marie."

Through the palms and dracaena dividing security from the other departments, Casey spotted the accounting staff going about their business more quietly than usual.

"Wesley told you, right?" Marie asked. "He was really into Jasmine. Probably wants to divert the blame from him, seeing as how it was his gun that killed her."

Casey caught the employees' stares. Great, everyone at Mainland would know before the day was over. "How do you know about the gun?"

"Noel's lawyer found out." Marie crossed her arms. "Maybe you should ask your source why he made up that shit about an engagement."

Casey smacked her hands on the desk. "How many times do I have to tell you that I'm done investigating?" Her voice rose. "I'm going to email everyone and post a copy on the bulletin board. Should I pin one to your shirt so you'll remember?"

A giggle came from the end of the room.

The cherry patches on Marie's cheeks darkened. "You think Noel's guilty, don't you?"

"I don't know what to think."

Marie was a master at manipulation and generating sympathy. Everyone at work took her side after each of her three divorces, believing what she'd said about being victimized by "vindictive" men. No one had heard the ex-husbands' stories.

"I know about your altercation with Eisler yesterday," Marie said. "Did you check his alibi?"

"What about Eisler's alibi?" Stan said as he stepped out of his office.

"I'm trying to convince Marie that I'm not investigating Jasmine's murder anymore because of what happened last night."

"Anymore?" Stan put his hands on his hips.

"Could we talk privately?" Casey asked.

"Sure."

Ignoring Marie's scowl, she marched into Stan's office and shut the door. Too edgy to sit, Casey paced the room. How much should she tell him? He wouldn't be pleased to hear that she'd been interviewing people and lurking outside Birch's home. Stan had worked hard to earn the co-operation of police departments throughout the Lower Mainland. He wouldn't want his team interfering with a murder investigation.

"I got an anonymous call yesterday, warning me to stop investigating, or Summer would die."

Stan recoiled. "Is Summer okay? Where is she?"

"At school. I'm picking her up and taking her to Lou's mom's tonight. Barb's offered to let Summer stay there as long as she needs to. They've got a security system and a rottweiler, and two of Lou's buff younger brothers still live at home."

"Did you tell Corporal Lundy about the threat?"

"Yes." He'd lectured her about the danger of meddling in police business. "Please don't tell anyone, including Marie, where Summer is."

"Okay, but it sounds like you've worried the killer, so exactly how much snooping have you been up to?"

Casey highlighted the interviews with people on Birch's mail route and her talk with Noel. When she reached the part about visiting Birch's trailer, Stan whistled and scratched his beard. She stopped the story there.

"Why was Marie asking about Eisler's alibi?" he asked.

"If I tell you, you could wind up in an awkward position."

"Tell me anyway."

Casey gripped the back of the wooden chair. "It seems that no one knows where Eisler was the morning Jasmine died. He also came to my house on Sunday and asked where Jasmine's grave was."

Stan leaned forward. "You're joking."

"No. He said he wanted to send flowers, but since Marie and Lou were with me, that's all he said, though I wonder if he wanted to say more." She watched Stan push his keyboard away and rest his elbows on the desk. "The night before Jasmine died, Eisler asked her out for a drink, which she refused. Apparently, that wasn't the first time he'd called her."

"Can you back this up?"

"Roberto de Luca can. She told him about Eisler's last call that night, and Wesley told me about other calls he'd made."

"Rude Wesley Axelson?"

"He and Jasmine were friends."

"Eisler, huh?" Stan blew out a big breath of air. "Married and on the executive team. How stupid is that?"

"I've heard that he's taken to disappearing without telling anyone where he's going." Casey paused. "Yesterday he overheard me talking to Roberto about the murder and basically ordered me to shut up about it."

Stan's gaze drifted to the bonsai on his desk. Casey could almost see his mind thinking things through. She turned to the window and watched buses coming and going in the depot. Above the garage, someone had painted over the "Remember Jasmine" sign, as if memories could be so easily banished.

"Let me ask you something," Stan said. "Do you think Marie's brother is innocent?"

"I have no idea." Casey glanced at the door. "But as long as the murder's unsolved, this isn't a fun place to work."

"You got that right. I'll see if I can find out where perma-tan man was that morning, but this is strictly for my own peace of mind."

"Absolutely, and thanks."

"Just take care of Summer and pray the killer's found fast."

"I will." She stood. "By the way, would you like one of Jasmine's gerbils, hamsters, or guinea pigs?"

He gave her a brief smile. "I'll ask my wife."

"Thanks." Casey stepped outside.

She'd barely made it back to her desk before Marie said, "I've been thinking."

"Please don't."

"The shooter wore a ball cap and sunglasses," Marie went on. "It could have been a woman. If *you* made inquiries about Gabrielle's abili, no one would know."

Why wouldn't this idiot listen?

"So could you or Noel's lawyer."

"I've told you before, the lawyer costs too much." Marie scribbled something on a piece of paper. "Gabrielle knows my name and voice, but *you* could talk to her. Give a false name and make up a story to find out where she was when Jasmine was shot."

She placed the paper next to Casey's keyboard. "Here's the landlord's number. You met Paval when we collected her pets. He has Gabrielle's home number."

"Why would he have it?"

"After Jasmine died, he thought he should break the news to Hannah, so he got her number through directory assistance, and Gabrielle answered the phone. It turns out Hannah's still recovering from her stroke at some rehab facility. Gabrielle barely cared that her half sister had died, which is all the more reason to check her out."

"You just don't listen, do you?" Casey began working on her timesheet.

"Just this one last thing, Casey, and then I promise to make sure everyone knows you're done helping us."

Bloody unbelievable. "What if Gabrielle's the killer, Marie? How will that protect Summer?"

Marie's mouth twitched. "Don't talk to her directly. Ask someone she works with."

"Where does she work?"

"I don't know if she even has a job. I just assume she does."

Tension shot across Casey's sore shoulders and her goose egg throbbed. "Please, Casey," she mumbled. "Where's the justice for Noel and Jasmine?"

Admittedly, she was curious about Gabrielle's alibi, yet she had to think about Summer. Casey looked beyond the plants. Human resources personnel had returned from lunch and everyone at the end of the room was still unusually quiet.

"Can I ask you something?" Casey kept her voice low. "And I want the truth."

"What?"

"Can Noel walk with crutches or any other device?"

"He's never had any interest in trying, I swear."

Judging from Marie's downcast eyes and the resignation in her voice, she seemed sincere. So, how could Noel have pulled himself up, retrieved two pistols and a rifle from a high shelf in Wesley's closet, and then carried them to his van without help?

"Is there more evidence against Noel you didn't tell me about?"

"I told you everything and, like I said, it's all circumstantial. The stolen van, the gun found near his property. Everything."

Again, Casey thought of the threat. "Sorry, but I have to think of Summer, and you, above all people, should understand that."

"Wouldn't it be better for all our kids if the killer was caught fast? With your skills, you can make that happen. You can't just selfishly walk away. I mean, I'm the first to admit I'm a coward, but you're not."

Placing her hands on the arms of her chair, Casey rose. Her heart thumping, she moved close to Marie. Uncertainty clouded Marie's eyes and she stepped back.

"That is not the first time you've called me selfish, and I really resent it," Casey said. "I am *not* selfish. I've already done more for you and your brother than anyone else around here. And don't ever use Summer to manipulate me, understand?"

"Fine." Marie headed for her desk. "Whatever."

Casey tried to focus on her timesheet, but she was too furious to think. She had to get out of here. Scrunching the paper with the landlord's number into a ball, she marched out of the room. While Casey jogged downstairs, it occurred to her that Marie might have a point about helping find the killer fast. Looking over her shoulder, waiting for the bad guy to be caught, wasn't her style. Should she at least phone Paval? No one would have to know, and she really was curious about Gabrielle's alibi. Why else would she still be carrying this ball of paper?

In the lunchroom, Casey poured herself a coffee and sat at the back of the room. She removed her cell phone from her purse, flattened the paper, and memorized the number. After she'd come up with a suitable story to tell Paval, she started pressing digits.

Paval answered on the second ring. After pleasantries were exchanged, Casey asked him if he knew Gabrielle's phone number. "We have Jasmine's personal belongings in her locker, and my supervisor said I should contact next of kin. Since Jasmine's mother's been ill, I thought I'd try Gabrielle."

"I doubt she'll pay to have anything delivered to Parksville."

David Eisler sauntered in at the other end of the room. When he spotted Casey, her muscles tensed. She looked out the window. Half a dozen conversations were going on in here, so he wouldn't be able to hear her from this distance.

"Casey, are you still there?" Paval asked.

"Yes, do you know if she's employed?"

"I've no idea, but since she showed up on a weekend, she could be. All I have is a home number. Give me a minute and I'll get it for you."

Eisler stared at her as if he expected her to do something wrong. At last he turned away and poured himself a coffee.

When Paval returned and recited the number, Casey scribbled it on the sheet. Eisler started toward her, but three drivers at a table said something to him and he stopped. Casey swept the paper into her purse and held her breath.

"Thanks, Paval, and just one more thing: did Jasmine ever say anything about moving away?"

"No, but I wouldn't be surprised if she'd wanted to get away from her ex, and she did talk about spending time with her mother."

"That reminds me, did you ever see a woman with Birch during these stalking episodes?"

"There had been someone with him a couple of times over the past month, but this person always stayed in the car. I can't honestly say if it was a him or her."

Eisler was still with the drivers. Since Paval knew a lot about what went on in his building, she said, "Did Jasmine ever mention a man named David Eisler calling her, or coming by her place recently? He has light brown hair, a tan, and nice clothes."

"Hmm, my wife said something about a man in a suit lurking by the building's entrance about a week before the murder. Ursula saw him when she was getting the mail and asked what he wanted. He said he was looking for Jasmine, so she assumed he was one of Jasmine's nightclub acquaintances."

Casey kept her gaze on Eisler. "Did he give a name or say anything else?"

"I don't know. You should probably ask Ursula."

"Is she around?"

Eisler's conversation ended and he headed for her. Damn.

"She's working days this week. Today she's meeting a friend at the Silver Groove after work."

The club Ursula had mentioned when Casey first met her.

"Thanks, bye."

As Eisler drew nearer, she sat up straighter. "Miss Holland." Eisler's icy tone reached the table before he did.

"Mr. Eisler." She sipped her coffee.

Eisler rarely sat with people. He seemed to prefer standing and looking down at them.

"Are you feeling better after yesterday's mishap on the M10?"

"Pretty much." She picked up her coffee and stood.

"Have you completed an injury report?"

"I will this morning." She'd felt too lousy to complete the form yesterday and had forgotten about it until now.

Anxious to get out of here, Casey left the room. She couldn't shake the feeling that Eisler had another reason for approaching her and that it had everything to do with Jasmine.

# FIFTEEN

**FOR SUMMER'S SAFETY, THE PRINCIPAL** had allowed Casey to park close to the door so Summer could enter the car quickly. As she waited inside the school's exit, Casey watched, through the glass in the door, for anyone who looked like he shouldn't be on the grounds. Her cell phone rang.

"Hey, it's Lou. Mom says you can bring Summer over anytime."

"Great." Barb's house was only five minutes from her place. "I'll take her after supper."

"Think she'll want to go?"

"Given that Winifred moved in yesterday, she'll be running out the door." Casey scanned the grounds. "Would you like to go dancing tonight? Summer will be safe and neither of us have early shifts tomorrow, and the club I have in mind plays your kind of music."

"Disco? Really?"

"Totally." Casey grimaced. Much as she loved Lou, she didn't share his taste in music.

"I thought you hated disco."

"Yeah well, things have been stressful lately, and I wanted to make up for dragging you to Birch's trailer." The strain Casey had sensed in their relationship since she'd agreed to help Marie hadn't eased, and the danger to Summer had made things worse. "We could use a fun night."

"I'm kind of tired. How about a rain check?"

Casey glanced down the empty hall. "That's not going out, and this is Thursday, so maybe the place won't be too crowded."

"Is going out that important to you?"

The bell rang and kids began rushing out of classrooms. "There's another reason, which is to talk to Jasmine's landlord's wife about David Eisler."

Casey spotted a frowning Summer shuffling down the hall. She hadn't been happy when Casey told her she couldn't hang out with friends after school, but Casey wanted her close to home.

"What about Eisler?" Lou sounded edgy.

"Ursula Gallenski apparently talked to a man at her building who wanted to see Jasmine. Based on Paval's second-hand account, it sounds like him, but I need to talk to her to be sure."

"I thought you'd quit investigating."

"It's just one simple question."

"We need to talk about this."

"Oh, Summer's coming, I've got to go."

Lou could talk all he wanted, but he wouldn't change her mind. One way or the other, the truth about Eisler had to come out.

**"MUST YOU USE** the back door?" Winifred glared at Casey as she and Summer stepped into the kitchen. "It's very disruptive."

Utensils covered the counter, and Winifred was wiping out a drawer.

Casey wrinkled her nose at the smell of bleach. "Since I park my car out back, it's also very convenient."

"Where's Cheyenne?" Summer scanned the kitchen and hallway.

Winifred kept wiping. "In the basement, where she belongs."

"Thanks a bunch, Grandma." She dumped her backpack on a chair and headed downstairs.

The Winifred invasion was twenty-four hours old and she'd already overstayed her welcome. Cheyenne bounded into the room and jumped up on Casey.

"Her leash was tied to the stair railing," Summer said, glaring at Winifred.

"Animals don't belong in kitchens or bedrooms. They're filled with disgusting germs and parasites."

Summer rolled her eyes. "Casey thinks it's okay, right, Casey?"

"Well, let's compromise." She calmed the dog down. "How about if Cheyenne stays out of the kitchen during meal times?"

"See?" Summer stuck out her tongue at her grandmother.

"Summer, stop it," Casey said.

"What on earth is the matter with you?" Winifred stared at her grand-daughter. "You were never this rude before Casey became your guardian."

Summer's smug expression vanished. "It's not because of Casey. And it's not because of school or my friends."

Winifred tossed her sponge on the counter. "Are you on drugs?"

"No!" Summer's lower lip quivered. "You don't get it."

"All I *get*, as you put it, is that you're more belligerent everyday." Winifred plunked her hands on her hips. "Why is that?"

A tear rolled down Summer's cheeks. She started to say something else, but stopped and paced around the table. Part of Casey wanted to intervene, but part of her wanted to hear what Summer had to say.

"Answer me," Winifred said.

"You never talk about Mom!" Summer's anguish tore through the room. "You act like she's dead! No one's called her in weeks, or even asked if I want to talk to her."

Guilt warmed Casey's face.

Winifred said, "Your mother doesn't call us either—"

"You've never once said her name since she went to prison," Summer went on.

"Are you trying to tell me that mentioning your mother's name now and then will improve your manners?"

While Summer began to sob, Casey slumped into a chair. Just as she'd feared, Summer hadn't really accepted or adjusted to life without Rhonda. She'd hoped that the camping trips, shopping excursions, sports, and tons of movies during those first few weeks had helped Summer; but since school started, they'd both been busier. New friends had entered Summer's life. It had been easier to blame those girls for Summer's actions than to understand what was really happening.

"Acting out while your mother's away won't solve anything." Winifred pointed her finger at her grandchild. "You might as well make the best of it, young lady."

"How can I?" Summer shouted. "She's a thousand times better mom than you are!"

Winifred's eyes blazed. "She's not a real mom at all. She doesn't know the first thing about giving birth or watching a child die like I have!"

"Winifred, no!" Casey leapt to her feet.

Winifred's eyes bulged as if surprised by her own outburst. Casey wanted to slap duct tape over the stupid woman's mouth. Winifred knew that Rhonda had never wanted Summer to hear the truth.

"What's she talking about?" Summer turned to Casey. "Mom gave birth to me."

Oh lord, what was she supposed to say?

"No," Winifred answered, crossing her arms. "She didn't."

Summer gasped. "What?"

Casey wanted to explain, but it felt like someone had kicked her in the ribs. She rushed to Summer and started to put her arms around her, but Summer pushed her away.

"Tell me!" Summer's gaze darted from one to the other.

Cheyenne whimpered and nudged Summer's hand.

"I had another daughter, ten years younger than Rhonda." Winifred's mouth quivered. "Anna died of a heroine overdose two months after she gave birth to you. She was eighteen."

Casey gripped the back of the chair while the color drained from Summer's face. The old bat hadn't approved of Rhonda's desire to keep the past a secret. Helpless to stop what was about to unfold, she braced herself.

"Anna tried to take care of herself when she was pregnant," Winifred added. "Right after your birth, she picked up that filthy habit again."

Summer slumped into a chair. "Who's my dad?"

"No one knows." Winifred fumbled through her pockets, as if looking for something. "You had health problems at first, but with professional help, you recovered. When Anna died, Rhonda adopted you."

Summer jumped up and dashed out of the room. Cheyenne bounded after her.

Casey's heart pounded so hard she could only take quick shallow breaths. "How could you do that?"

Winifred picked up her cleaning rag. "It's wrong to live with deceit."

"It was Rhonda's call to make, not yours!"

"Rhonda's not here! My daughters aren't here because they made bad choices." She glowered at Casey. "Do you actually think you're competent enough to control that girl?"

"Are you?" Casey's voice rose. "I mean, your track record isn't too great, is it?"

"And you have no record at all!" Shades of red mottled Winifred's face. "You're destroying Summer!"

"She's a grieving twelve-year-old who misses her mom. I know what that's like."

The bitterness and resentment toward Mother was still vivid. Casey wished she'd ended their estrangement when Mother offered her the chance.

"Do you have any idea how agonizing it is to watch that bright, beautiful child unravel?" Winifred's eyes glistened. "It was hard enough losing one daughter to drugs, and a husband who had nothing to say to me even as he took his last breath." Her voice wavered. "But to have my oldest child kill another human being in one insane moment is unbearable."

Casey recoiled. This was the first time those words had been spoken in this house, the first time she'd seen a tear spill from Winifred.

"I devoted my life to my family." Winifred removed a tissue from her apron pocket. "And all I got was shame and heartbreak. I don't want Summer to turn out like them." Her hand shook as she wiped her eyes. "Rhonda wasn't in the proper frame of mind when she made you guardian. A judge should decide who's best qualified to raise that child."

Casey's jaw clenched. "Is that a threat?"

"I'm just saying that Summer's guardianship should be re-evaluated."

"Rhonda would have something to say about that."

"Rhonda's lost her right to have a say in Summer's upbringing, and I will not let that child become as unstable as her mother."

"I don't want to hear that crap, and especially not anywhere near Summer."

Winifred looked taken aback. "How can you forget and forgive what Rhonda's done?"

"Stop it!" Fury roiled in Casey. She had no right to throw the past in her face. "Let's get one thing straight, you're only in this house because I'm allowing it. I was hoping you and Summer would find a way to connect, but if you don't start offering more support and less criticism, you're out of here."

Winifred plunked her hands on her hips. "No one speaks to me that way."

"I just did." Casey charged out of the room. By the time she reached the second floor, she was out of breath and shaking. "Summer?" She tapped on the door. "Can we talk?"

"No!" Something struck the door hard.

Casey flinched. "I'll be upstairs if you change your mind."

Inside her apartment, Casey leaned against the door and closed her eyes. Tears slipped between her lashes and trickled down her face. How on God's earth was she supposed to handle this?

The whistling guinea pigs caught her attention. Casey retrieved carrots and lettuce from the fridge. While she replenished water and pellet dishes, she took deep yoga breaths to ease the tension, but it wasn't enough.

Once the animals were fed, she hopped onto her stationary bike and pedaled fast as memories of things Rhonda and her parents had kept from her eventually surfaced. Casey shoved them back. This wasn't the time for self-pitying nostalgia. She was building up a sweat when a light rap on the door made her stop.

"Come in." Casey got off the bike.

As Summer stepped inside, followed by Cheyenne, relief and trepidation bombarded Casey. A bulging backpack hung from Summer's shoulder. She'd put on pink lipstick, mauve eye shadow, and a ring of black eyeliner around pain-filled eyes. It was too much makeup for a twelve-year-old, but this wasn't the time to criticize her.

"You don't have to knock anymore, remember?"

"I'm still not used to it."

Meaning she hadn't yet accepted that they were officially a family now, and that Summer was welcome to come and go as she pleased up here. When she remembered, Casey kept the door open, but she also had a hard time breaking habits. Now that Winifred was living here, though, she kept it closed.

"In the car, you said I can stay with Lou's mom. Can I go there now?"

Not until they'd talked a bit. When Casey's marriage ended and she moved here, Summer was nine years old. They used to drink cocoa and talk through all sorts of stuff. But this child's monster-under-the-bed worries had evolved into real-life hurts. Goodnight kisses and soft assurances wouldn't make them go away.

"Can I eat something first?" Casey asked. "I'm starved."

Summer hesitated, then shrugged off her backpack and slumped into the rocking chair. Cheyenne sniffed at the guinea pig cages.

"I didn't know you owned makeup," Casey said.

"It's Mom's. When I put it on, it's like she's with me."

A lump rose in Casey's throat.

"Was Grandma telling the truth about my birth?"

"Yes." Casey's legs felt weak and she sought refuge on the sofa. "Your mom thought the truth would upset you."

Summer began to sob. Casey hurried to the bathroom, grabbed a couple of tissues, and rushed back.

"It doesn't matter anyway." Summer blew her nose. "That person's dead and Mom isn't, even though everyone acts like it."

Casey saw the accusation in Summer eyes. "I'm so sorry, sweetie, but given the way her last phone call went on your birthday, I was afraid mentioning your mom would upset you all over again."

Summer watched Cheyenne settle in front of the cages. "Why hasn't Mom tried to contact me?"

"I don't know." Rhonda was the one who broke off communication; said she wouldn't call again until she'd gotten her act together.

"She doesn't even know my new friends." Summer stared at the floor. "I haven't seen her in over four months."

At the time, Casey thought Rhonda had done the right thing by pleading guilty to spare Summer the anguish and humiliation of a trial, but her decision had given Summer virtually no time with Rhonda after her arrest.

"You never told me why you stopped hanging with your old friends."

Summer's face grew scarlet and she gazed at the floor. "Like I had a choice."

"Oh." Casey's heart sank.

"They said mom was insane and that I might be too."

Casey leaned back against the sofa, her stomach in knots. She'd been too afraid of the truth to come right out and ask.

"I want to go see Mom," Summer said, looking up.

Oh geez, would Rhonda want that? "I have a mailing address. Maybe you should start with a letter."

"No, I want to see her. Please?"

"Oh honey, I don't know."

Summer covered her face with her hands. More guilt shredded Casey's peace of mind. She stood and wrapped her arms around Summer.

"I'm sorry," she murmured. "This is all a mess, isn't it? You haven't mentioned your mom since your birthday, so I really thought you didn't want to talk about her. Then I started wondering if no contact might be better."

Summer stifled her sobs. "Don't you miss her a little?"

"Yes." Yet the anger was still there, lurking in the back of her mind, appearing in unsettling dreams.

She hadn't forgiven Rhonda for what she'd done, and hadn't had much to say during any of her three phone calls. By letting Rhonda become a taboo subject, though, she'd made things worse. Casey's eyes filled with tears. How could she have let this happen? Hadn't her own father made her adulterous mother the forbidden topic when he kicked her out of the house? God, she was only a year older than Summer when Mother was banished and became the unseen specter who was always there yet never acknowledged.

"Can't we at least phone her?" Summer's voice was small and fearful.

"Okay." She wiped her eyes. "I'll do it tomorrow when we're less emotional." She just prayed that Rhonda would want to talk to them.

"Do you hate being stuck with me?" Summer asked.

"What? Heavens, no. It's just that I don't know what I'm doing most of the time."

Ralphie stood on tiny hind legs and placed his paws on the wire mesh cage as if waiting to be picked up. Casey lifted the critter and gently stroked him while Cheyenne watched with great interest. Someone knocked on the door.

"If that's Grandma, I don't want to see her."

Casey sympathized. "Who is it?"

"Lou."

She hadn't expected him for another two hours. Still carrying Ralphie, she opened the door.

"I thought I'd come early," he said, smiling tentatively.

"And you brought a six-pack. Thank you." She could use one.

Stepping inside, his smile faded when he spotted Summer.

"Hey, Lou," Summer mumbled.

"Hi, I hear you're going to stay at my mom's; the land of pool tables and big-screen TVs."

Summer attempted a smile. "Can't wait."

"Want us to keep you company at Barb's tonight?" Casey returned Ralphie to his cage. "We could change our plans." She'd told Summer she'd be out with Lou at the Silver Groove. Summer hadn't seemed to care one way or the other.

"No, go. I need to do homework. Just promise you'll call Mom tomorrow, okay?"

"Sure."

"I might as well start the stupid homework now." As she headed for the door, Cheyenne followed. "Call me when you're ready to go."

"I'll call you when dinner's ready. I've decided to whip up a pot of chili."

After Summer and Cheyenne left, Lou removed his jacket. "What happened?"

"Winifred blurted the truth about Summer's birth, and now she wants to see Rhonda."

"No wonder she looked upset." Lou put the beer in the fridge, leaving two out. "Are you sure that having Winifred here is a good idea? She seemed pretty hostile when she found out I had a key to the back door."

"That's her natural state, only she's more natural than usual today." Casey removed a pack of hamburger from the freezer, popped it in the microwave, and hit defrost.

"Why did Winifred bring up her birth now?"

"They were arguing and it came out; seems the old bat's still furious with Rhonda for everything." She removed an onion and mushrooms from the fridge. "Spilling her daughter's biggest secret was payback."

"Must be tough for you, coping with all this family stuff," Lou said, handing one of the cans to Casey.

"Why? Just because I couldn't handle issues with Mother, it doesn't mean I can't deal with Summer and Winifred."

"Whoa, where did that come from?"

"Sorry. I was thinking about Mother before you came by." Shortly after Mother died in the car crash, Casey told him about her regrets in one long tirade of rage and grief. "I'll call Rhonda tomorrow. See what's going on with her."

"Good idea." As he drank, Casey noticed the TWO BEERS AND I'M NEGOTIABLE logo on his T-shirt. Was he actually wearing that to the club?

"I've been thinking about Eisler," he said, "and you're right to ask the landlord's wife about him, but wouldn't it be easier if you just phoned her tomorrow?"

"I thought if we bought her a beer, she'd be more open. Ursula's not the nicest person in the world." Casey began washing mushrooms. "Could you get the large pot out and pour in a little oil?"

Lou opened the cupboard. "I think tonight's also about refusing to let some nameless coward dictate your actions."

Casey sighed. She didn't want to discuss motive right now.

"When it comes to skills and integrity," he went on, "you worry about everyone's opinion too much."

"No, I don't." She chopped mushrooms. "Not really."

"What will you do if Ursula confirms that Eisler was at their apartment building?"

"Tell Stan and Corporal Lundy, and let them deal with it."

"And that's all you need to do, right?"

Casey sensed Lou watching her, but she wouldn't acknowledge him. She'd had enough advice, judgements, and recrimination this week. Too many bloody people telling her what she should and shouldn't do.

# SIXTEEN

**WHILE LOU MANEUVERED THROUGH THE** Thursday night traffic, Casey peered at his side mirror for the umpteenth time.

"No one's tailing us," he said, glancing at her. "I've checked as much as you have."

"I know." Still, she was uneasy. Someone could be following. On their way to Barb's earlier tonight, she'd constantly watched the mirror. Even escorting Summer out of the house and into Lou's vehicle had frazzled her nerves.

"Do you think I should call Summer?" she asked.

"She'll be fine with Mom."

"I'm worried about her mental state."

"Mom will help. She's raised five kids and has been through a lot. Besides, I told her everything Winifred said."

"Really?" Why would he do that? "When?"

"While you and Summer were settling Cheyenne in."

"I'm not sure Summer wants anyone to know. She's barely had time to absorb the news." Casey looked at the stores. "She was working too hard to be upbeat."

"That's why I gave Mom a heads up. I wasn't sure how long Summer could keep faking it before she crashed."

Whatever; no point in making an issue of it. This was supposed to be a fun night mixed with a little fact finding. On the other hand, not making an issue of things had become a habit. She'd kept things she'd found hard to discuss to herself. She'd avoided dating Lou for a long time because she hadn't believed she was any good at love. Her bloody ex had accused her of emotional distance; told her she'd never get close to anyone until she resolved issues with her mother. Hours before Mother died, she'd tried to reconnect with her. It hadn't gone well. Casey hadn't let it go well.

"There's the club," Lou said, making a right turn into a parking lot across the street.

When they reached the club's entrance, two tall women emerged. Despite their pink wigs and beaded dresses, their Adam's apples were obvious under the bright lights.

Lou gripped Casey's arm. "You're kidding me, right?"

"Not me." Smiling, she urged him forward.

"Am I going to need a tiara and a pair of sling-backs to get in?" he asked.

"I doubt it. See those guys?" Casey pointed toward a bearded man escorting what definitely looked like a woman. "If you don't like the place, we won't stay along."

Inside, her eardrums were assaulted by "Car Wash" blasting from speakers. Too bad she hadn't brought earplugs. While they edged past crowded tables and clusters of people standing around in pastel suits and shiny dresses, Casey looked for Ursula Gallenski. Lou led her to an empty table on the far side of the room, near a hallway that led to the bathrooms.

They were barely seated before a server in a hot pink mini-skirt with matching headband approached and took their drink orders. In a corner of the room, the DJ stood on a platform surrounded by strobe lights. Casey spotted a crowded bar at the back of the room. Men dominated the bar and looked anywhere from twenty to over fifty years old. Some of the guys were holding hands. Others were either alone or in small groups and ogling the women. When the song ended, the DJ announced a short break. Canned music, quieter than the DJ's brain-shaking noise, began to play. Their server appeared with two beers. Casey paid before Lou could retrieve his wallet.

She picked up her glass and studied the colorful, crowded room. "How odd."

Lou spluttered as he swallowed his beer. "Ya think?"

"I've never been to a club with such a mix of gay and straight couples, not to mention a shared love of sequins, feathers, and disco."

Lou glanced at the room. "It's packed for a Thursday night."

Casey gazed at the enormous silver ball above the dance floor. A rainbow of lights flashed over patrons shimmying to "You Make Me Feel Like Dancing" on the floor. It was all so gaudy, so seventies tacky.

"What do you think of the décor?" she asked.

"Cool." His head began to bob.

A young woman strutted past them, wearing clear plastic, high-heeled sandals with lights in the heels. Every time she moved, blue and red lights flickered.

Lou said, "I'm buying you a pair of those for Christmas."

"Please don't."

"Come on, it'd be worth it to hear what Stan would say if you sauntered into work in blinking heels. You're a size eight, right?"

"I'm not telling."

Given the amount of strutting and preening happening on the dance floor's perimeter, people were as interested in being seen as they were in dancing. Women seemed particularly engaged in a notice-me competition. Rhinestones and beads wound through hairdos shaped like birds wings. Two women in short, lime dresses and matching shoes wore sparkles on their faces and chests.

"This explains all the wigs and mini-skirts I saw in Jasmine's closet, right next to her church-going dresses," Casey said. "I never pictured so many sides to her."

"Jasmine spent a lot of time trying to find herself."

Casey watched him. "What was missing?"

"A sense of belonging, I think."

"She always seemed so ultra-cool at work; like she had it together."

"It was an act." Lou gaped at a young woman with muscular legs and bleached blond hair that reached her butt.

Casey put down her drink and tried to recapture his attention. "How do you know it was an act?"

"She asked me out for a beer in August, after we'd both had a crappy shift. She was really down about her mom."

"Why didn't you tell me?"

"I knew you two didn't get along, and I didn't want you to feel worse."

He was right. She would have felt lousy, even more than she did right now. Jasmine had been dead two weeks, and Lou hadn't once mentioned that he'd already known about her birth mother. Once again, though, why make an issue of it?

"Was she down because her mom was sick?" she asked, her tone casual.

"Pretty much. After her mother's stroke, Jasmine wanted to go see her, but her mother kept putting her off, saying she didn't want Jasmine to see her paralyzed and feeble." He shook his head. "Jasmine had begun to think that her mother didn't want to meet at all."

Three young guys in striped spandex sauntered past them. The man nearest Lou winked at him. Lou developed a sudden interest in his beer.

"That's what happens when you wear a TWO BEERS AND I'M NEGOTIABLE shirt, especially on someone as cute as you," Casey remarked.

"You're really enjoying this, aren't ya?"

"It's getting better."

"Dancing Queen" began to play, transforming the floor into a congested, psychedelic swirl. When everyone started to sing, the whole scene became suffocating. Ursula emerged from the bathroom, wearing a red feather boa and purple dress. Hadn't there been a boa just like it in Jasmine's bedroom? Ursula had her arm around a woman who looked far too sad to be clubbing.

"That's Ursula." Casey pointed to her. "The one in purple."

"Really? Is she pregnant?"

"Yep." Ursula spotted Casey, who gave her a quick nod. "She doesn't look surprised to see me."

"Or that thrilled." Lou's finger tapped the edge of his glass.

"That's fine, just as long as she talks." Casey waved Ursula over and watched her speak to her friend. "I wonder if she could pinpoint any of the guys Jasmine went to dinner with."

"Does it matter? You're here only to ask about Eisler, right?"

He was doing it again, damn it. Telling her what she should and shouldn't do. Making sure she didn't become too involved. The friend headed toward the washroom while Ursula ambled toward them.

"Paval said you might drop by." She plopped into a chair, grinned at Lou, and then looked at his shirt. "How many beers have you had?"

"Just this one." He raised his glass.

After Casey introduced him, Ursula asked, "Do you take good care of Casey, Lou?"

"She's good at taking care of herself."

"Paval takes excellent care of me." She patted her belly. "He'll be a great dad."

"You must be excited," Lou said.

Ursula's smile lasted one second. "Paval loves kids. He's wanted one of his own for ages, so what the hell?"

Casey already felt sorry for the baby. What kind of mother decided that she might as well get pregnant because she has a great househusband? On the other hand, it wasn't her business. She needed to focus on Jasmine. "Were you and Jasmine often here at the same time?"

"Not if I could help it." Ursula waved at a couple of women nearby. "I brought her here after she first moved into our building and introduced her to people, but she was so snobby that I never did it again. I figured she kept coming back for the rich guys."

Casey caught Lou's disapproving expression. Did he honestly believe that people who saw the dark side of Jasmine were wrong?

"Did your husband say why I wanted to talk to you?"

Ursula's gaze bore down on Casey. "To ask about the guy who showed up at our building last month, looking for Jasmine." She rested her elbows on the table and gave Casey a slinky smile. "My price for information is a soda water with a twist of lemon, and twenty bucks."

Lou flagged down a server.

"I've only got ten on me," she replied.

Ursula rolled her eyes.

As Casey handed her the cash, Ursula said, "He was a tanned, skinny guy with short brown hair and manicured nails. Wore a suit and walked like someone had shoved a stick up his butt."

This definitely sounded like Eisler. She and Lou exchanged solemn glances.

"Did he give you his name?" she asked.

"Nope. Just said he wanted to see Jasmine. I told him to buzz her apartment."

"Did he?"

"Nah." Ursula leaned back in her chair. "The twit took off."

When "Jive Talkin'" started playing, Ursula and Lou began bobbing their heads. An older guy escorted a young woman in white vinyl boots and a teeny yellow skirt onto the dance floor. When the entire room started singing again, Casey cringed. Oh, dear god, she was in disco hell.

Lou paid for the soda while Ursula glanced at the washrooms, presumably to see if her friend was around, which she wasn't. When the song finally ended, Ursula raised her glass to Lou. "Cheers." After taking a gulp, she gave Casey a bemused look. "So, was Tight-ass one of Jasmine's admirers?"

"Apparently."

"That explains his lovesick face."

"Did you see this guy more than once near her apartment?"

"Nope, but Pav and I are too busy to keep track of everyone."

Paval seemed to know what was going on with tenants, though. "Your husband told me that Jasmine's half sister, Gabrielle, showed up at your building two days before Jasmine died. Did either of you see Gabrielle near your building after that Sunday?"

"I didn't, and Paval would have told me if he had." She gave Casey a shrewd look. "So, are Tight-ass and Gabrielle your murder suspects?"

"I don't have suspects. I'm not investigating."

"Then why are you here?"

Lou slipped his hand under his chin and peered at Casey.

"It's a work issue." She shrugged. "Too boring to explain."

"Yeah, well, I heard the cops are pretty interested in Noel Merryweather," Ursula said, "which is a good call."

"Why?" Casey asked.

"The night before Jasmine died, Pav and I saw him zoom out of the building like his chair was on fire." Ursula sipped her drink. "The guy looked mad as hell and stank of wine."

"How could you tell? Your apartment isn't near the door."

"We'd been out for a walk and bumped into him outside. His van was parked in the handicapped spot out front." Ursula looked around the room. "Jasmine had a way of pissing people off. A couple of them are here." She nodded toward the bar.

"How do you know she pissed these guys off?" Casey asked.

"I told some of her dates about her death, and you know what?" She leaned close to Casey. "They didn't give a shit. It seems that little Miss

Too-Good-for-the-World was happy to let men take her out to dinner, but she wouldn't put out."

Lou's upper body went rigid. "So they didn't like her because she wasn't a tramp?"

"No, sweet pea, they didn't like her because she was one hell of a tease. A taker."

"Excuse me." Lou stood and headed for the bathroom.

Ursula watched him leave. "Don't tell me your boyfriend's a Jasmine fan."

Casey bristled. "They got along."

"Is that so?" She raised a painted brow. "What did she want from him?"

"A boyfriend for Marie Crenshaw."

"Fight for him, honey. He seems like a keeper."

"I intend to, but let's talk about losers, like Jasmine's ex. He would hang around the building, right?"

"All the time." She examined her silver nails. "When it came to men, Jasmine made some really bad choices. That chick was playing a dangerous game, and I should know; I've been down that road." She sipped her drink. "Never dreamed that hers would lead to death."

"Did her ex ever have a woman with him when he came by the apartment?"

Ursula played with her straw. "I drove past his car in early September, and saw some chick wearing a ball cap and sunglasses in the passenger's seat."

"Making it tough to ID her."

"Damn straight." Ursula turned and spotted her friend standing a few feet away, wiping her eyes. "I gotta run."

"Your friend seems upset."

"If you had a husband who'd cheated on you, wouldn't you be?"

"I did, and I was for a while."

Ursula turned to her. "Were you pregnant at the time?"

"No."

"She is, which reminds me; one Saturday last month, when Jasmine left her kid with Paval, Birch and his friend were sitting in his car, watching. Instead of following Jasmine, they stayed to watch Jeremy, who was with Paval outside. It freaked Paval out so he took the boy in. Birch left after that, but it made me wonder if the jerk was more interested in Jeremy than Jasmine."

Casey spotted Lou edging past Ursula's friend.

"By the way, Birch's passenger also wore a dark jacket," Ursula said. "I heard that the killer wore a dark jacket, ball cap, and sunglasses. Curious, ain't it?"

"It is." Casey's skin prickled.

# SEVENTEEN

CASEY IGNORED THE CHATTER OF passengers on the M6 bus while she scanned the sidewalk for anyone who might be carrying a fist-sized rock. The last hit happened on September twenty-seventh and she'd worked this route several times since without incident. Today was October fifteenth. The rockhound had either found a new hobby or had had few opportunities.

Casey rubbed her freezing hands. The temperature had dropped since the rain began and Wesley again refused to switch on the heater. It didn't help that she was sitting right behind the center door where cold air wafted in every time it opened, but if she needed a quick exit, this was the place to be.

The M6 approached the Columbia Street and Blackwood intersection, which was the beginning of the rockhound's turf. Casey sat up straight and took a deep breath. Two young women ate McDonald's fries, offering a welcome change from the usual rotten banana smell.

Behind Casey, a group of teens burst out laughing, presumably at some joke. After the rockhound's last strike, management had tried eliminating passenger pickups along this stretch of Columbia until further notice, but dozens of complaints had forced David Eisler to change his mind. He had insisted, however, that notices be posted throughout the M6, stating that the company wouldn't be liable for personal injuries.

Unfortunately, riding the M6 had become some sort of sport for thrill-seeking teens who—despite Wesley's warnings—chose seats next to the sidewalk. Tonight, six annoying boys and three girls joked and laughed behind her.

Casey studied pedestrians' clothing, height, weight, bags, purses, and umbrellas. She looked for hands in pockets. Wesley slowed for a man waiting at the stop just beyond the Fourth Street intersection as four males sauntered down Columbia. Two wore tuques, another wore a wide-brimmed hat, and the fourth man was hatless.

Casey slid to the edge of her seat, and her muscles tensed up. No one in the group lagged behind. As Wesley eased the bus to the stop, a dozen people exited the SkyTrain station a few strides away. Some headed for the M6 while others walked down Columbia Street.

Through the stream of people, Casey noticed a man with a long beard standing in front of a closed shop. The dark hoodie was pulled low over his forehead. Witnesses had never mentioned a bearded rockhound, but descriptions were varied enough to make her think the perp wore disguises.

As the doors opened, the bearded man headed back toward the Blackwood intersection. Casey watched his retreating back and studied his loping gait. The guy was tall, his shoulders slightly stooped. He removed his hands from his pockets. The doors closed. A half second later, the sound of tinkling glass made her duck.

"Shit!" a passenger shouted.

More voices erupted with "What the hell?" Nearly everyone jumped to their feet.

"Damn!" Casey raised her head enough to see if the perp was running up Fourth like he had last time.

No one was running or even turning up Fourth, but the group of four guys was now three. The man with the wide-brimmed hat had disappeared, and where had the bearded guy gone?

She straightened up. "Anyone see anything?"

People shook their heads. There was no time for more than a quick glance at the window. Casey rushed down the steps, crunching glass fragments under her feet. This was new. No rock had done this much damage before.

"Hold it, Casey!" Wesley shouted. "That sounded like a gunshot."

She hesitated. The noise had sounded different from the last strike, but a gun? She looked up and down the street. No one seemed in a hurry. She rushed up to the group of three who'd stopped and were now staring at the small hole in the window. God, it looked like Wesley was right. She turned to the guys.

"MPT security." She flashed her ID. "Where's your friend?" The men, all twenty-something, gave her blank stares. "There were four of you together, and he had a wide-brimmed hat."

"He wasn't with us, but I saw him," one of them replied. "I thought he was going to pass us, but I guess he dropped back."

Casey wished she hadn't focused on the bearded guy. Another bloody mistake.

"He ran into the station," another replied.

Casey looked at the SkyTrain entrance. The perp could have cut through the station and left through the Fourth Street exit. If he'd done so, it would be nearly impossible to find him.

"Did any of you see his face?"

They shook their heads.

"His hat was brown," one of them said, "and the coat was either dark blue or black."

"Casey?" Wesley called out. "We've found the bullet."

"The suspect went into the SkyTrain station, so I'm going to check it out."

"Don't. He could still be there."

"The transit police or security will be around." She turned to the guys. "Could I grab your names and phone numbers in case we need a written statement?"

It took only a few seconds to scribble down the info and then enter the SkyTrain station. Several steps beyond, a narrow escalator led up to second floor offices. Ground floor shops were closed for the night. She rushed past the stores, farther into the station. Two men in suits were using the ticket machines, but there was no sign of any transit police. Casey ignored a sign prohibiting entrance without a ticket. As she jogged to the escalator, her phone rang.

"Hello?"

"That was your last warning," a male voice whispered. "Stop investigating Jasmine's murder."

The blood rushed to her face. "I'm not!"

Was the freak stalking her? She heard traffic noise at his end of the line, and then nothing. She looked up and down the escalator. No one was on a cell phone. Sweat trickled down her sides and she shivered. Desperate to make sure Summer was okay, she speed-dialed Barb's number, but Barb was on another call.

Casey stepped onto the platform. Two lines ran through this station. The shooter might have already hopped onto a train, but in which direction? It was after ten, and at least a dozen passengers were waiting for the automated rail cars. Two women chatted near the steps.

"Excuse me, ladies. I'm with MPT security." She showed them her ID. "Did either of you see a man in a dark coat and brown, wide-brimmed hat come up here?"

The women looked at each other. "We followed someone like that up the escalator," one of them said. "He stayed on the platform about two seconds, and then headed back down."

"Did you get a look at his face?"

Both shook their heads.

A SkyTrain security attendant approached Casey and she again displayed her ID. "Did you see a man who might have come up here less than five minutes ago? He was wearing a dark coat and brown, wide-brimmed hat." She spotted an elderly couple edging closer to her. Both were short, their wrinkled faces curious and apprehensive.

"I saw him come up here then leave right away," the attendant replied. "I didn't get a good look at him. What's he done?"

"Excuse me, but we couldn't help overhearing," the elderly woman said. "We saw the man with the hat, too. He seemed rather flustered, didn't he, Fred?" She glanced at her companion who nodded his bald head.

"Could you be a bit more specific?" Casey asked.

"Well, he was turning every which way, and his hands were in his pockets," she replied, reaching for Fred's hand. "He left almost as soon as he got here."

"Did you see his face?"

"Just a bit, really." When she turned to her companion, her loose plastic bonnet hat didn't quite move with her. "He could have been young, couldn't he, Fred?"

"Young." Fred nodded.

"Was he light skinned, dark skinned?" Casey asked.

"He was a tall, white fellow," she replied. "Clean shaven."

"Tall," Fred agreed. "Clean shaven."

"He was shorter than me," the attendant said.

"Did any of you notice other markings like a mole, tattoo, or piercings?" Everyone shook their heads.

Casey turned to the attendant. "The station has a few closed-circuit TVs, right?"

"Yeah, but you can't see footage without authorization."

Casey removed a notebook and pencil from her jacket pocket, and then smiled at the elderly woman. "May I have your names and phone numbers, please?"

"I'm Elsie Watson. This is my husband, Fred."

After she and the attendant provided the information, Casey handed the attendant her business card. "If you see him again, call me. Are any transit constables around?"

"He's around somewhere." The man reached for his two-way radio. Seconds later, he said, "There's a lady here from MPT security who's looking for a guy in a dark coat and wide-brimmed hat. See anyone like that?"

Casey heard him say that he had. "I'll be right down."

She hurried off the platform and onto the escalator. At the bottom, a transit officer stepped through an open entryway at the back of the station. The man barely glanced at her ID.

"Your guy took off out there." He nodded toward the way he had just come. "He seemed kind of nervous, so I asked if he was all right. He said he was fine and rushed outside, but I had a bad vibe about him, so I followed him as far as Church Street."

Church Street was on the other side of the SkyTrain entrance. A road only one block long that ran from Columbia up to private property. "Was he heading toward Columbia?"

"Yeah."

Casey stepped up to the entrance: a wide, rectangular gap in the thick cement wall. No doors or gate. She peeked outside and saw a set of steps leading up to the lane.

"What's up with the guy?" the officer asked.

"He shot a bus window."

"No shit."

"How old would you say the man was?"

"Don't know, he wore his hat low; but he was clean-shaven and about five foot ten."

Casey stepped outside and looked around. A light rain spritzed her face.

"There are plenty of hiding places," the officer added.

A New Westminster police officer appeared from the Columbia Street entrance. The officer glanced at Casey before turning her attention to the transit constable.

"We received a report about an armed man entering the station," the officer said.

"My driver reported it," Casey replied.

The transit cop described his encounter with the suspect. The tall, bulky officer turned to Casey. "You need an escort back to the bus, ma'am?"

"No, it's right out front." The implication that her presence wasn't needed irritated Casey. "I gathered information from witnesses on the platform."

"Did you get their names and numbers?"

"Yes."

"Go back to your bus and wait for me there."

Casey marched outside. By the time she returned to the M6, more New Westminster police had entered the bus. Wesley and an officer were on the sidewalk.

"Did you see him?" Wesley asked her.

"No, but he called to tell me that this was my last warning."

"How did the freak know you were here?"

"Good question." Casey wiped her perspiring forehead. Had someone at Mainland told him her schedule, or was the caller a coworker? "It's possible that the bullet came from a gun that was used on a colleague's house. The Vancouver police have a file on the incident."

The officer peered at her. "You're the security guard?"

"Casey Holland, yes."

"So, Miss Holland, what makes you think the incidents are related?"

She didn't want to waste time discussing this. "It's a long story."

"The station's only a short walk away." His voice adopted a hard edge. "Want to tell me there?"

Sighing, Casey sat down. "It began when a colleague was murdered in Coquitlam on September twenty-eighth."

"The one whose house was shot at?"

"No, another one."

"Really?" He opened his notebook.

She kept her story brief. When she told him that two Glocks were stolen from Wesley's place, the officer raised his hand. "Stop."

He looked at Wesley. "Didn't you say your name was Wesley?"

Wesley gave him a curt nod. The hostile glance was reserved for Casey.

"So," the officer said to Wesley, "one of your weapons killed a colleague?"

He let out a puff of air. "Uh-huh."

The female cop joined them as Casey finished highlighting events since Jasmine's death. When she finished, both officers were staring at her.

"Let me get this straight," the male officer said. "Your coworker was shot at and warned to stop investigating the Birch woman's death, and you've also been warned twice, correct?"

"Yes."

"Then why haven't you stopped?"

"I just told you I have." Casey struggled to keep her anger in check. "I was doing my regular job tonight and, like I said, we've already told everyone at work that I'm done asking questions."

The cop tried not to smile. "It looks like someone didn't get the memo."

Casey glared at his snickering partner. "If I'm getting warnings to stop investigating, then isn't it possible that I'm on the right track?"

The smirks vanished. "Let the professionals handle it, ma'am," the female cop said. "There's probably lots going on that you know nothing about."

Casey was fed up with the woman's condescension. As the officers started to leave, Casey said, "Maybe you should put a rush on that ballistics test. If it did come from the same weapon that shot holes in Marie's house, the Vancouver cops and IHIT will want to know."

Neither officer acknowledged her as they left the M6.

"They think we work in a freakin' nut factory," Wesley muttered.

Casey sighed. "They could be right."

The problem was, one of the nuts might be a killer, and the danger to Summer might have just escalated. Casey retrieved her cell phone and tried Barb's number again.

# EIGHTEEN

**AS CASEY DROVE TO NOEL'S** house, she tried to ignore her aching shoulders. After last night's drama on the M6, her muscles were still knotted. When Noel called this morning to invite her to lunch as a thank you for helping him and said Marie would be there, she'd accepted. If they both heard what happened last night, maybe Noel could convince Marie to stop badgering her to investigate.

Casey checked the rearview mirror for glimpses of lurking strangers. Despite Barb's and Summer's assurances last night that they were fine, Casey hadn't stopped worrying. It took another call to Summer this morning to keep worry from turning to panic.

Stan had his concerns, too. Before she met with him this morning, she'd heard a shouting match between Stan and David Eisler through Stan's closed door. Eisler was saying that she was bringing too much trouble to Mainland and should be suspended. Stan had stood his ground, thank god. By the time Eisler flung open the door and charged out, he was red-faced and scowling. He'd glared at Casey and started to say something, but took off when Stan stepped out of his office.

"I had to tell David about the shooting," he'd said. "He thinks you'll be safer if you weren't on any buses right now. I have to agree with him, but it's not a suspension." Stan could be diplomatic when he wanted to be.

Casey pulled into Noel's driveway. Marie's vehicle wasn't there. She stepped out of her Tercel, walked up to the door, and was about to ring the bell when the door opened.

"Hello," he said. "Good to see you."

"You too." Casey tried not to glance at the biceps bulging under his black T-shirt. Today, his long blond hair was tied back. Sam wagged his tail and nuzzled her hand.

Casey stepped inside. "Something smells wonderful."

"Baked salmon. Marie said you eat a lot of salmon sandwiches, so I figured this was a safe bet. By the way, one of her kids got sick, so she bailed."

Uh-oh. "Aren't they staying with your mom?"

"Yeah, Marie's spending the weekend there."

Leaving her alone with Noel. Damn.

He shut the door. "Can I take your jacket?"

The phone rang in a nearby room.

"Go ahead," Casey said. "I'll hang it up."

As he wheeled his chair down the hall, Casey opened the closet door and noticed a bicycle helmet, assorted gloves, and elbow pads on the low shelf. At the far end, a royal blue ball cap partially covering a pair of sunglasses made her freeze. The killer had worn those things.

Still, September twenty-eighth had been a sunny day. Lots of people would have worn sunglasses, and blue ball caps were common. Not many of them would have been wearing a dark jacket, though. Casey spotted a black windbreaker hanging from the rod. Her heart started to pound.

Stay calm. Don't jump to conclusions. If Noel was guilty, wouldn't he have gotten rid of these things? Wouldn't the cops have confiscated them? On the other hand, Marie was the one who'd asked her to investigate. Noel had tried to dissuade her, and he'd neglected to mention the marriage proposal. Oh god, what if he'd hired someone to take a shot at her last night?

She heard Sam's nails click on the hardwood floor. Casey shut the door just as Noel turned the corner.

"Are you okay?" he asked. "You look a bit freaked out."

"I was thinking about something that happened last night, and was hoping to tell you and Marie at the same time."

"Let's go in the living room." He paused. "Don't you want to remove your jacket?"

"Actually, I'm a little cold."

If she had to make a quick exit, what excuse could she come up with for leaving? Summer was at Barb's, Lou was at work. With any luck, one of them would call; and she was expecting a call from Rhonda. After phoning the prison yesterday, she'd learned that Rhonda was in the infirmary with the flu. She'd left a message asking her to call as soon as possible.

In the large open area that was both living and dining room, Casey spotted the beautifully laid table. Crystal water goblets, wine glasses, and black plates shone below halogen lights. Noel had even uncorked a bottle of wine and put out white linen napkins with black napkin rings. She didn't even own a napkin ring.

"This is beautiful, but you shouldn't have gone to so much trouble." She removed her cell phone from her purse and checked for messages.

"I wanted to show you my appreciation." He watched her. "Are you expecting a call?"

"Yes, it's an important family thing."

"Would you like some wine?" Noel asked.

"No, thanks."

Casey sat on the edge of the sofa while Noel angled his chair so he could see both Como Lake and her. Grateful for the coffee table between them, she looked for signs of weapons on her host. The pockets in his trousers could hold a knife. The side pockets in his wheelchair could hide several knives and a small handgun. He might even have a weapon tucked between his back and the chair.

"What happened last night?" Noel asked.

"Someone took a shot at me while I was on one of our New Westminster buses." Casey rubbed clammy hands on her jeans. "A minute later, I got a call telling me that this was my last warning and that I'd better stop investigating Jasmine's death."

"Holy shit." Lines creased Noel's brow. "What do you mean by last warning? How many others were there?"

"Just one, but the caller threatened Summer's life." Casey watched Noel's face grow pale. Could a person fake losing the color from their face? "Only Mainland staff would have access to my schedule and they're not supposed to give it out."

"Maybe someone staked out buses leaving the yard." Noel looked at Sam who'd settled next to his chair.

"I picked up the bus in Burnaby."

"My lawyer said that Wesley Axelson owned the gun that killed Jasmine." He raised his hands as if to ward off a response. "I'm not saying he's the killer, but Wesley was Jasmine's friend, and the weapon does connect him to this mess."

Deflecting suspicion wasn't helping things. "Has your lawyer heard anything about the silver car that was seen speeding away?"

"Not that I know of." He scratched Sam's head. "It's been two and a half weeks since Jasmine died. Leads are going cold."

The longer Noel looked at her, the more unreadable his expression became. Casey leaned back against the sofa and tried to appear relaxed.

"Why didn't you tell me about the threat to Summer?" he asked.

"I thought Marie would." She'd blabbed about everything else.

He watched her. "I think you've been avoiding me because of the marriage proposal."

Casey felt her cheeks grow warm.

"Marie told me you confronted her about it," he added.

She looked at those gorgeous blue eyes. "Is it true that she didn't know?"

Noel nodded. "I didn't want to tell her until I had an answer. As for you, well, it would have made me look guiltier." He paused. "Do you think I am?"

What should she say?

"Your opinion matters to me," he added.

Especially if he was a killer. Casey turned her attention to the window. Heavy clouds hung above the lake. Any moment, the rain would start to fall. "How long had you been in love with Jasmine?"

Noel stroked Sam. "I wasn't, at least not in a starry-eyed crazy way, but I did love her and wanted to take care of her and Jeremy."

"Was her rejection the real reason you fought that night?"

"Partly." His expression grew somber. "She said she couldn't cope with a handicapped husband."

Man, evidence was mounting against this guy. "I thought I was the only one who'd experienced Jasmine's insensitivity."

His brief smile seemed resigned. "Let's face it, she had bad moments. That's what happens to abused children who don't get therapy. She was angry and starved for love and acceptance."

Casey shook her head. Too bad that all she'd seen was the angry, hostile part of her.

"You never said if you thought I was guilty," Noel mumbled.

Her shoulders stiffened. "I don't know." She studied his crestfallen face. "Maybe I should go."

"No, wait." He leaned forward. "Please, we're getting everything out in the open. I don't want to stop now."

Asking about the jacket and cap in his closet was a risk, but he was practically shoving the opportunity at her. Casey walked toward the trophy display across the room. "Did you win these before or after your paralysis?"

"After."

Casey glanced at the front door. She could reach it in six or seven quick strides. "Here's the thing." She crossed her arms. "I just saw a black jacket, royal blue ball cap, and sunglasses in your closet. It's pretty much what Jasmine's killer wore."

He almost looked relieved. "That's what's bothering you?"

"Uh-huh. Why didn't the police take these things away?"

Noel swept his hand over his head. "They weren't here." He cringed, as if expecting a sharp response. "Marie was washing the jacket at her place."

"That sounds bad, Noel."

"I know, but my van had been stolen and Sam was out of food, so Marie offered to drop some off on her way to work. It was the morning Jasmine was killed."

"Oh."

"She saw the jacket and ball cap on the floor by the closet and wanted to know why they smelled like wine. I told her I spilled some. The truth was that Jasmine had thrown a glass at me during the fight. Marie offered to get the stain out of the cap, so she took everything."

Ursula had said Noel reeked of wine when she and Paval bumped into him that night. "Would anyone from Mainland have seen you in those clothes?"

"Sure, Jasmine, Marie, and I went to the pub with MPT staff a few times."

"Did you ever meet Mainland's VP, David Eisler?"

"No, but Marie pointed him out once." Noel rubbed his chin. "I caught him staring at me in the parking lot last month when I was picking Jasmine up."

"I heard that he phoned Jasmine the night before she died. Were you there when he called?"

Noel blinked a couple of times. "Now that you mention it, we were arguing when the phone rang. She answered it, so I went to the bathroom. By the time I came back she was off the phone and looking furious. I assumed it was because of me."

"She never said who she'd been talking to?"

"No, and I didn't ask. Too caught up in the fight."

Convenient. "People say Eisler was hot for Jasmine and that he doesn't have an alibi. Also, the landlord's wife said she met him at their apartment building a few days before her death. It seems he wanted to see Jasmine."

"I wouldn't put much stock in what Ursula says. She and Jasmine didn't get along. What I would pay attention to, though, is something I should have mentioned before; something you won't want to hear."

"Go on."

Noel hesitated. "While Jasmine and I were fighting, she blurted out that she was in love with Roberto and that he had a key to her apartment."

Oh, crap. "And you didn't you tell me before because . . ."

"It's not cool to accuse people without proof, and it would make me look bad. Are you sure you wouldn't like some wine?"

"Not yet, thanks."

"Mind if I start?"

"Not at all." She watched Noel roll for the table and pour himself a glass of what looked like rosé. "I was thinking about the photos you mentioned, and I wonder if Roberto took them."

"He said he didn't." Although he could have lied. "Did the issue with the key tick you off?"

Noel swished the wine in his glass. "I was willing to build a life with Jasmine. He wasn't."

He made it sound as if he'd been doing her a favor. "Didn't you find it strange that she took your ring while she was in love with Roberto and dating other guys?"

"I didn't realize how deeply she felt about him until she gave the ring back," he answered. "Anyway, Marie says there's a new suspect; some girlfriend of Birch's."

"Maybe, but no one knows who she is yet. Did Jasmine ever talk about moving?"

"No, but I wouldn't be surprised if she'd decided to, since she really wanted to get away from Birch." He sipped the wine. "What if the girlfriend shot Jasmine to give Birch a solid alibi? Birch saw me in the ball cap and jacket a couple of times."

"With sunglasses and her hair pushed up under a ball cap, a woman could be mistaken for a guy from a distance," Casey said. "Speaking of female suspects, your sister asked me to check out Gabrielle O'Reilly's alibi, and I have her phone number, but I don't want to call her, so can I give it to you?"

"Sure." Noel tapped the rim of his glass. "It's more than a little freaky that the killer knows enough about me and Wesley's guns to set us up. The killer has to be someone we've both had contact with a few times, which rules out Gabrielle and Birch's girlfriend, unless the girlfriend works at Mainland."

"Possibly." Although she still hadn't completely ruled out Noel. Should she sit back and wait in fear, or help nail the suspect before the freak shot Summer? Was there a way to establish Noel's innocence once and for all?

"Maybe it's time I stopped acting like a doormat and did more to save my ass, like taking a closer look at Gabrielle and MPT staff," he said. "After all, I don't have to work with them."

"True." But what would he find?

# NINETEEN

**"SORRY, CASEY, BUT YOU'RE BACK** supervising the kids with Marie," Stan said. "We're too short-staffed."

Casey slumped in her chair and watched him straighten his tan tie with the pink triangles. She kept her gaze on that god-awful tie so she wouldn't have to look at Marie sitting next to her. She was being unusually quiet. Casey had argued that this was Marie's case, not hers, and that Marie could easily handle what would probably be a subdued bunch of kids after that last fight, but Stan disagreed.

"Look, it's not my fault that the parents threatened to complain loudly and publicly about Mainland if we didn't pick up their kids again," Stan said. "Eisler promised parents two security staff for a couple of days. Anyhow, it took some effort, but I got him to agree that your presence would send a strong reminder to those boys about fighting."

"Fine." She just hoped Marie wouldn't whine about her brother's situation all through their shift, or beg for more help.

"How's the goose egg, anyway?" he asked.

"It's still tender, but there've been no more headaches." She sat forward. "Did anyone address the real problem between these kids, which is that the white kid, Scott, is smitten with a girl from the other group and that the girl might feel the same?"

"I was told that all concerned parties had a meeting, but I wasn't given details." Stan's phone rang. When Marie stood he said, "Wait here a minute. There's something else you both need to know."

Marie strolled to the window, keeping her back to Casey. Casey yawned, wishing she could have slept in. After her lunch with Noel, the rest of the weekend had been a marathon of errands, housework, cage cleaning, and essay writing. Never far from her thoughts, though, was Friday night's ominous warning. Troubling as well was her turmoil over Rhonda and Summer.

Casey had hoped that Friday's phone message to Rhonda would

prompt a quick response, but it hadn't. She'd called again yesterday and learned that Rhonda was still in the infirmary. When she explained the situation to Summer, the poor kid tried to sound optimistic. Casey knew what Summer was thinking: that Rhonda was avoiding them.

Stan hung up and leaned back in his chair. Casey tried to stifle another yawn.

"Tired?" he asked.

"Yeah, busy weekend, stressful week."

"If things go well today and tomorrow, you can skip the rest of the week."

"Thanks."

"How's Summer doing?" he asked.

"Okay. I've moved her to a safe location."

Marie turned to face her. "With her grandmother?"

Summer's whereabouts were none of her business. "No."

Casey didn't understand why Winifred had chosen to remain in the house. She knew Summer might not be back for several days, even weeks. Part of Casey was tempted to ask her to leave, but Winifred seemed determined to scour the entire house. Maybe it was helping her work out some stress. Whenever Rhonda had been under stress, she scrubbed the kitchen floor incessantly. Winifred's thing was vacuuming.

"To stop more rumors from spreading," Stan said, clasping his hands together, "you girls should know that Eisler's alibi is solid."

"What?" Marie approached his desk. "Are you sure?"

Stan gave her a look. "Would I be saying this if I wasn't?"

"Then what the hell was he doing the morning Jasmine died?" Marie asked.

"First off," Stan said, pointing at her, "do not take that tone with me."

She slumped into the chair. "Sorry."

Casey got up and opened a window for fresh air.

"Secondly, what I'm going to say is confidential, you got that?"

"Yeah," Casey answered, noticing Marie's nod.

"Eisler was at a job interview, which the cops verified."

"Damn," Marie murmured.

"Excuse me?" Stan said, frowning.

"Well, surely you can see it from my perspective."

Casey crossed her arms. That was the problem. Marie only saw things from her perspective. Even before the crisis with Noel, everything revolved around her needs and worries.

Stan checked his watch. "The M10 is pulling out in fifteen minutes. Be on it."

Anxious to get away from Marie, Casey hurried out the door and jogged downstairs. She marched past the lunchroom, and then entered the women's locker room. The room was empty. As she approached her locker, she spotted RAT BITCH scrawled across the door in burgundy lipstick.

"You've got to be kidding!" Marie yelled from the other end of the room.

Casey walked over and saw the same words on Marie's locker.

"Who would do that?" Marie kicked the locker below hers.

Good question. Although Casey had let everyone know she wasn't looking into Jasmine's death anymore, some coworkers still kept their distance. Rumors of a killer among them had hardly inspired a warm fuzzy feeling. Clearly, certain people blamed her and Marie for starting them.

"Have you seen that shade of lipstick on anyone?" Casey asked.

"No." Marie glared at the words. "I wonder when this was done."

"We can ask the cleaning crew if they saw anything."

Cleaners worked between 5:00 and 7:00 AM and this room was never locked, so anyone could have come in. The main entrances were unlocked at seven and locked after six at night. Casey removed a tissue from her purse and rubbed it on the lipstick.

"You won't get it off that way," Marie remarked.

"I just want a color sample."

"The tube could be wrecked, and who'd be stupid enough to wear that shade now?"

"You never know. Lipstick's expensive. Check out the garbage can."

Marie marched up to the can by the door and looked inside. "Nothing." She returned to her locker. "The shade's vaguely familiar. I just can't remember who I've seen it on. It shouldn't take us too long to figure it out."

"Us?"

"Don't tell me you're going to sit back and do nothing?"

"I'm not wasting time over a cheap shot," Casey said. "If I happen to see a similar shade on someone, I'll make a note of it, but that's all. I've had more than enough trouble for one week."

Marie's expression softened. "I heard about the shooting Friday night. Aren't you going to do anything about that?"

Casey returned to her locker and shoved her purse inside. "Not if it means risking Summer's life."

"The killer doesn't believe you're off the case, so why not keep searching for him?"

Casey had been debating that question all weekend.

"Catching the freak before he gets us is the best way to protect our kids," Marie continued. "Come on, Casey, it's not like you to sit around waiting for a bunch of cops to save the day. You're smart enough to be discreet."

Casey marched out of the room. She got as far as the lunchroom entrance before Marie caught up. "Noel's really depressed. He figures he's about to be arrested. If there's a trial, he'll have to sell his house to pay legal costs." She grabbed Casey's arm. "We're out of money and we've tried banks loans, but . . ." Her mouth trembled.

A group of maintenance guys and clerical workers left the lunchroom. When they saw her and Marie, conversation stopped and they slowed their pace. None of the women were wearing burgundy lipstick.

"You're the only one who can help us," Marie said, oblivious to her coworkers.

Two female drivers, neither wearing lipstick, headed their way. The big tall woman, Ingrid, gave Marie a hard stare. Ingrid had been employed at Mainland six months and Casey had never worked with her. From what she'd heard, though, Ingrid wasn't much of a team player.

"What I want to know," Casey said to Marie, "is why you've been so eager to have me check people out when you've been withholding key information?"

"What are you talking about?"

"You had Noel's dark jacket and royal blue ball cap when the murder happened." Casey knew she shouldn't mention this in front of others, but she'd had enough bullying.

Marie's face reddened. "I was so upset by Jasmine's death that I forgot I had his stuff until after the funeral. Anyway, that just proves Noel's innocent. His jacket was swishing around my washing machine when Jasmine was shot."

"So, you made Casey scrounge for suspects here." Ingrid crossed her arms. "And you shouldn't have agreed to help, Casey."

Great. More people telling her what she should and shouldn't do. "I'll make my own decisions, thanks."

"What's wrong with trying to find the truth?" Marie asked. "Certain people around here have lied about their alibis."

"That doesn't make them killers," Ingrid shot back.

"It doesn't clear them either. Has anyone bothered to ask Roberto where he really was the morning Jasmine died? Because he sure in hell wasn't at the dentist."

Casey inhaled sharply. Was Marie trying to piss off more staff, and how had she found out?

"Why doesn't someone ask Wesley how his gun happened to be the murder weapon?" Marie went on.

"Stop trying to get your brother off at staff expense!" Ingrid shouted.

"Noel is innocent! Jasmine was in love with Roberto, but he didn't love her. Wesley was crazy about her, but she didn't love him." Marie scanned the grim faces. "Do I need to draw you people little pictures?"

Casey cringed. "Let's go, Marie."

Three more employees joined the group circling her and Marie.

"You didn't want Jasmine marrying your brother, did you?" Ingrid said. "Everyone knew she went out with anything in pants."

"Liar!" Marie's face was now crimson. "I wish she had been my sister-in-law."

"Since you're into accusing people," a mechanic said, "maybe we should wonder about you. You just said you had a dark jacket and blue cap when Jasmine was shot."

Marie's eyes blazed. "How dare you accuse me of murdering my best friend!"

"Isn't that what you're doing to Wesley and Roberto?" a secretary asked.

"Roberto doesn't have a credible alibi and Wesley's gun killed her!"

Casey shook her head. "Marie, let's go."

"What's your alibi, Marie?" Ingrid asked.

"I was doing the bloody laundry!"

When the group laughed, Marie swore at them and stomped outside.

Casey's mind whirled. Marie couldn't be a killer, could she? Sure, Jasmine hadn't told Marie everything, but if Marie was guilty, then why keep asking for help? Had she hoped Casey would prove her brother's innocence and leave it at that?

Pain flared up deep inside Casey's head and she winced. Damn, not a migraine. Not now. She stepped outside into the cool October sunshine. Marie was yakking at Lou in the parking lot; something about filing a complaint with human resources. Gee, that would really help.

When Lou saw Casey, he walked toward her. She hadn't seen or spoken to him since Saturday night. He'd only stayed for two hours. Both of them had been tired and neither had had much to say. Truth was that they'd hardly talked since Thursday's excursion to the Silver Groove four days ago. Usually, he called every day, but not yesterday.

"How are you doing?" he asked.

"Okay. And you?"

"All right. Are you coming bowling tonight? A few of us are getting together."

"I'll try."

Marie looked from Lou to Casey, then back to Lou. "It sounds like you two haven't seen each other in ages."

Casey ignored her.

"Did I tell you how much Noel enjoyed lunch with you on Saturday?" Marie said, glancing at Lou.

Casey shrugged. "It was just a goodbye lunch. Since I'm out of the picture, he and I won't be meeting again." And that's exactly what she'd told Lou. Taking his hand, she headed toward the M10.

"Noel was hoping to call you socially." She trailed after them. "I mean, you two hit it off and he needs all the support he can get."

Casey noticed Roberto walking toward a bus.

"Hey Roberto!" Marie called out. "Did you know that my brother asked Jasmine to marry him?"

Roberto strolled toward them. "She showed me the ring and asked me not to say anything."

"When did she show it to you?"

"The day before she died."

Marie grimaced. "Were you jealous?"

"For shit's sake, Marie." Roberto's eyes narrowed until they were almost squinting. "Jasmine and I were just friends. How many times do I have to say it?"

"Your dentist alibi doesn't hold up."

Casey wanted to ask if he had a key to Jasmine's place, as Noel claimed, but this wasn't the time.

"We're done here." Roberto charged toward the garage.

"Time to go, Marie," Lou said. "Let's hope you're more tactful with the kids."

Marie stomped toward the M10 bus.

# TWENTY

CASEY PULLED INTO HER PARKING spot at home and tried to ignore her growing migraine. The aspirin she'd taken earlier had dulled it a bit, but the pain was returning with a vengeance. Neither her goose egg nor today's uneventful shift on the M10 was the cause; it was the escalating tension among Mainland staff.

Word had gotten around about this morning's nastiness between Marie and coworkers and now most employees were avoiding Marie. Some even glared at her. A few colleagues gave Casey sympathetic nods, while others had steered clear of her as well. Judging from Marie's blazing eyes and pinched lips, their behavior ticked her off. Casey didn't see much hope for a truce. There were too many questions and too few answers. Here she was, reduced to looking over her shoulder every five minutes, running from danger like a scared rabbit.

A sharp pain exploded in her head and her vision blurred. Casey scrunched her eyes shut. Oh, crap. She usually didn't get migraines this severe, but when she did the only remedy was medication and sleep.

Casey stepped out of the car. Her open door tapped Winifred's green Buick. Man, would the old crone never leave? Casey had told her about the shot and the caller's warning Friday night, hoping the news would send Winifred packing.

Winifred was at the stove, stirring something beefy-smelling in the soup pot. Casey's stomach grumbled. As she started toward the hallway, Winifred said, "My lawyer thinks we have a strong case for obtaining guardianship of Summer, especially since some bloody maniac's trying to kill you."

Casey's jaw clenched as she turned around. "We'll see what Rhonda says about this."

"I don't care what she says. We wouldn't be in this mess if she hadn't killed someone, and if you didn't go around making people want to kill you."

"What a nice thing to say. No wonder Summer doesn't want to live with you."

Winifred spun around. "How dare you talk to me that way."

"How dare you try to take a child who doesn't want to be with you." Casey's patience evaporated. "And why are you still here?"

"Someone has to keep this place from becoming a condemned pigsty." Winifred turned to the pot.

Casey's heart pounded in her chest. "You're no longer welcome in our home, Winfred. I want you out by the end of the day."

"I will not be ordered about by you."

Lou knocked on the door and peered through the window. Grateful for the distraction, she waved him in.

Lou looked at the scowling Winifred. "Nice to see you again, ma'am."

Winifred huffed as Casey led Lou down the hallway, up the stairs, and into her apartment.

"Winifred's talked to a lawyer." She shut the door. "The old bat's going after full custody."

"You need to tell Rhonda."

"I know."

The guinea pigs started whistling. Wincing at the noise, she placed her fingertips on her temples.

"Are you okay?" Lou asked.

"Migraine." She headed for the refrigerator. "There's still a beer in the fridge, if you want."

"No, thanks. You need to rest, so I won't stay long." He joined her in the kitchen. "Let me help." He took the lettuce and carrots from her. "How's Summer doing?"

"She's enjoying your mom's big-screen TV." Casey rubbed her temples again. "I called her before I came home. Summer wanted to know if Rhonda had phoned, and then asked if she could call the prison. I said no because I want to talk to her mom first."

"Is she okay with that?"

"Not really." Casey sat on the cushioned seat in the bay window.

Lou glanced at her phone on his way to the cages. "Your message light's blinking."

Casey pressed the button. Two seconds later, Rhonda's voice filled the room. Casey froze. Lou spun around.

"Sorry I took so long to call back," Rhonda said, her voice weak. "I caught a rotten bug. Anyway, you said Summer needs to talk to me. I hope my baby's okay." Her voice cracked. "I'll call between seven and eight tonight. Make sure Summer's there. Bye."

"She sounded shaky," Lou said.

Casey looked at her watch, but couldn't see the time through her tears.

Lou gave her a comforting hug. "Tough to hear her after all these weeks, isn't it?"

She nodded and pulled a tissue from her pocket. Ralphie stood on hind legs, propped his paws against the wire, and whistled so loudly that Casey covered her ears. Lou gave him a piece of carrot.

When the phone rang, she grabbed it.

"Hi, it's Noel. I tried Gabrielle's number all weekend, but there was no answer."

"She might have been away. Maybe she'll be back tonight."

"Do you know where she works?"

"I don't even know if she has a job." She watched Lou feed the animals.

He paused. "Is life any better at Mainland?"

Was he truly concerned, or just lonely for conversation? Or was Noel as interested in her as Marie had implied? "It got worse today. Marie argued with a couple of drivers and interrogated Roberto. She needs to back off, Noel."

Lou turned to the guinea pigs.

"I was afraid she'd go off the deep end."

"Me too, but if she doesn't learn to control her emotions and her mouth, she could get herself suspended."

"I'll talk to her. Keep me posted on any new developments, okay?"

"Sure, bye."

Lou headed back to the fridge. "Noel wasn't asking you to keep investigating, was he?"

"He wanted me to know that his own efforts weren't going anywhere."

"Does this mean you'll still help him?"

"I've been debating that all weekend." She returned to the window seat. "Marie said that since the killer thinks I'm investigating, I might as well keep going. Maybe she has a point. The sooner we get this psycho, the safer Summer will be."

"I don't know about that."

When Lou disappeared behind the fridge door, Casey sighed. Whenever he didn't like what he was hearing, he kept busy. "For a few moments today, I wondered if Marie was the killer, seeing as how she had the ball cap and glasses at the time Jasmine was killed, but I can't see her arranging for someone to shoot a bullet into her son's room."

"You're right, she wouldn't."

"Still, I'm not sure she and Jasmine were as close as Marie wanted people to think. I mean, both Noel and Wesley knew stuff about Jasmine that she didn't."

Lou closed the door and wandered toward her. "I've been working up the courage to ask you something. It's why I came over." Trepidation clouded his face. "Part of me thinks I'm making something out of nothing, but then . . ." He looked away.

Lou's discomfort was making her edgy. "What do you want to know?"

He cleared his throat. "Is Noel Merryweather as interested in you as Marie said?"

So that was it. In the four months they'd been a couple, Lou had never shown insecurity or jealousy, but then she'd never been physically attracted to another man during that time either. He had seemed a little distant on the M10 today. Casey had noticed that he'd kept looking at her, but not in a happy-you're-with-me way. More in a I'm-not-sure-about-you way.

"Noel hasn't asked me out or anything, but if he did, I'd say no." He didn't look convinced. "You realize Marie's trying to use her brother to come between us, don't you?"

"Kind of, yeah." Lou gripped her hands. "You know she and I will never happen, right?"

"Yes. Noel and I will never happen, either."

"Are you sure?"

"Totally." Again she saw the doubt. "This isn't like you."

"It's just that you sound kind of funny whenever you mention his name."

"I do?"

"It's subtle, but it's there."

She'd had no idea. "If I sound funny, it's mainly because he's part of something you didn't want me involved with."

"You said mainly." He paused. "What's the other part?"

"Well, he is a charismatic, good-looking guy."

"Then you're attracted to him?"

If she lied, he'd probably sense it. "Physically, yeah, a bit; but not emotionally. Obviously, I don't trust the man."

"If you did, would that attraction become emotional?"

"Lou, you're the one I want to be with." She smiled when he embraced her. "I know I'm not good at saying so, but you really do mean the world to me."

"I should have told you the same more often too, hon, especially when I've been so worried about us. I mean, things have been kind of weird lately. The last thing I need is competition."

"You don't have any." Man, she'd never seen him so insecure. Casey closed her eyes and again rubbed her temples. She wished Marie had never introduced her to Noel.

"Can I get you something for the migraine?"

"No, I'll take a couple of pills and rest in a minute."

"I guess you won't be going to bowling practice tonight?"

"Sorry, no."

Lou watched her. "Are you sure I can't do anything for you?"

"Yeah."

He walked to the door and then kissed her. "Feel better, sweetheart."

"Thanks." She listened to him jog down the stairs until her phone rang. Casey flinched, and then hurried to pick it up before her head exploded. "Hello?"

"Is this Casey Holland?" a frail female voice asked.

"Who is this?"

"I'm Hannah O'Reilly, Jasmine Birch's mother."

# TWENTY-ONE

**HANNAH O'REILLY WAS CALLING HER?** What could she possibly want?

Casey plunked into the rocking chair. "Uh, hello."

"Have I called at a bad time?" The woman sounded uncertain. "Marie Crenshaw said I should contact you."

"This is fine." She'd kick Marie's butt tomorrow. "I'm not sure why she referred you to me, though."

"She said you've been looking into my daughter's murder. The police won't tell me much, you see." Hannah cleared her throat. "Marie said you went to her ex-husband's place to check on my grandson, but that you didn't see him."

Casey closed her eyes and massaged her forehead. She'd really let Marie have it. "I couldn't get close to Birch's trailer because he was home, and I only went as a favor to Marie. I'm not investiga—"

"I hear that Birch has an alibi," Hannah interrupted, "which is troubling, given the disgusting way he treated her. She wrote me about it, in detail."

Casey opened her eyes. "Emails?"

"Letters. I had a stroke, you see, so talking on the phone became difficult. I asked Jasmine to write down everything I missed while she was growing up. I was afraid of another stroke, and wanted to know everything about her. The experience has been, well . . ." A sob broke through Hannah's words.

"I'm sorry," Casey murmured. "I can't imagine what you're going through."

"Thank you. I'd planned to have her visit, but then this stupid illness happened. I was too proud to let her see me as an old, drooling invalid, so I asked her to wait until my rehabilitation was nearly over. Jasmine was making plans to come here when . . ." Another sob.

Poor woman. Giving up a daughter, and then finding her again, only to lose her this way had to be unbearable.

"Marie also said you saw a woman with Birch in that trailer."

Casey rested her head against the chair. "Yes."

"About a month ago, Jasmine called and said she'd seen a woman in Birch's car."

"Did Jasmine recognize her, by any chance, or describe her to you?"

"No, but she did say that Birch used to flaunt his girlfriends in her face, although he didn't this time. Anyway, I have a very special request to make, dear."

"Oh?" She didn't like the sound of this.

"Since you worked with Jasmine and would therefore know many of the people she mentioned in her letters, would you read them?"

"I, uh, don't quite understand why you'd want me to."

"If Birch truly is innocent, then someone else shot my daughter."

Casey's head pounded and she felt queasy. "I don't—"

"According to the letters, Jasmine had conflicts with a few people, and one or two of them were from Mainland Public Transport."

Casey gazed at the rodent cages in front of her bookshelf. She envied those little guys, eating, resting, and playing; no complicated decisions to make. As she headed for the bathroom, she said, "Did Jasmine mention anyone she was especially worried about?"

"No one, other than Birch."

"Shouldn't you give the letters to the police?"

"Marie said the RCMP suspect her brother, so why would they listen to me? And I just can't believe Mr. Merryweather killed her. Jasmine wrote so many kind things about him."

Presumably, Hannah hadn't heard about the returned engagement ring. Hadn't it occurred to her that Jasmine had only written what she'd wanted her mother to know and that her viewpoint might be biased?

"Mrs. O'Reilly, Noel told me that he and Jasmine argued the night before she was killed. You see, he proposed to her and she turned him down."

The line was silent a few moments. "I still don't believe he shot her," Hannah replied. "Birch wanted custody of Jeremy and now he has it. This is what matters. Has anyone considered the possibility that his mystery girlfriend shot my daughter? Even if I'm wrong, some other clue could be in those letters."

"Couldn't Marie read them?" Casey removed two pills from a bottle in the medicine cabinet. "She knows the same people I do."

"I asked her, of course, but she said it would be too upsetting. She's also very worried about her brother and the threat to her children."

Yet Marie had no qualms about putting her and Summer in more danger. "Did she mention that we were also threatened, my child and me?"

"Oh dear, I'm so sorry." Hannah sounded close to tears. "I know this is asking too much, but Marie assured me you're an excellent investigator, and I'm desperate, Miss Holland."

"What about a private investigator?"

"I need someone who knew Jasmine and her colleagues."

"Okay, well, how about you mail the letters to me?"

"I couldn't! Birch works for the post office and the letters could go missing. A courier could also lose them. They're are all I have of Jasmine, and they musn't leave Parksville."

Great. Wonderful. Casey swallowed the pills and some water.

"Miss Holland, I know this is a lot to ask, but could you come here and read them? I'll pay all your expenses."

Was she kidding? "Wouldn't it be cheaper to have the letters photo-copied and the copies sent to me? Or you could fax them."

"I don't have access to a copier, nor do I want anyone at this facility to know about my private life. Oh, my god!" Hannah said. "She's here, I have to go."

"Who's there?"

"Please come to Grantwood Manor." She sounded panicky. "You must take the letters before she finds them!"

"Before who finds them?" What in hell was going on? "Hannah? Are you all right?"

"Gabrielle will destroy the letters if she sees them. Please come as soon as you can." The line went dead.

The daughter? How was Casey supposed to drop everything and leave? Rhonda would be calling tonight. Surely Hannah could hide the letters from Gabrielle. She'd done so up to this point. Why did she have to, though?

Should she even go to Parksville? Summer was safe at Barb's, and Stan had told her she could take a break from the M10 after tomorrow. What about the rockhound assignment, though?

Casey slid under her comforter, then phoned Barb. Each ring sent shock waves through her skull, forcing her to hold the phone at a distance. Finally, Barb answered.

"It's Casey. How's Summer?"

"She's great. In fact, she's playing pool with my youngest right now."

"Good. I need to tell her that Rhonda called and left a message. She's calling back between seven and eight tonight, and wants to talk to Summer."

"Don't worry, we'll get her there safely."

"Thank you. May I talk to her?"

"Sure, and while I fetch Summer, you can talk to Lou. He just dropped by."

Should she tell him about Hannah? He wouldn't want her traipsing off to Parksville, but to leave without telling him would make things worse between them.

"How are you feeling?" Lou asked.

"I took meds and I'm in bed, so I'll be fine." She hesitated. "Listen, I just got a call from Jasmine's mother. She asked if I'd read some letters Jasmine wrote her."

"Why?"

After Casey explained, she said, "She wants me to come to Parksville to read them."

"Are you going?"

"Still deciding, but she practically begged me." She didn't want a lengthy debate about it.

"Here's Summer," he murmured.

"Did Mom really phone?" She sounded excited.

"Absolutely. Barb's going to bring you over." Casey closed her eyes. "Remember, I'd like to talk to your mom first, okay?"

"I guess. So, are you gonna tell her about the freak who wants to hurt me?"

"I have to be honest, Summer. Besides, your mom always helped me sort things out."

"You won't talk forever, right? I have tons of stuff to tell her."

What if Rhonda changed her mind and didn't call? What if she called and it went badly? "You know, something could come up and she might not be allowed to phone us."

"I suppose." She paused. "Lou just left the room and he seems kind of down. Is he mad at you?"

Summer had her mother's way of probing into personal issues. "Not that I know of."

"But he didn't stay with you tonight."

"I have a migraine and I just had a strange phone call from the mother of the lady who was killed. She wants me to come see her in Parksville, but I don't feel right about leaving you for a whole day."

"You should go; maybe even stay overnight. I'm fine here."

Casey smiled, but even this made her head throb. "Are you trying to get rid of me?"

"No, but Barb's totally awesome, and this place is cool."

Meaning better than here. Casey felt a pang of jealousy. "Good."

"If someone needs help, you shouldn't turn your back on them," Summer said. "That's what you and Mom taught me."

She thought about Hannah and little Jeremy. "Even if it means endangering yourself and those you love, like I've done to you?" Not to mention turning colleagues into enemies.

"Totally. You gotta do what you think is right, no matter what."

God, she sounded like Rhonda, when Rhonda had been at her best. "So, oh Wise One, what if you've lost sight of what's right and what's wrong?"

"You gotta go with your instinct, right? Isn't that what you always say?"

"I'm not sure my instinct's been working all that well lately. Anyhow, I should get some sleep before your mom calls."

"Uh, Casey? If she doesn't call, we can phone again, right?"

"We'll reach her no matter what."

"'Kay." Summer cleared her throat. "When I was talking about how you have to help your friends, I was also thinking about Mom."

"If she needs me, I'll be there for her."

"Me too."

But would Rhonda want their help? Would she want to deal with them at all?

# TWENTY-TWO

IN MAINLAND'S LUNCHROOM, CASEY STIRRED her third coffee of the morning, and it was only eight-thirty. She wished she hadn't spent most of the night stewing over Rhonda's phone call. Even now, too much of it replayed in her mind, like Summer's tearful rant about Winifred. "All she wants me to do is chores and homework, and I don't want Grandma living here!" She'd finally plunked the phone in Casey's hand. By the time Casey had finished telling Rhonda about Summer's deteriorating behavior, Winifred blurting the truth about Summer's birth, and her investigation into Jasmine's murder, Rhonda was the one in tears.

"I'm going through enough shit, Casey, and now you're telling me my baby's in danger? What am I supposed to do about it from here?"

Casey hadn't known what to say. Her assurance that Summer was safe with Barb had seemed so lame that she'd felt ashamed and incompetent. Summer had asked to speak to Rhonda again. This time, the topic was school. Seconds later, Summer was shouting, "My friends are not losers!" Before Casey knew it, Summer was running out of her apartment and Rhonda was fuming. After she'd calmed Rhonda down, Rhonda promised to call back soon and deal with Winifred then.

"What's the matter, kiddo?" Stan asked as he approached. "Is that bump on the noggin still hurting?"

Casey looked up. She didn't want to talk about Rhonda. "No, I got a call from Jasmine's mother last night."

By the time she finished telling him about Hannah's request, they'd left the lunchroom and were standing in front of the exit to the parking lot. Through the plate glass window next to the doors, Stan watched Mainland's latest pre-owned acquisition pull out: a two hundred and seventy-five horsepower beast that could hold seventy-two passengers and two wheelchairs. The bus had been recently washed, making the silver and black stripes along the green side shine.

Casey looked for Lou's old black pickup, but it wasn't here. The M10 was due to pull out in fifteen minutes.

"Do you think I should go to Parksville?"

"I can only tell you which bus to work on and when," he answered. "Since Marie's kids are away, I'll put her on the rock-throwing case until it's safe for you on the M6 again."

"Did you say you're giving Casey time off to go to Parksville?"

The sound of David Eisler's voice made them turn around.

"What of it?" Stan asked.

Eisler glanced at staff wandering past them. "Step outside, both of you."

Stan rolled his eyes while Casey led the way, irritated that Eisler had been eavesdropping when she'd purposely kept her voice low. Outside, he didn't stop walking until they were too far from the doors to be overheard.

The VP zeroed in on Casey. "Why are you going to Parksville when we're short-staffed?"

"Why should you care?" Stan shot back.

"Jasmine's mother lives there," Eisler said, turning to her. "I thought I told you not to pry into a murder investigation."

Her jaw clenched under his withering stare. "She invited me, and there's nothing to investigate in Parksville."

"There must be a link or she wouldn't have asked you." Eisler stood straighter, as if to appear taller, yet he still barely reached Stan's shoulder. "Since you didn't respect my request to stay out of the investigation, you're fired for insubordination and sabotaging what was a pleasant working environment."

"What the hell are you talking about?" Stan asked.

"She was involved in an altercation with staff about murder suspects."

"That was Marie, not me."

"It was both of you! I heard every word."

Part of Casey wanted to scream at the moron, but why give him more reasons to fire her?

"I decide which of my staff are fired, not you," Stan said.

"You're not running this show, Stanley."

Even under the beard, Casey could see Stan's face redden. He hated it when people used his formal name.

"It looks like you won't be running things much longer either," Stan replied. "I know about your job interview the morning Jasmine died."

Casey saw Eisler's hands curl into fists.

"Not what I'd call productive time for Mainland Public Transport," he added. "So maybe you should fire your own ass, you fascist little twerp."

Eisler's lips grew white "Maybe I should fire your ass, too."

Casey spotted employees staring at them.

"Well, Davey, old buddy, that works both ways," Stan crossed his arms and smiled. "What do you think Gwyn will say when I tell him you've been job searching on company time?"

Before Eisler could respond, Casey said, "Do the police know that you went to Jasmine's apartment looking for her?" The shock on Eisler's and Stan's faces was worth the risk. "Some of the staff know you'd been calling her at home, David. Jasmine told people and I imagine phone records will corroborate that."

"It seems we'll have lots of news for Gwyn when he gets back from holiday," Stan remarked.

Eisler's perma tan darkened. "You never did have much class, did you, Stanley? But then, you belong in this dump, so why should I expect otherwise?"

"Casey stays," Stan said, "and stop bloody eavesdropping!"

"That wasn't my intention," he shot back. "I came to tell you that the company's lawyers just learned that the bullet fired at Casey came from the same gun that shot holes at Mrs. Crenshaw's house. A Glock twenty-seven, which I'm told is owned by Wesley Axelson."

"Lawyers, huh?" Stan remarked.

"Someone has to protect the company's interests; obviously, you're not up to it and never will be."

"Look who's talking."

Eisler ignored him as he focused on Casey. "See what happens when you meddle?" Anger seethed through his words. "Keep it up and you'll get yourself killed." He marched toward the door.

"Good luck with the job hunt!" Stan shouted.

Casey noticed the surprised looks on employees' faces. Word would be out about it by lunchtime, which was probably what Stan intended.

"Miserable toad," Stan muttered. "When are you leaving for Parksville?"

The question caught her off guard. "I haven't said I'm going."

"I've known you a long time, kiddo, and you'd never turn your back on a plea for help."

It wasn't that easy. There were critters to feed, an essay to finish, a class tomorrow. On the other hand, Lou could feed the animals and she could take the essay with her. "Do I still have a job?"

"You bet." He watched her. "Be careful over there, okay?"

"I will, and thanks." Maybe getting away would be good. Marie might call it selfish and even cowardly to take off, but survival, psychological and physical, sometimes required selfish acts. "I'll leave after tomorrow morning's class, stay the night, and take a ferry back first thing Thursday."

Wesley stepped out of the building and headed for one of two buses still in the yard. He spotted Casey and Stan, and gave them a curt nod.

"Aren't you usually at the gym in the mornings?" she called, and walked toward him.

"Too many guys called in sick."

There'd been a lot of sick calls lately. People not wanting to work at a place with horrible morale. Two of Mainland's admin staff greeted Casey and Stan on their way into the building. She'd noticed a couple of other friendly greetings this morning. Were staff finally believing that she wasn't investigating Jasmine's death? If this was really true, would she be even going to Parksville?

"Wes, we just found out that the bullet in the bus came from the same gun used on Marie's place," Casey said. "A Glock twenty-seven."

"Shit, it's probably mine."

"So I heard," Stan said as he joined them.

Wesley looked at her. "You told him, too?"

"No, Eisler did." She detected a glimmer of respect on that big hairy face.

Wesley rolled his eyes. "They were ripped off from my apartment," he told Stan. "Two Glocks and a rifle. The thirty-five was used on Jasmine."

Roberto pulled his Corvette into a parking stall. The moment Roberto stepped out, Wesley charged toward him. "Your alibi's shit, de Luca!"

Casey cringed.

Roberto slammed the door shut. "Mind your own damn business."

He squinted in the sunlight as Wesley moved to within arm's length of him. Compared to Wesley, Roberto was short and spindly. Wesley could have Roberto on the ground and writhing in two seconds.

"Your gun killed Jasmine," Roberto said. "Maybe you're the liar."

Casey held her breath. Who'd told him about the gun? Wesley flexed his fingers and narrowed his eyes. He looked like he wanted to tear Roberto's head off. Why was Roberto poking the bear? He'd never win a fight with Wesley.

"You weren't at no dentist when Jasmine died," Wesley said.

Roberto started to walk away.

Stan leaned close to Casey and whispered, "Is that true?"

"I think so." She saw Marie drive into the lot.

"She was my friend!" Wesley shouted, following Roberto toward the garage at the far end of the yard. "For some dumb reason she loved you and you treated her like shit! I ought to kick your ass from here to hell."

Roberto gave Wesley the finger and kept walking.

Wesley started after him, but Stan moved fast and grabbed his arm. "Violence will get you fired, Wes. Eisler's probably watching right now."

As far as Casey knew, Stan was the only man at Mainland who could touch Rude Wesley Axelson without getting hurt, but Stan was a big guy; a former pro football player not intimidated by anyone.

"Where were you when Jasmine was shot, de Luca?" Wesley yelled.

"Ask the cops!"

Casey counted six staff members who'd stopped to listen. Worse, Marie was heading toward Roberto.

"If you have an alibi," Marie said, "why did you tell people you were at the dentist?"

"Because it's got nothing to do with Jasmine!"

Marie plunked her hands on her hips and gave him the same impatient look Casey had seen a million times. "We'll find out sooner or later, so you might as well talk."

Casey groaned. Marie couldn't afford to make more enemies. Didn't she care that she had to work with these people, and that the tension she created affected everyone?

Wesley yelled, "Tell her, you piece of crap!"

Stan stayed close to Wesley.

Roberto spun around. "I was with a married woman. Happy now?"

"All morning?" Marie asked. "Who is she?"

"She's not with Mainland. That's all you need to know."

"And we're supposed to believe you?" Wesley said.

"Ask the cops."

Casey believed him. Some of Roberto's trysts had bothered his conscience enough to confide in her. He'd been with married women before and had skipped work more than once for a hot romance.

"What about your alibi, Wes?" Roberto asked. "How many guys did you pay to say you were at the gym that morning?"

"Those jerks wouldn't lie for me."

Also probably true. Casey recalled the competitiveness and animosity between wrestlers.

"I'm shocked, seeing as how you're such a nice guy," Roberto remarked, and headed for the garage.

Wesley swore and charged toward the buses.

"It looks like Roberto and Wesley have alibis too." Casey turned to Marie. "And let's not forget Eisler's job interview."

"Do you actually think Wesley's telling the truth?"

"Yeah, I saw him in action at the gym. Those guys aren't friends, they're rivals. If anyone saw a way to throw him in jail, they might just do it."

"I talked to the janitors and they said the message wasn't on our lockers when they were cleaning."

Casey wasn't going to waste time worrying about it. She wandered toward the M10, wondering where Lou was.

"Only two female drivers worked the early shift," Marie said, keeping up with her, "and three clerical workers started at eight-thirty. I showed them a sample of the color and two of them said that Ingrid sometimes wears a dark shade like that. I think I've seen it on her too."

"What can you do about it?"

"Report her for harassment and defacing company property," Marie said. "Did you get a phone call from Hannah O'Reilly last night?"

"Yes, and why did you give her my name? What's wrong with you?"

Lou roared into the depot and screeched to a halt.

"Sorry, but I can't travel far from my kids. They're upset enough about not being able to come home. At least Summer's old enough to understand."

Lou jogged up to them.

"Morning, Lou," Marie said. "Casey got a call from Jasmine's mother last night."

Casey fumed. Would she ever stop stirring things up?

"I know." He stopped at the entrance. "I'd like to talk to Casey privately a minute."

Marie looked disappointed. "A minute's about all you have or we'll be late."

As she boarded the M10, Casey and Lou strolled out of earshot.

"Are you going to Parksville?" he asked.

"I think so, yeah. I'm worried about Hannah. She was scared that Gabrielle would destroy the letters, which makes me wonder if there's something nasty about her in them."

"What about Summer?"

"She's okay with me going."

"I'm not sure I am." Lou's gaze was intense. "You'll be on your own over there."

"As long as you and Stan are the only people who know when I'm leaving, I'll be fine. I'll make sure I'm not being tailed. By the way, the ballistics test came back. The bullet in the bus came from a Glock twenty-seven; the same gun used on Marie's house."

"Shit."

"Roberto has a new alibi, verified by the cops. It seems he was having fun with a married woman."

"Come on, you two!" Marie shouted.

Lou shook his head. "Who's doing this?"

"I don't know. All the more reason to find out what Jasmine wrote in those letters."

"What if you run into Gabrielle? Isn't she a suspect too?"

"Since we've never met, she won't know who I am."

"When are you leaving?"

"After class tomorrow. Will you feed the critters while I'm gone? It will only be twenty-four hours, and I swear I'll make it up to you. I'll make everything up to you, promise."

Lou studied her a moment, then kissed her cheek. "Tell me how later."

# TWENTY-THREE

**CASEY TOOK A DEEP YOGA** breath, realizing too late that she'd just filled her lungs with the smell of antiseptic. She blew the air out fast and shook the tension from her shoulders before knocking on Hannah O'Reilly's door. The door was one of a dozen lining the spacious corridor inside Grantwood Manor, although "manor" was too grand a word for this single-story structure. The immaculate lawn and vibrant rose gardens separated by footpaths were impressive, though.

Despite Stan's and Summer's support, Casey had had second thoughts about coming here; however, Hannah phoned again last night and tearfully begged her to come read the letters as soon as possible. It seemed Gabrielle suspected Hannah of hiding something, and Hannah was convinced that Gabrielle would soon search her room.

Casey knocked on the door, and looked up and down the hallway. If it wasn't for the telltale hospital smell, this place could be mistaken for a hotel. Landscape paintings were strategically spaced between sconces illuminating the corridor.

"Just a minute," a woman answered.

Once Casey had exited the ferry and begun the half-hour drive north to Parksville, misgivings about this trip had started to magnify. By the time she'd cleared Nanaimo's long sprawl of big box stores, shopping malls, fast food joints, and other businesses, anxiety had really kicked in.

The doorknob turned slowly. When a tall, white-haired woman with Jasmine's sapphire eyes peered at her, Casey was taken aback. She'd pictured Hannah as a stooped, feeble old lady, not this erect, confident-looking woman. The only evidence of her stroke was a slight droop on the right side of her mouth.

"Casey?"

"Yes, hi."

"Welcome." Hannah stepped back. "Please come in."

Casey entered a spacious room containing bedroom furniture and a sitting area at the far end. An alcove off the sitting area contained a small sink, bar fridge, and toaster oven. French doors opened onto a large, enclosed courtyard filled with orchids, gardenias, and other tropical flowers.

"This is far nicer than I would have expected from a government facility," Casey said.

"Actually, it's a private care facility, which essentially means that the place is an overpriced transition house. Residents here don't need full nursing care, but they still can't quite manage on their own yet."

Not cheap, Casey thought; yet Parksville was a picturesque, oceanside resort town with enough golf courses and activities to attract plenty of well-off retirees.

"Come, let's sit down." Hannah strolled past the wheelchair by her bed and chose a cushioned chair at the round glass table. Judging from her smooth gait, she didn't need the wheelchair, at least for short distances.

Casey spotted the flat-screen, wall-mounted TV above a chest of drawers opposite the bed. The walls were mauve and the quilt on Hannah's twin bed was dark purple with yellow and white flowers. An oil painting of lilacs hung above the bed. Violet plants sat on tabletops. Casey wondered if every room was a tribute to the many shades of purple, or whether Hannah had customized it with bedding and flowers.

"Coffee?" A pot, two cups and saucers, and a plate of sugar cookies were on the table.

"That'd be great, thanks."

"Would you mind pouring? My arm isn't quite strong enough to lift a full pot. It took both hands just to get the stupid thing to the table."

Casey began to pour. "I'm glad you called me back last night. I was worried about you."

"I realized that I must have sounded like a frantic nut after my initial call." Hannah clasped her hands together and rested them on the table. "I was just so shocked to spot Gabrielle coming down the hall." She nodded toward the courtyard. "She rarely visits these days."

Casey saw a row of windows at the end of the courtyard and recognized the lobby. "I'm sorry if this sounds nosy, but why do you think Gabrielle would destroy your letters?"

"She thinks I'm losing my memory and have forgotten about my grand-son. She wouldn't want me to have any reminders of Jeremy or his mother."

"She didn't get along with Jasmine?"

"She doesn't want to share a million-dollar inheritance with her nephew. She's resentful enough that her brothers will each inherit the same." Hannah slurped her coffee. "As long as Gabrielle thinks I'm weak and forgetful, she's less likely to snoop into my affairs." Hannah slid the cookie plate toward her. "Help yourself."

"Thanks." While Hannah slowly poured cream into her coffee, Casey noticed an eight-by-ten photo of four school-age children on the night table. "Nice looking kids."

"My grandchildren."

Casey drank the coffee. Good and strong. "I guess Jasmine was your first child?"

"My third, actually. Her two half brothers are older and Gabrielle is three years younger. I know this sounds odd, Miss Holland."

"Call me Casey."

"And I'm Hannah." She sipped her coffee. "My parents were conservative, religious people. When my husband died and I was left to manage our farm, they kept throwing eligible men my way, hoping I'd find a new husband. When they ran out of church people they resorted to reliable farmhands."

"It doesn't sound like much fun."

"Oh, I had my moments." Her mouth drooped further when she smiled. "I fell in love with one of them and became pregnant, but he ran off. My parents wouldn't have anything to do with me unless I gave up the baby." Hannah gazed at the courtyard. "I desperately needed their support, so I left my boys with my sister and brother-in-law for a few weeks and had Jasmine in Vancouver. Then I gave her away."

"That must have been so difficult."

"You have no idea." She placed her hand over her mouth and lowered her gaze. "Two years later, I married again and had Gabrielle. When my husband died, I began the search. Of course, I had no idea Jasmine had been looking for me as well." The corners of her mouth were turned so far down they nearly reached her chin. "I suppose losing her twice is God's punishment for giving her up in the first place."

Casey noticed a senior hobbling toward a rattan chair in the court-yard. "How many letters did Jasmine write?"

"Thirty. Once I was well enough, we spoke on the phone, of course, but I asked her to keep the letters coming. She wrote beautifully detailed letters; said it helped her put things in perspective."

Crap, this would require more reading than she'd anticipated. "I'd probably only need to read those concerning her work. Did Jasmine write much about her colleagues?"

"A fair bit, yes. She wrote a lot about her friend, Marie Crenshaw." Hannah looked at Casey. "Jasmine was trying to help Marie sort out a complicated love life."

Casey smiled. "Marie has three ex-husbands. Complicated describes her life well."

"Apparently, she'd chosen number four, although he's already in a relationship."

The smile faded. She had a feeling Hannah knew about her and Lou. "Did Jasmine write about her own love life?"

"Yes, and I'm afraid her choice of husband was terrible. Jasmine probably sympathized with Marie because she too craved a loving relationship."

"Most people do."

"Indeed. Gabrielle's craving for love is just as strong and her choices have been no better than Jasmine's. She doesn't even bother introducing boyfriends anymore because she knows I'll probably disapprove."

The strength and bitterness in her voice again struck Casey. So little about Hannah seemed vulnerable. Had the fearful tone in her phone calls been a ploy to bring her here?

"I'll have to kick her out of my house when I go home in a few days," Hannah added, dabbing a spot of drool from the corner of her mouth. "After my stroke, she moved out of her apartment to save money. I doubt she wants to resume paying rent, but God knows neither of us wants to live under the same roof again."

Casey looked away. This was more than she wanted to hear about Hannah's family problems.

"I'm sorry for being so personal, Casey, but I believe in frank, honest discussion, and the truth is that my daughter's one of the greediest people I know."

"It's okay." Casey smiled. "Does Gabrielle have a job?"

"She's a secretary at a management consulting firm here in Parksville."

The firm wouldn't be hard to track down. Once the summer tourists and residents left, Parksville's population was about twelve thousand. How many consulting firms could there be?

"Hannah, did you know that Gabrielle visited Jasmine two days before the murder? It was Sunday afternoon."

Hannah dropped the tissue she'd been holding. "No, I did not. What happened?"

"I wasn't there, so I'm getting this secondhand, but Gabrielle essentially told Jasmine to stay out of your life."

Her sapphire eyes developed an icy glow. "She did, did she?"

"Do you remember what state of mind your daughters were in between Sunday, the twenty-sixth, and the morning Jasmine died? Did Jasmine seem troubled by anything?"

"I spoke with her that Sunday morning and she didn't sound bothered by anything, and I didn't see Gabrielle at all that week; just spoke on the phone with her after the murder."

Had Gabrielle been on the mainland when Jasmine died? The implication was too awful to raise. "I understand that Jasmine was thinking about moving to Parksville."

"Yes, during that last phone call on Sunday, she asked me what I thought of the idea. I told her I loved it and invited her and Jeremy to live with me. She certainly sounded appreciative, but there was Noel, and she'd been building friendships with a couple of coworkers she was very fond of."

"Do you know their names?"

"One is foreign . . . Roberto, I think. Anyhow, I intend to be Jeremy's caregiver now. The sooner I get him away from that violent drunk and the tart he's with, the better for my grandson. My lawyers will find out who she is." Hannah stood awkwardly and opened the French doors. The scent of gardenias wafted into the room. "Gabrielle won't know any of this until Jeremy's in my house and the locks are changed."

"She's that difficult?"

Hannah studied a palm tree near her door before turning back to Casey. "Please understand, I do love my daughter, and she was helpful after my stroke, but I'm well aware of her dark side. I've rescued Gabrielle from destructive relationships, supported her after she was fired once, even bailed her out of jail for marijuana possession, but she'll soon learn that the free ride's over. Jeremy needs me now."

Casey couldn't tell who was more manipulative, Gabrielle or her mother.

"You look disconcerted, my dear," Hannah remarked. "I've learned the hard way that it's crucial to learn to protect what's yours before others take it away." Her expression became solemn. "Jasmine had a dark side, and I'm afraid she wrote unflattering things about you."

Casey nodded. "We started off okay, but she became distant. I never knew why."

"Judging from her letters, she was influenced by Marie."

Hardly a surprise. Hannah rose, walked to the night table by her bed, and lifted out a bundle of pale yellow envelopes. She gave them to Casey.

"The letters are sorted from her earliest memories to the present. I'd like you to read them all, to understand who my daughter was."

Double crap. "On the phone, we talked about photocopying them. Would you like me to do that now and return the originals today?"

"Why don't you deliver everything first thing tomorrow in case Gabrielle shows up, which is always in the afternoon."

Casey placed the bundle in her bag. Man, this was going to be one long night of reading.

"If you find a clue to the killer, please let me know straight away, dear."

There was a quick rap on the door and a young woman barged in. Casey inhaled sharply as she recognized the same face, dark braided hair, and double-D chest she'd seen in Elliott Birch's trailer eight days ago. This time, the woman was wearing glasses and a blue silk blouse instead of a white T-shirt.

The woman glared at her. "Who the hell are you?"

"Casey Holland, and you?"

"Gabrielle!" Hannah hobbled toward her, suddenly looking like a frail old lady. "How lovely to see you again."

Casey's stomach lurched.

# TWENTY-FOUR

→

**"MOTHER, ARE YOU ALL RIGHT?"** Gabrielle grasped Hannah's outstretched hands. "What are you doing out of your chair?"

Casey pressed her lips together to keep from blurting something stupid, like how Birch's lover was Gabrielle and that she'd just earned number one spot on the suspect list.

"I was feeling a bit stronger today," Hannah answered, "and wanted to show Casey what I could do. See?"

Casey's heart pounded, but she kept her expression impassive as Hannah hobbled toward her wheelchair. In seconds, the woman had gone from able-bodied woman to feeble stroke patient. Her shoulders had become rounded, her right hand curled and claw-like, and she leaned slightly to one side. Even her voice had reverted to the weak tone Casey had first heard on the phone.

"Is Casey a therapist?" Gabrielle asked.

"Oh dear, I'm so forgetful." Hannah turned to Casey. "This is my daughter, Gabrielle."

"Hi." It was the only word she could speak under Gabrielle's intense scrutiny.

"I thought you were too busy to come by today," Hannah said to Gabrielle.

"I finished my work early, so they let me leave." She helped her mother into the chair.

"Thank you. Would you get me a blanket, dear?"

Gabrielle reached for the mauve blanket at the end of her mother's bed. After she'd fussed over Hannah, she turned to Casey. "If you're not a therapist, then why are you here?"

Casey smiled at cold, cobra eyes. "I'm here because of Jasmine and her son." She loved the way Gabrielle's belligerent face became apprehensive.

"How did you know Jasmine?" Gabrielle asked.

"We worked at the same place."

Those cobra eyes didn't blink. "So, you just popped over to Parksville to chat with my mother?"

"I invited her here," Hannah said.

Gabrielle gaped at her mother. "You don't know this person."

"I knew they'd worked together, and I wanted to know more about Jasmine's life." Hannah adjusted her blanket. "Casey's been terribly helpful. I can put this whole ordeal behind me now."

Man, this woman deserved an Oscar. "I should get going." Casey headed for the door. "Nice to meet you, Hannah."

"Thanks so much for coming by," Hannah said.

"Are you going back to Vancouver right away?" Gabrielle asked.

Casey heard the tension. "Soon." She opened the door and gazed at the O'Reilly women. "It's a shame Jasmine didn't grow up in your family. I think she would have fit right in."

She rushed down the corridor, eager to put some distance between herself and a possible killer. When had Gabrielle hooked up with Birch to destroy Jasmine? If she'd known about them, surely she would have told someone, unless Jasmine had learned the truth just before she was killed. Was this the reason she'd been so irritable those last couple of days? In the lobby, Casey glanced over her shoulder. No sign of Gabrielle. Outside, she ran to her car, tempted to catch a ferry right away. Still, she'd promised to photocopy the letters and return them before she left town. Hannah needed to know about Gabrielle and Birch as well.

How would she take the news? A lot of moms would deny the truth; maybe lash out at the messenger. Hannah was hard to predict, though. She claimed to know Gabrielle's darker side, but could she see her own daughter as a murder suspect? Would Hannah demand the letters back and tell Casey to get lost?

She looked in her rearview mirror. Gabrielle would probably tell Birch about their encounter. If he and Gabrielle had killed Jasmine, would he take his anger out on Summer? Casey peeled out of the parking lot and headed to her oceanside hotel ten minutes away. She didn't breathe easy again until she'd entered her ground floor room and locked the door.

She called Lou's mom and got voice mail. Casey checked her watch. Five o'clock. Barb had told Casey and Summer that supper was between five and six, and that she never picked up the phone during that hour.

"Hi, it's Casey," she said after the message beep. "Listen, I've stepped into a mess here in Parksville." She kept her voice calm. "Make sure Summer doesn't go anywhere on her own until I get back, okay? I'll call and explain more later."

She called Lou's cell. While the phone rang, she sat on the bed and gazed at the pine furniture, the blue and green squares on the bed-spread. No answer there either. Casey left a quick message, describing her encounter with Gabrielle and asking him to check on Barb and Summer.

Casey walked to the window. A handful of people strolled along the beach on this cool October day. A seagull strutted along the water's edge, stopped and cried, then flew away. Corporal Lundy needed to know about Gabrielle and Birch. Maybe he could ask a Vancouver city cop to patrol Barb's street tonight. Casey removed the bundle of letters from her bag and retrieved Lundy's number. He answered on the second ring.

"I have news." She described the connection between Gabrielle and Birch, Gabrielle's potential inheritance, and her fear for Summer's safety.

"How did you find all this out, Miss Holland?"

"By accident."

"What kind of accident?"

He wasn't going to like this. "Jasmine's biological mother asked me to visit her here in Parksville, and while we were talking, her daughter showed up. I recognized Gabrielle right away because I've seen her with Birch before; kissing him, in fact." Before he could ask where she'd seen them, Casey added, "A few weeks before Jasmine's death, her landlords saw someone in the car with Birch when he was stalking her. They never got a close look at the face, but it could have been Gabrielle."

"Are you still in Parksville?"

"Yes, which is why I'm worried about Summer. Could you ask the Vancouver police to keep an eye on the house?" She gave him Barb's address. "Do you know if Gabrielle has an alibi?"

"That comes under the none-of-your-business heading, Miss Holland. I'll do what I can for your ward, though. Meanwhile, I suggest you return home and stay out of our investigation."

"I've been trying, Corporal, but people keep dragging me into it."

"Try harder." He hung up before she could give him the name of Gabrielle's employer.

Casey tossed her phone on the bed. He was the one who should be bloody trying harder. She picked up a phone book from the table's bottom shelf and flipped through the yellow pages, looking for management consulting firms with four names. One company fit that description. Casey jotted down the company name and phone number on a hotel notepad.

If she called the company and came up with a good reason for asking if Gabrielle was working the morning of September twenty-eighth, a receptionist might be able to help, but it would be tricky. Casey checked her watch. Twenty past five. She wanted to call Hannah and tell her about Gabrielle right now, but Gabrielle might still be there. Casey called the employer. A perky recorded voice announced they were closed for the day and would re-open at 9:00 AM.

Casey picked up a brochure that boasted about Parksville's beaches, parks, golf courses, and nature walks. Several resorts offered special romantic getaway packages. She thought of Lou and loneliness overwhelmed her. Might as well grab a meal, read some letters, and try to understand a complicated woman she really hadn't known at all.

BY THE TIME Casey had poured over five heart-wrenching letters about Jasmine's childhood and marriage, she'd lost her appetite. Understandably, Jasmine hadn't gone into graphic detail about the sexual abuse she'd suffered, yet her pain was clear, and because of this Casey felt like a sleazy voyeur.

"*After my adopted parents died,*" Jasmine had written, "*I was afraid I'd never have a family again and didn't think the depression would ever end.*"

A feeling Casey knew all too well. After Dad's passing, medication and therapy eventually got her through months of depression. Jasmine's remedy had been to marry Elliott Birch, which only made things worse. Refusing to be victimized again, she'd left him.

Casey pushed away her half-eaten clubhouse sandwich. She'd been sitting in the hotel's restaurant for what felt like ages, and it was now dark outside. With any luck, Gabrielle would have left Hannah by now. She'd already called Barb back and had updated her on recent events.

Casey picked up her phone, took a calming breath, and called Hannah. When Hannah answered, Casey said, "Are you alone?"

"Yes, thank heaven." Hannah's voice was strong again. "God, I hate her surprise visits. Two in one week. She probably lost another boyfriend."

"I don't think so," Casey replied. "I have something to tell you about your daughter, and it's not good."

Hannah hesitated only a moment. "Go on."

"Gabrielle was the woman I saw with Birch in his trailer. I recognized her right away." She waited for a response. "Hannah?" Oh no. Was the poor woman having another stroke? "Are you all right?"

"I'm fine." Her voice was quiet. "Just surprised."

"I'm sorry, I had no idea who Gabrielle was until you introduced us."

"I understand, Miss Holland, and I respect your honesty."

Back to last names. Hannah was ticked and Casey didn't blame her. "If you confront her about it, I'd appreciate it if you left my name out of this."

"She'll want to know how I found out."

"Please understand that I'm not accusing Gabrielle of anything," Casey said. "I simply saw her kissing Birch in his trailer the night I went to check on Jeremy."

"When was that, exactly?"

"Eight days go, on the twelfth." Casey stared at her iced tea. "Maybe they've split up since then."

"I'll have someone look into it. If she's still with Birch, I'll know soon enough."

Would Hannah confront Gabrielle before then? "Do you still want me to read the letters?"

"Yes, of course."

Twenty-five more to go. Part of her wished Hannah had said no.

"I'm glad you told me," Hannah added. "The more I know, the better I can protect my grandson. Goodbye."

Casey picked up letter number six.

→    →    →

**WHEN SHE RETURNED** to her hotel room an hour later, she didn't know whether to feel angry, sad, or relieved that she finally knew why Jasmine had hated her.

"*I like to help people,*" she'd written. "*My friend Marie said a girl named Casey stole the man she was in love with. Casey puts on a nice act, but Marie says it's phony. Casey always acts like she owns the place.*"

Apparently, Marie had convinced Jasmine that Stan gave Casey better assignments because she was his favorite. Casey tossed the letters onto the bed. The rest would have to wait till after she'd had a long hot bath. She removed her runners and socks, then started to pull off her T-shirt when someone knocked on the door.

Who the hell was that? Only Lou knew where she was staying. She'd drawn the curtains when she came in, but they weren't heavy enough to keep the room's lights from showing through.

The second knock was louder and more insistent. Worry sent a shiver through Casey. Pulling the shirt back down, she tiptoed toward the door and peered through the peephole. Gabrielle. Adrenaline surged and goose bumps rose on her arms. She stepped to the side, away from the door. Had the woman seen her drive away? Had Gabrielle scoured parking lots in search of an old red Tercel?

"What do you want, Gabrielle?"

"I need to talk to you. Please, it's urgent."

"Has something happened to your mother?"

"She's fine. Could you open the door?"

Casey didn't want to see those cobra eyes again. "I was about to take a bath. Can you phone me in an hour?"

"I'm here now and this won't take long."

Not long at all to fire a Glock twenty-seven. "I don't see why it can't wait."

"I'm not leaving until we talk. I'll camp outside this door all night if I have to."

Crap. Threatening to call security would be pointless. This was a small, cheap place, probably without security. Casey grabbed her cell phone, stuffed the letters in her bag, and then shoved the bag in a drawer. She peeked through the drapes on the right side of the door. Gabrielle appeared to be alone and empty-handed, but this didn't mean a companion wasn't waiting nearby, or that she wasn't hiding a weapon.

"You can't contact my mother again!" Gabrielle yelled through the door. "She was so upset after you left that I thought she'd have another stroke. What did you say to her?"

Hannah hadn't sounded upset on the phone. "Ask Hannah."

"She's already forgotten most of it."

Sure, right.

"She might ask you about Jasmine again," Gabrielle went on. "Don't tell her anything, understand?"

"Casey will talk to whoever she wants," a familiar voice said loudly.

Oh god, it was Lou! If Gabrielle was armed he could be in trouble. Casey opened the door, barely aware of the cool, salty air wafting into the room.

"Hey, darlin'." Lou stepped past Gabrielle.

"This is Gabrielle O'Reilly," Casey said to Lou. "Jasmine's half sister."

From the recognition and wariness on Lou's face, he remembered her from Birch's trailer. He put down his backpack.

"Jasmine wasn't family, she was trash," Gabrielle stated. "All she wanted was Mother's money."

"Is that what you plan on telling the cops when they ask for your alibi?" Casey asked.

"I have an alibi." Her cobra eyes glowered.

"Good," Casey said, crossing her arms, "because they know about your affair with Elliott Birch."

Gabrielle recoiled. "You're full of it."

Lou squeezed Casey's arm, a warning not to pursue this, but she didn't want to stop. If the woman had a weapon, she would have revealed it by now, and Casey had no intention of letting her leave without obtaining information.

"We saw you in his trailer eight days ago," she said.

Gabrielle's eyes practically popped out of her head. "You were spying on me?"

"Of course not, I didn't even know who you were until this afternoon."

"What the hell were you doing there?"

"Walking my dog."

Gabrielle bit her lower lip. "Have you told my mother?"

"Ask her."

"Don't play games with me!"

"I'm not the one who's been playing." Casey raised the phone still in her hand. "You have three seconds to leave before I call the cops."

Gabrielle didn't move. "What will it take to keep you from telling anyone? I have money."

"All I want is the truth about you and Birch." She felt Lou's arm slip around her.

"We fell in love," Gabrielle said, "but Mom would have disowned me if she found out."

Given the way Gabrielle kept fidgeting, Casey figured she was lying. "How and when did you and Birch meet?"

"When I saw Jasmine for the first time, she and Elliott were standing at the front door, arguing about their kid. Jasmine didn't know who I was."

"When was that?" Casey asked.

"A month and a half ago."

Not true. Marie had said she'd been with Jasmine when Gabrielle approached and introduced herself two days before the shooting. Birch hadn't been anywhere around at that time.

"After Jasmine took off, Elliott and I started talking." Gabrielle shoved her hands in her pockets. "He was devastated that he couldn't see his son more often."

"A custody battle would have been tough to win," Casey replied, "what with Birch's drinking and domestic violence history."

Lou squeezed her arm a little harder.

"What are you talking about? He's a great dad, and he's never hit me."

Give it time, Casey thought. "Word is he's still a suspect in Jasmine's murder, that he had someone else shoot her."

"That's ridiculous!" Gabrielle stepped back. "Don't contact my mother again!"

Casey shut the door and turned the deadbolt. "Think we struck a nerve?"

"Just a tad." Lou plunked onto the bed. "You took a huge chance."

"I know, but that woman clearly has plenty to hide." She sat next to

Lou. "If Jasmine had found out that Gabrielle was involved with Birch and had threatened to tell Hannah, it'd be a strong motive for murder."

"You need to tell Corporal Lundy."

"I already have." She put her arms around Lou. "I don't want you to take this the wrong way, and notice how cheerful I sound, but what are you doing here? Did you get my message?"

"Yeah, and I was already on my way." He smiled tentatively. "I got a couple of guys to take my shifts." He squeezed her hard. "What was Hannah like?"

"Kind of creepy." After she highlighted their conversation and told him about Hannah's transformation after Gabrielle arrived, she described the contents of Jasmine's letters, including the part about Marie.

"In Marie's world, my feelings don't count," Casey said. "She told Jasmine I was a driven, career-minded prima donna who wasn't interested in marriage or family."

"Since you and I don't live together," Lou replied, "I guess it only added to her fantasy."

As his gaze met hers, guilt blanketed Casey. After her divorce, but before they became a couple, she'd told him she wasn't any good at marriage. Had he wondered if she'd changed her mind? Had she?

"Marie doesn't understand that I can't imagine living without you." Casey placed her hands on each side of his face. "How much I love you."

He wrapped his arms around her. "I love you too. Always will."

A lump formed in her throat. "We've had some bad moments lately, but it'll be better."

"Totally."

She kissed him until her whole body tingled. When they finally pulled apart, she said, "Who's looking after the critters?"

"I put a ton of food in their cages." Lou rubbed her back. "They'll be fine, and we'll be back before noon tomorrow if we catch an early ferry."

She stroked his cheek. "I really was trying to help Hannah, but the person who most needs help is Jeremy. The little guy's surrounded by manipulative adults who probably don't deserve him."

"You can't help everyone, especially when you have Summer to think about."

"I guess." Casey hesitated. "You know I only want to do what's right for her, don't you?"

"Yep."

"I helped Marie and Noel because she practically begged me. I didn't plan to launch my own murder investigation."

"I know that too."

"If you know so much," she said, smirking, "then what am I thinking now?"

He looked at her bare feet. "That you want to soak in a hot tub?"

She laughed. "I bought a bath bomb in a gift shop down the street."

"Cool. Do those things really explode?"

"Your question will be answered once you're naked."

"I was hoping you'd say that." Lou kissed her again.

# TWENTY-FIVE

"OH!" CASEY SWIVELED IN THE passenger seat of her Tercel and waved a photocopy of Jasmine's final letter at Lou. "Listen to this. '*Last week, I caught my landlord's wife in my apartment when I came home from work early. Ursula said neigbhors had heard Muffin (my cat) scream-ing and thought he was in trouble. But Muffin was asleep on my bed—I checked!!! I think Ursula stole my amethyst pendant and earrings. They were a present from Noel.*'"

"It doesn't look good for Ursula." With his eyes half closed and his hand on Casey's thigh, Lou slouched farther down the driver's seat of the parked car.

"True, and what with Birch stalking Jasmine and Jeremy, no wonder she wanted to move away." Casey scanned the letter. "She doesn't say whether she phoned the cops."

"I doubt she did. Jasmine didn't trust cops because they didn't do much about Birch harassing her."

"They might have had something to say about all the animals in her apartment too."

As the blue and white Queen of Coquitlam ferry glided into the harbor, Casey scanned the dozen lanes of cars, trucks, RVs, and buses waiting to board. Half of them were empty as travelers stretched their legs. As much as she wanted to see Summer, part of her regretted having to end this romantic interlude. She stroked Lou's arm.

"I had a great time last night, and this morning."

He gave her a sleepy smile. "Me too, but the real world calls."

"And whines and demands and bullies." Casey flipped through copies of letters she hadn't had time to read.

On their way to the terminal, she'd returned the originals and a full set of copies to Hannah. With Hannah's permission, she'd made an extra copy of the letters she hadn't had time to read. She'd also told Hannah about Gabrielle's visit last night.

"Typical of my daughter to try intimidation," Hannah had said. "I hope you didn't cower."

"It's not my style." And then she'd left.

With Lou behind the wheel, Casey had time to read the remaining letters, which mainly covered Jeremy's development and her pets. She'd also written about Paval's helpfulness.

Casey took another look at one of the pages. "In some letters she's really positive. Writes about what good friends Wesley and Noel are, and her infatuation with Roberto."

"Is that what she called it?"

"No, but she didn't use the word love either. Here she says, '*He's the coolest, friendliest, most fun guy I've ever gone out with.*'"

"Sounds like something a teenager would say."

"Part of her was naïve and immature." The other part was sarcastic, critical, and just plain mean. Casey scanned another sheet. "She trashes a couple of tenants and parishioners over petty issues, and does the same to some Mainland staff."

"Which ones?"

"Me and a few administrative staff, all of them women. I think she saw them as competition, especially where Roberto was concerned."

"Hannah asked you to read the letters despite what Jasmine wrote?"

"She's more shrewd and open-minded than her daughter was." Casey continued reading. "Jasmine apologizes to her mother for venting, then writes '*You're the only one I can talk to.*'" Casey paused. "She must have been lonely."

Lou nodded. "And insecure."

"Jasmine's disputes and complaints didn't seem serious enough for someone to want to kill her. Unless something else was going on, something she didn't want Hannah to know."

"Did she write about Eisler?"

"Yeah, she said he was an annoying jerk who wasn't getting enough at home." Casey scanned more lines. "She tried searching the Gallenskis' bedroom for her pendant when she picked up Jeremy one afternoon." Casey turned to Lou. "When Marie and I went to Jasmine's apartment, I saw a red feather boa hanging in her bedroom closet. Ursula was wearing a red boa when we met her at the Silver Groove."

"She could have owned one as well."

"Or stolen Jasmine's." Casey returned to the letter. "Jasmine had planned to keep searching for her jewelry. Oh, and she hated Ursula. Said she was nothing but a cheap tramp . . . Whoa. Here's something: she says that both Gallenskis have stepped over the line and that she'd phone Hannah about it later." Casey looked up. "Hannah's last chat with her was Sunday morning, but Hannah said that Jasmine hadn't seemed especially bothered by anything."

"Maybe Jasmine had decided not to worry her."

"Or something happened after that call." Casey noticed the date at the top of the page. "She wrote this Monday, the day after her confrontation with Gabrielle. Must have mailed it right away. Interesting that she never mentioned Gabrielle's visit."

"Like I said, she didn't want to upset her mother."

"Maybe. So, what if Jasmine told Paval about the theft and he didn't believe her?" She watched the Queen of Coquitlam dock. "Maybe Paval was doing a little snooping and stealing himself. The Gallenskis have a master key to every apartment and Paval seems unnecessarily friendly with tenants."

"It's possible, I guess; though it could all be Ursula's doing. Maybe Jasmine didn't actually say anything to Paval, but confronted Ursula instead. Ursula might have been worried about losing her husband and going to jail."

"If a tenant had accused either Gallenski of theft, Paval could have lost his job." Casey folded the letter. "Paval would have known Jasmine's schedule because he babysat Jeremy, which means Ursula could have found out from him, or she could have just followed Jasmine to the church that morning."

"What about your work schedule?" Lou asked. "How would she have heard about it?"

"By calling the office and posing as a friend. Witnesses said the shooter was a man, though." Casey watched people return to their vehicles. "I can't picture Paval doing that, but I can picture Ursula hiring someone to take a shot at me."

"Wouldn't the cops have checked everyone's alibi in the building?"

"They would have asked most of them where they were that morning, but I doubt there were enough officers to follow up on every alibi unless they had a good reason to."

"I'm thinking the Gallenskis should move up on your suspect list."

"Definitely." Casey glanced at cars driving down the ramp from the ferry's upper parking level. "If Jasmine complained about Ursula to Paval, he might have threatened to evict her. Maybe that's what prompted her decision to move." Casey's eyes widened. "The photographs!"

"What?"

"The ones I found in Jasmine's locker of her sleeping, and Jeremy in the tub." She looked at Lou. "What if Paval or Ursula took them?"

"Why would they do that, unless they were kinky?"

"Maybe they are. The guy spends his days babysitting and pet-sitting for tenants, and he talks about them like they were family. It's a bit strange."

"Not if it means extra income. Apartment managers don't make much, and he has a baby on the way."

"Somebody should interview the tenants," Casey said. "See if they've had photos snapped or items missing from their suites."

"Give the cops the letters; let them figure it out."

She opened her mouth to say something but stopped. Things were good between them again. Why jeopardize that? Still, the answers were close. She could feel it.

"Thanks for riding back with me." Casey placed her hand over his. "Your company's made the trip so much fun."

"Thank my sister for teaching over here and offering to drive my truck back this weekend." Lou stared past Casey. "Shit, is that who I think it is?"

Casey turned and spotted Gabrielle walking through the lanes of cars. "Oh, my god."

Gabrielle stopped at a vehicle three lanes away and one car ahead of theirs.

"Holy crap, she drives a small silver car." Casey stuffed the letters in her purse. "I wonder if that's the vehicle Corporal Lundy's been looking for. We need to get the plate number."

"Why is she heading for the mainland on a Thursday afternoon? Didn't you say she was a secretary?"

"Yep. Last night's chat probably freaked her out, which means we're going to be riding with a murder suspect." She retrieved her cell phone. "I need to make sure Summer's okay."

"Tell Mom to watch for Birch's brown Dodge Dart. Maybe she can get my brothers to check out the neighborhood."

Casey listened to the phone ring. No one was picking up.

# TWENTY-SIX

**THE MOMENT CASEY SPOTTED WINIFRED'S** Buick at the back of Rhonda's house, tension shot through her shoulders and knotted her stomach. Why was the old bat still here? She parked next to the Buick. After yesterday's chat with Gabrielle, the last thing she needed was another confrontation. Still, Casey had told Winifred to leave and she bloody well meant it.

She yanked her overnight bag out of the trunk, wishing Lou hadn't had to return to work right away. After dropping him off at Mainland, she'd rushed over to Barb's to see if everything was okay. It turned out that Summer and Barb had left for school early to grab breakfast at McDonald's, and Barb had forgotten to bring her cell phone, which was why Casey's call hadn't been answered.

Casey trudged up the steps to the kitchen door, skirting a bag of garbage on the top step. It wasn't like Winifred to leave garbage sitting around. Inside, the kitchen was spotless. The coffee maker hadn't been turned on. The house was silent. Maybe Winifred had gone for a walk or was taking a nap. Maybe she was hiding in a closet waiting to ambush her with legal documents.

Casey started down the hall toward the front of the house. She peeked in the living room. No Winifred. She started up the staircase and listened for signs of life. At the second floor landing, she glimpsed the two closed bedroom doors at the front of the house. Summer's room was on the left. Winifred was using Rhonda's room on the right. Casey turned around. All was quiet from the two tenants' rooms.

Reluctant to face Winifred, Casey hurried upstairs and into her apartment. A chorus of whistling guinea pigs greeted her. Tiny paws pressed against the bars as the guinea pigs stood on hind legs, while hamsters and gerbils scampered back and forth.

"Hey, kids." She glanced at her blinking message light. She would have preferred to listen to the messages right away, but until the critters settled down, she wouldn't be able to hear anything.

Casey fetched the veggies and then refilled pellet dishes and water bottles. She picked up Ralphie and let him nibble the carrot in her hand. He grasped the carrot while his mouth worked at breakneck speed. For a rodent, he was awfully cute.

The telephone rang. Casey answered and heard Marie say, "Good, you're back."

Anger surged through her as she thought of Jasmine's letters and the bull Marie had told her.

"First, Stan wants you on the M6 with Wesley tonight and tomorrow night. He'll call you about it, but I thought I'd give you a heads up."

Casey sat down and placed Ralphie on her lap. "I thought I was off that assignment for safety reasons."

"Yeah, well, Eisler received a note from that rock-throwing nut yesterday."

"Really? What'd he say?"

"That he didn't shoot at the bus, but that he wouldn't stop throwing rocks until Mainland shaped up, whatever that means. Anyway, I can't work nights because I need to go see my kids, so Stan's putting you back on."

Casey stopped stroking Ralphie. If the rockhound knew about the shooting, had he been there when it happened? She hadn't seen or heard anything in the media about the incident. She recalled the people she'd seen: the three guys who'd been walking by when the shot was fired, and the old man with the long beard and hoodie pulled low over his forehead.

"What happened in Parksville?" Marie asked. "Did you meet Hannah?"

No point in denying she went. Marie wasn't stupid. "You didn't tell anyone I was going, did you?"

"No one at work knows, and Noel's discreet."

Casey sighed. The stupid woman had told the police's prime suspect.

"Did you read Jasmine's letters?" Marie asked.

"Yes, and I read some of them to Lou too. He came over and spent the night. Wasn't that sweet?" She'd feel ashamed for rubbing Marie's nose in it tomorrow, but right now revenge was sweet. "It turns out that Parksville's a great place for hot sex."

"We were talking about letters." Her voice was sharp. "Stay on topic, Casey."

"I am; Jasmine wrote about you." She gripped the receiver. "You told her I stole Lou from you. You also told her I was Stan's favorite and got the best assignments. How could you lie like that, Marie? What the hell is wrong with you?"

"She must have misinterpreted—"

"Stop it! You were playing her and that's not only disgusting but selfish." Casey returned Ralphie to his cage. "Get this straight: Lou's with me and we're staying together because that's what we both want."

"Not even you can predict the future. You thought your marriage would last forever and look what happened. Everyone knows you're not anxious to try that again."

"I don't recall discussing marriage with you or anyone else at work." Rhonda and Lou were the only ones who knew about her insecurity. "If Lou wanted to be with you he wouldn't have gone all the way to Parksville to tell me that he loves me."

"I didn't call to talk about Lou, for shit's sake. I thought you'd want to know that Paval found a new tenant for Jasmine's place, and he's been selling her stuff cheap."

"Is that legal?"

"Hannah gave him permission to get rid of the furniture. She's already had someone pick up photo albums and other personal stuff. Anyway, I remember you liked her footstool with the sunflowers, but you'll have to collect it today. Whatever's left goes to charity first thing tomorrow."

"Making money off her death's a bit cold, isn't it?"

"That's what I told Ursula. She said Jasmine owed them a week's worth of babysitting so it balances out, but yeah, it's beyond tacky." Marie hung up.

Casey wondered if the footstool was still available. Should she go out there? It was nearly one o'clock. And she needed to catch up on homework. Besides, Ursula was a suspect. Getting close to her again wouldn't be smart. On the other hand, she'd sure like to know if the Gallenskis had crossed the line with other tenants. If she could talk to some of them . . .

Casey watched the animals munch their food and thought again about Jasmine's letters. When it came to wanting something or solving problems, Jasmine had been a take-charge person. When her parents died and the rest of the family disowned her, she moved on. Got a job, left an abusive marriage, and sought her biological mother. She'd taken charge of her life, made plans.

Casey remembered when she used to be like that, and she knew that passivity crept in the day she started parenting a grieving, angry teenager. She'd spent the past four months tiptoeing around, hoping Summer would learn to deal with Rhonda's absence, but clearly she hadn't. Time to face reality, regain control of her life. Marie had been a good start. Winifred's turn next.

Casey marched out of her apartment and jogged down to the second floor. She rapped on Winifred's door. "Winifred, it's Casey. I want to talk to you."

No answer. Casey pressed her ear against the door and listened. She heard a noise. "I'm not leaving until we talk, so you might as well open the door." She crossed her arms and counted to ten. "That's it, I'm coming in."

She turned the handle. The door was unlocked. Casey stepped inside the darkened room and gasped when she saw Winifred on the floor, beside the bed. Blood covered some of her face and one eye was swollen shut. Oh god, how long had she been here? Bending closer, Casey felt Winifred's breath on her cheek. Casey checked her pulse. It was there, but not that strong.

"Winifred, can you hear me?"

"Mmm."

"Can you breathe okay?"

"Hurts."

"What happened?"

Winifred moaned. Her swollen eyelid twitched. "Attacked."

"Did you see the person?"

"No."

"Can I check to see where you're injured? I have first aid."

"No."

"I'll call 911." Casey yanked the comforter off the bed, draped it over Winifred, and then called for help on her cell. She tried to answer the dispatcher's questions, but knew too little to be of much use. "Winifred, do you know how long ago this happened?"

"No."

"The suspect could still be nearby," Casey said to the dispatcher. "Send the police right away." She turned to Winifred. "Winifred, did you see any part of your attacker, like clothing, hair, a tattoo? Anything that could describe him?"

"Dark clothes . . . hat."

"A wide-brimmed hat?"

"Mmm."

"Brown?"

Winifred groaned.

Nausea roiled in Casey's stomach as she repeated Winifred's description to the dispatcher. She spotted closed suitcases in front of the bed, an unopened purse on top of them. Winifred must have been preparing to move out when she was attacked. Since Summer wasn't here, the killer must have carried out his threat on the next available victim.

"Winifred, you've got a gash on your cheek. Do you want me to wash it out and get some disinfectant?"

"No."

Aside from Marie and Noel, the only other suspects who knew she'd gone to Parksville were Gabrielle and possibly Birch. Gabrielle probably told Birch everything that had happened over there, and hitting women wasn't new to him.

Panic shot through Casey. Was he still in the house? Winifred moaned again. Casey swallowed back her fear while she stared at the open bedroom door. Her gaze darted to the closed closet door. She held her breath and listened for sounds, but the pounding in her ears made it tough to hear anything.

"Casey?" Winifred squinted at her.

"I'm here."

"Your fault," she mumbled.

# TWENTY-SEVEN

RUSH HOUR HAD BEGUN AS Casey drove east toward Coquitlam, but she didn't mind the slowing traffic. She needed to think before she met the Gallenskis. She called them twenty minutes ago to see if the sunflower footstool was still available. Ursula warned her that she'd only hold it for an hour. Casey wasn't thrilled to see Ursula again, but staying alone in the house was worse. Winifred's assailant was out there somewhere, probably waiting for her or Summer.

The paramedics thought some of Winifred's ribs might be broken. They'd also found large dark bruises on her lower back, where she could have been kicked. Casey told the police that Elliott Birch could resort to something that vile and suggested they contact Corporal Lundy about him.

Explaining things to Summer had been tougher. When she heard about Winifred, she cried. She'd wanted to visit Winifred at the hospital, but with a killer running loose Casey had said no.

"I can take care of myself," Summer had insisted. "And Lou and Barb and you can protect me. Don't hospitals have security anyway?"

"It's not that simple."

And on it went until Casey cut things short by saying she needed to call Rhonda. When she heard about Winifred, Rhonda said, "What kind of coward would attack an old woman, and why on God's earth was Mother still at the house? What if the psycho's waiting to get Summer?"

Rhonda had then demanded Barb's number so she could tell Summer to stay away from the hospital. She'd also decided to take a more active role in parenting her daughter. Casey's job was to simply ensure that Rhonda's rules were followed. Her diminished role as guardian made her feel incompetent.

She pulled up in front of the Gallenskis' apartment building and scanned the street for Gabrielle's Jetta or Birch's Dodge Dart. What if she'd missed something in the rearview mirror? By the time Casey shut off

the engine, her body was so tense that a tap on the shoulder would cata-
pult her through the front entrance. She needed gum. Chewing would at
least unclench her jaw. She popped a piece in her mouth, stepped out of
the car, and jogged up to the door. The sound of Ursula's voice over the
intercom already annoyed her.

"This is Casey."

"You got the cash?"

"Yes." Geez, this wasn't a drug buy, for heaven sake.

The intercom buzzed and Casey entered a lobby cluttered with boxes
and full plastic bags. A woman and two guys were pushing a sofa toward
the door.

"Moving day, huh?" Casey asked.

"Yeah, thank GOD," the girl replied.

"It's that bad here?"

She barked out a laugh. "You could say that."

"Really? I was thinking about moving in." The tenant headed for
the door.

"Please, I need to know. I'm about to give them a damage deposit."

The girl turned around. "Stuff goes missing around here."

"From the laundry room?"

"From your bloody apartment. Coins or a five dollar bill; things they
don't think we'll notice."

"Has it happened to others?"

"Two that I know of." The girl headed for the door. "Run while you
can."

"Thanks."

Casey continued to the Gallenskis' apartment. Ursula answered the
door dressed in blue jeans and a T-shirt that barely covered her bulging
stomach. A sudsy bucket and a pair of yellow rubber gloves sat by the
door. Casey tried not to smile. She'd never pictured Ursula as the cleaning type.

"You look busy," Casey said.

"People moving out, people moving in." Ursula removed a key from
the board by the door. "I hate these losers." Ursula handed her the key.
"Bring it back when you're done. Someone else is supposed to drop by,

so leave the door unlocked." She put on the gloves. "You won't take off without paying, will ya? I'll be in suite three-ten."

"Of course not."

"Right, you're one of the good guys." Ursula watched her. "I heard you've been tracking down the skanky half sister."

Casey frowned. "Who told you that?"

"That dingbat Marie told Paval."

Just great. "Why would she tell your husband?"

"They're friendly. Why, I'll never know."

So, Ursula now knew about her interest in the murder. Damn, damn, damn. Casey stepped into the corridor. "I'll get the stool."

"What did that cold witch have to say?" Ursula asked.

A suspect would want to hear what she knew. "Gabrielle warned me to stay away from her mother." Paval walked up to her, carrying a basketful of clothes. A tiny baby slept on top of the clothes. "Cute bundle you got there."

"Warm laundry puts them right to sleep." His smile faded. "Did I hear you mention Gabrielle O'Reilly?"

"She threatened Casey," Ursula said. "I think that chick's more than capable of blowing someone's head off."

"I told Corporal Lundy that Gabrielle and Birch are a couple. She's the one you spotted in his car."

Ursula didn't look surprised. Paval, on the other hand, seemed baffled. "How do you know?"

"I saw them together, and Gabrielle admitted it yesterday. She claims she wasn't in Vancouver the day Jasmine died. Anyway, she's on the mainland now. We rode the same ferry over."

"She's here?" Ursula asked. She put her hand on her swollen belly and avoided Casey's gaze.

The longer Casey watched her, the more nervous Ursula seemed. "Did you know about Birch and Gabrielle?"

"No, what a stupid thing to say." She started to leave.

Paval stood in the doorway. "Did you recognize Gabrielle in Birch's car?"

"All right, I did, yeah. I thought they'd hooked up to hurt Jasmine and maybe even take Jeremy. It looks like they decided to kill her instead."

"Did you tell the police?" Casey asked.

"What for? It would only be my word against theirs."

Maybe Ursula had seen Gabrielle up close and decided to blackmail her. She might have already stooped to stealing from tenants. "I'd better get that stool."

"It's twenty bucks." Ursula held out her gloved hand.

"Let her see it first, darling," Paval said, "then we'll work out a fair price."

"Look, Pav, I'm trying to do everything I can to put money aside. You know maternity benefits won't cover what I get from tips. We can't slide into poverty either. I'm not going through that shit again."

The phone rang.

"I'll get it." Ursula put down the bucket and removed one glove.

"Be right back," Casey said, and started down the hall.

She unlocked Jasmine's apartment and stepped into a room reeking of garbage and over-used kitty litter. The red shag looked dirtier than she remembered. The only furniture in the living room was the sunflower footstool and a broken wooden chair.

The chill Casey had felt her first time in this apartment returned. She hated being here. It was as if Jasmine's essence still hovered. She glanced at the dark kitchen cupboards and yellow countertop, a throwback to the seventies when this building was probably constructed. Casey headed for Jasmine's bedroom, curious to see what else was left.

The bed and bureau were gone, as were her disco clothes, wigs, red feather boa, and even her shoes. In Jeremy's room, she found a box of clothes and a crucifix on the wall. Otherwise, the room had been picked clean. Poor Jeremy. His life had changed so much. Was he still waiting for his mom to come and get him?

Feeling a bit queasy from the apartment's stench, Casey headed for the bathroom, flipped on the light, and tossed her gum in the garbage. She sat on the edge of the tub and took slow deep breaths. Reminders of Jasmine were everywhere: a toothbrush in a red plastic cup, mascara and lipstick by the sink. Bath toys cluttered the top of the toilet tank.

Jasmine hadn't been the world's best housekeeper. The tile grout around the tub was black in places. Blue decals on the bottom of the green tub were also stained. Staring at the decals, Casey recalled the photo of Jeremy. He'd been sitting in the bathtub and grinning up at the camera. But hadn't the picture seemed much brighter? Casey looked at the two swag lamps on each side of the sink. The wattage wasn't strong.

The sound of a closing door made Casey jump. The other buyer? She hoped this person didn't want the stool. Casey left the bathroom and flinched when she saw Elliott Birch walking toward her.

Birch stopped and gaped at her. "You were at the funeral."

Her heartbeat quickened. "Yes."

"You're a friend of that Crenshaw bitch."

"We're coworkers, but no one would call us friends." Crap, he was blocking her path to the living room. "Are you here for the sale too?"

"I'm picking up the rest of Jeremy's stuff, but I ain't paying for nothin'."

His black hair, which had been slicked down at the funeral, was disheveled. Casey leaned against the wall and crossed her arms, hoping to look more at ease than she felt. "How's your son doing?"

His eyes narrowed. "What's it to ya?"

"Just making conversation." Birch's stare rattled her. Why wasn't he saying anything about her confrontation with Gabrielle? Surely he knew about it.

"What are you doing here?" he asked.

"I came to buy the footstool." She nodded toward the living room.

Watching his hands, she strolled toward him. If he reached in his pockets she could be in deep trouble. Birch was shorter and thinner than her, but still dangerous. Her heart pounded so hard her chest hurt. She walked closer, but he didn't move. When she was close enough to touch him, he turned and let her pass. Casey marched toward the stool, feeling his gaze on her back. She lifted it and turned so she could examine the piece while keeping Birch in view.

"Why do ya want that shit?" he asked. "It's dirty."

"Dirt can be removed." Moron. "I like sunflowers and it's beautifully embroidered."

"Yeah well, I suppose everybody's good at one thing." Birch hurried to the door, blocking her exit. "When are you and Crenshaw going to stop acting like cops? Gabby told me about you and Hannah." He looked like he wanted to flay her. "If you tell her mother about us, I swear you'll regret it."

If Birch had a weapon, he would have waved it at her by now. Maybe he preferred his fists. "Seeing as how you didn't kill Jasmine," she said, holding the stool chest high, "you've got nothing to worry about."

Birch laughed. "Damn straight."

What was he hoping to do? Marry Gabrielle so he could cash in on the inheritance when Hannah died? Casey flung open the door and hurried down the hallway. She looked over her shoulder. Birch wasn't following. As she rapped on the Gallenskis' door at the far end of the hall, Birch stepped out of the apartment, carrying the box she'd seen in Jeremy's closet.

Ursula was still on the phone when she opened the door. Somewhere in the apartment, Casey heard a baby start to cry.

"I gotta go," Ursula said into the receiver. "Bye." She looked at the stool. "You still want that thing?"

"Yes, and I just had a run-in with Elliott Birch." She spotted Birch coming down the hall. He turned and headed toward the building's entrance. "He's leaving right now with a box and said he isn't paying for anything."

Ursula spun around. "Pav, Birch is here and he's taking off!"

"Would you pick up the baby while I deal with him?"

After Paval rushed out the door, Ursula held out her hand. "Where's my twenty?"

"The stool has a couple of stains, so I'll give you fifteen." Casey removed a twenty dollar bill from her wallet. "Do you have change?"

Ursula looked at her with contempt. "No wonder I'm still living in this dump. I have to get the baby, so wait here."

"How about I get the baby for you? It'll save time." It would also give her a chance to peek into the bathroom. Since Jeremy had spent a lot of time here, she had a hunch.

"Whatever." Ursula clumped down the hall. "She's in the room at the end."

Casey followed her until Ursula stepped into a bedroom on the left. Farther down the hall, Casey stopped at the bathroom. The lights were off. She continued to the second room containing two cribs, a chest of drawers, and a changing table.

The baby had spit up. Sour milk dribbled down her chin and onto her pink sleeper. Casey lifted the child and headed for the bathroom. Once she'd switched on the light, she found a box of tissues on the counter.

She wiped the tiny face and moved closer to the green tub with its clean white decals. The wall tiles were spotless. Halogen lights made the room much brighter than Jasmine's bathroom. Had Jeremy's picture been taken here? Jasmine might have come to pick him up early, seen him playing in the tub, and borrowed Paval's camera. But what if she hadn't taken the picture?

Casey lifted the whimpering infant onto her shoulder and massaged her back. Given the sexual abuse Jasmine had suffered, the thought of a landlord taking pictures of her naked child might have enraged her. Was this what Jasmine meant when she wrote that Paval had crossed the line? Maybe Jasmine hadn't given Hannah details because the implication was too awful. She wouldn't have wanted to upset her ailing mother.

Paval appeared in the doorway. "Is everything okay?"

"Yeah, but babies make me nervous." She handed the child to Paval. "She spit up."

Casey watched Paval's liquid eyes. The first two times she met him, she assumed he'd been close to tears over Jasmine, but maybe he always looked this way. What if he and Jasmine had argued about the photo? A sexual abuse allegation would end his job, possibly his marriage, and launch a police investigation. Could he have killed her? Was he nasty enough to have beaten Winifred and threatened to kill Summer? He didn't know Summer existed, though, unless Marie had told him. A prickly, stinging sensation ran up and down Casey's arms, as if someone was grazing her skin with a bouquet of thorns.

"Here's your change." Ursula plunked a crumpled five dollar bill in her hand.

"That's exactly what I got out of Birch," Paval said. "The jerk was about to take a swing at me."

Casey picked up the stool and stepped into the hall. "Thanks for this." She hurried out of the building and looked for Birch's car, but he'd apparently taken off. Keys ready, she jogged to her Tercel, alert for trouble. Once inside, she locked the door, then called Corporal Lundy.

While the phone rang, Casey's thoughts swirled. Thefts, child abuse, beatings, murder. Was Paval responsible, after all? Dirty blue decals, clean white decals. Three weeks had passed since she'd seen those photos. She couldn't be completely sure which bathroom the photo was taken in until she saw the snapshot again. Casey tried to exhale her anxiety away. Don't jump to conclusions, girl. Ask Lundy about the photo first, and then see what was what.

# TWENTY-EIGHT

**WHY DID LUNDY HAVE TO** be on another line? Casey plunked her phone on the passenger seat and pulled away from the Gallenskis' building. She checked the time. Quarter to five.

Before she'd left the house, Stan had called to make sure she'd be on the M6 bus by eight. She'd have time to grab some food and then head for the library to work on her essay. Ordinarily, Casey didn't welcome shifts with Rude Wesley Axelson. Tonight, though, even his company would be better than staying home and listening to every creak in the house. Besides, if the rockhound could describe the shooter, she wanted to catch this nut fast.

Casey checked her mirrors for any sign of Birch's Dodge Dart. She didn't see his car or the silver Jetta, but they could still be around, waiting for her. By the time she reached the highway, her tense shoulders had begun to ache.

She first spotted the SUV following her on the Gallenskis' street while she was turning onto Foster. A quick left turn onto North Road and then a slow right onto the highway hadn't changed the SUV's pace. The vehicle kept three car lengths back, too far away to read the license plate. Still, she might be making too much out of this. The highway was less than five minutes from the Gallenskis' place and a heavily used route to Vancouver. On the other hand, what if her encounter with the Gallenskis had prompted the tail?

Did Paval prey on kids? Did Ursula know? Why hadn't she told anyone that she'd seen Birch and Gabrielle together? Blackmail was a possibility, given Ursula's money worries. Had she found out that Gabrielle's mother was wealthy, and assumed Gabrielle had access to cash? Was Gabrielle on the mainland now to deal with Ursula? Casey tried to ignore the dread slithering like a serpent inside her. She again glanced at her rearview mirror. What kind of car did Paval drive?

Her phone rang. She answered with her Bluetooth.

"This is Corporal Lundy. You left a message about the photos?"

"Yes, but first, I think someone's tailing me." Casey explained what had happened and where she was.

"It's rush hour, which means a lot of traffic," he said. "Are you sure?"

"No."

"Can you describe the vehicle?"

"Just that it's a dark SUV. There's another intersection coming up and an Esso station on the corner. I'm turning off." She switched on her right turn signal, cruised through the intersection, then pulled into the gas station. "The SUV's driving past."

"Good. From what you described, you were near Mrs. Birch's apartment building, is this correct?"

"Yeah, Jasmine's landlords are selling her furniture, so I bought a footstool I saw in her apartment when we were picking up Jasmine's pets; which reminds me, would you like to own a gerbil, hamster, or guinea pig?"

"Thank you, no. You mentioned something about a bathroom?"

"Yes. I stopped in hers to get rid of my gum and that's when I noticed the blue flower decals on the bottom of Jasmine's bathtub. The lighting wasn't good, but the landlord's bathroom has much better lighting and white decals."

"How do you know?" He sounded annoyed.

"I was in there, too, helping with a crying baby. So, now I'm wondering which room the photo was taken in. I know it's none of my business, but this is important."

"That's your professional assessment, is it?"

Casey sighed. "Do you know what type of car the Gallenskis drive, by any chance?"

"It's not a SUV or silver compact, and I want you to stay away from that building, understand?"

"Just one more thing: did you know that tenants have had things stolen from their suites?"

"Excuse me?"

"I bumped into a tenant as she was moving out. She said the landlords stole stuff from her apartment and that it's happened to others. Jasmine even caught Ursula in her apartment one day and thought she took an amethyst pendant and earrings." Casey watched drivers pumping gas. "Apparently, she searched the Gallenskis' bedroom, which could be how she found the photos."

"How did you know about the stolen jewelry when you told me the two of you weren't on good terms?"

"Jasmine wrote about it in a letter to her mother. Hannah wanted me to read the letters, so she invited me to Parksville. Jasmine also wrote that both Gallenskis had stepped over the line."

"Why did the mother want you to read the letters?"

"Because I know some of the people Jasmine wrote about."

"Why do I get the feeling there's more to it than that?"

How could she explain that Hannah put more faith in her interpretation of clues than she did in the RCMP's investigation? "Hannah wanted me to see if there was a clue to the killer among them. The only incriminating stuff was about the Gallenskis."

"Do you still have the letters?"

"Only the last seven. I didn't have time to read all of them over there, so she let me take copies home."

"Are the letters with you now?"

"In my purse."

"I'd like to see them."

"My shift starts in a few minutes; otherwise I'd bring them now."

Lundy muttered something she couldn't quite hear. "I want them here first thing in the morning."

If he needed them that badly, he'd offer to meet her at the M6 bus, or call Stan to arrange a later shift start. "I have a class up at SFU that finishes at noon. I could bring them after that."

"Our detachment's about fifteen minutes from there. I'll expect you by twelve-thirty and, as I said, stay away from that building."

"No problem." There wasn't a reason to go back. "Did you know that Jasmine was sexually abused by her grandfather when she was six years old? She mentions it in the letters. Any hint of inappropriate behavior with her child, like taking a photo of him naked, might have enraged her enough to threaten one or both Gallenskis with the police."

"I had a call from the Vancouver police about an assault in your house."

Why was he changing topics? "I asked them to phone you. Thought you should know."

"When was the last time you spoke with the victim?"

"We talked before I left for Parksville, and it didn't go well. Winifred and I weren't getting along, and since Summer's staying with my boyfriend's mother, I asked Winifred to move out, but she doesn't like being told what to do."

"I see."

"You should also know that Gabrielle O'Reilly's on the mainland. We rode the same ferry over, which is when I learned that she drives a silver Jetta. I have the plate number." Casey recited the number she'd memorized. "Oh, and another thing."

"Just one?"

Cute. "Ursula admitted that she knew about Gabrielle and Birch's affair before today, but she didn't tell anyone, including her husband."

"Which sounds like another reason to stay away from the Gallenskis and their tenants, Miss Holland. Don't go looking for trouble."

"That was never the plan, Corporal."

Casey tossed her phone on the seat. She should have said no to Marie's plea for help from the beginning; the same for Hannah O'Reilly. Instead, she'd tried to do the right thing. So, why did she feel so bad about everything? And why did she feel the worst was yet to come?

# TWENTY-NINE

CASEY WALKED INTO MAINLAND'S LUNCHROOM and spotted Roberto talking to an eighteen-year-old clerk by the coffee urn. When Roberto noticed Casey he waved, but kept yakking while the girl smiled at him with adoring eyes.

"Good, you haven't gone to class yet," Stan said as he caught up to her. "Amy said you'd be grabbing a coffee before you left."

"The rockhound didn't show up last night," Casey answered.

"I know, I read your report. Did the undercover guy ride with you?"

"Yep."

Stan had told her that the New Westminster police would only let Casey on the M6 if an officer was present and she wore a Kevlar vest. It had taken time to convince authorities that the rockhound and shooter were two different people, but they'd finally agreed to let her do her job, despite concerns that the shooter would try again, a worry Casey shared.

"Amy just took a message for you." Stan handed her a slip of paper. "She said the caller sounded upset."

Casey scanned the message. "Oh lord, it's from Gabrielle O'Reilly. She wants to meet me at Birch's trailer to talk about Jasmine." The last thing she needed was another confrontation. Gabrielle hadn't left a phone number.

"Shouldn't she be calling the cops?" he asked.

"Not if she's the killer." Casey poured milk in her coffee, aware that Roberto was moving closer to her.

"Is that possible?"

"She's one of my top three suspects. Even if Gabrielle's innocent, she's afraid her affair with Birch will get back to her mother."

"Sorry to butt in," Roberto said, looking at Casey. "Did I hear you say that Jasmine's half sister wants to meet you?"

"This is a private conversation." Stan stared at him. "Shouldn't you be changing oil or something?"

"I'm on a break." Roberto rubbed his hand on his coveralls and turned to Casey. "You said the sister's having an affair with Birch?"

Since she owed no loyalty to Gabrielle or Birch, Casey brought him up to speed.

Roberto gave a low whistle. "If Jasmine knew her ex was mixed up with Gabrielle, she would've gone nuts."

"As far as I know, she never mentioned Birch's love life to anyone, so maybe she hadn't a clue." Casey placed a lid on her coffee. "On the other hand, something had been bugging Jasmine those last couple of days. Maybe that was it, or at least part of the problem."

"You want some company to Birch's place?" Roberto asked. "I could take a late lunch."

"I'm not sure I'll even go." If little Jeremy was there, though, she'd sure like to see if he was okay.

"If you do, call me. I want to help."

Was this Roberto's way of telling her that he'd forgiven her for questioning his alibi, and for all the suspicion and misunderstanding she and Marie had caused? Or was he bored and looking for a little excitement? Roberto would love boasting about confronting a female desperado. Regardless of his motive, though, she could use the backup.

"If the half sister's trouble, don't go," Stan said.

"Don't you want to hear what the woman has to say?" Roberto asked her.

"I'm curious," Casey replied, "but Gabrielle has serious anger issues. Besides, I have Birch's address and could cross-check it for a phone number." Phoning Gabrielle instead of talking in person, though, would mean not seeing Jeremy.

"If you give me the address, I could meet you at Birch's place," Roberto said. "I've calmed many a she-beast in my time."

He didn't know about Winifred, didn't realize how violent things had become. "Thanks, I'll think about it."

First, she'd need to check out Gabrielle's alibi. If Gabrielle's employers confirmed she was at work that day, then maybe she'd see her.

Lou joined them as Stan said, "Casey, I know you can handle yourself, but this is different, okay?"

"What's going on?" Lou asked.

"Gabrielle." She handed him the slip of paper.

Lou frowned as he read the message. "It sounds like a trap. Isn't Birch finished work by then?"

"No, while I was interviewing people on his mail route, I learned that he never finishes before one-thirty." Casey checked her watch. "I'm late."

She rushed out of the room, aware that Lou and Roberto were keeping up with her.

"Shouldn't you tell Corporal Lundy about this?" Lou asked.

"Yes, and I'm popping by the detachment after class."

"What if I can get someone to take my shift so I can be there too?" Lou asked. "Safety in numbers, right?"

"I'd love it if Gabrielle turned Birch in," Roberto said, "which is why I want to be there."

"We don't know if this is about Birch at all," Casey replied.

She stepped outside as Marie pulled into the lot. Casey hurried to her Tercel. As she slid into the driver's seat, Marie called her name. Casey tossed her purse on the passenger seat and placed her coffee in the cup holder. Roberto and Lou stood near the driver's door, watching her until Marie nudged between them.

"Noel and I want to talk to you about what was in Jasmine's letters," Marie said. "To see if there's anything that could help his case."

"I have a copy of the last seven, which I have to take to Corporal Lundy in a couple of hours. Nothing in them incriminated Noel."

"What letters?" Roberto asked.

As Marie filled him in, Casey shut the car door and rolled down her window.

"Maybe Gabrielle wants to talk about them," Roberto said to Casey.

Marie frowned. "What's this about Gabrielle?"

"Nothing." Casey started the engine.

"Don't give me that." Marie looked at the men. "Something's going on. I can tell from the glances between you three."

Lou leaned in and kissed Casey. "Let us know what you decide."

"Decide what?" Marie demanded.

Casey shifted into reverse and released the hand brake.

Marie lunged forward and gripped the window frame. "I'm talking to you, damn it!"

"Come on, Marie." Roberto peeled her hand off the frame. "Let the lady leave."

"I have a right to know what's going on when my brother's life is at stake! What are you people keeping from me?"

Casey glanced up at the admin building and saw Stan standing at the open window in his office. Given how loud Marie was getting, she figured he could hear most of what was being said.

"Give it a rest, Marie." Lou frowned.

"No!"

"If anything comes of it, we'll tell ya," Roberto added.

Marie glared at Lou and Roberto. "She sure has you two wrapped around her finger." She turned to Casey. "It's not enough to play Mainland's hero. Now you've got to turn the men against me too? What the hell is wrong with you?"

"Marie!" Stan shouted. "In my office, now!"

As she stomped toward the building, the guys wandered off. Casey rummaged through her purse for gum and found the slip of paper with Gabrielle's work number. Before she could talk herself out of it, she put the car in neutral and made the call. A receptionist answered on the second ring.

"Good morning," Casey said, her tone businesslike. "Is Gabrielle O'Reilly in?"

"I'm sorry, Miss O'Reilly's out of the office today. May I help you?"

"Well, that's just bloody marvellous. We were supposed to schedule a meeting, but I haven't heard from her. Do you know where she is?"

"No, I'm sorry, I don't."

Casey sighed loudly. "I've scheduled three appointments with her over the last six weeks and Miss O'Reilly canceled all of them."

"I-I'm sorry, I don't know what to say."

"Can you answer me one simple question before I decide whether to pursue this matter legally?"

"Uh, I, don't—"

"Miss O'Reilly was supposed to meet me at my office at 11:00 AM on September thirtieth, but she never showed. Is it possible for you to determine if she was at work or absent that day?"

"I could, but I should talk to my boss first."

"I'd rather they not be involved just yet, as this is a personal matter that could have a negative impact on my children and future dealings with your firm. All I'm asking for is a tiny piece of information."

"Okay," the perky voice answered. "Let me check."

"Thank you." Casey held her breath. If the girl talked to higher-ups, it'd be game over.

She looked around the parking lot until the receptionist came back on line a couple of minutes later.

"Gabrielle was away on September thirtieth. She took vacation days on Monday, Tuesday, and Wednesday of that week."

"Thank you."

"You're welcome."

Jasmine died on Tuesday, September twenty-eighth. Gabrielle could have killed her. It looked like a trip to Birch's trailer was a really bad idea.

## THIRTY

CASEY JOGGED UP TO HER car in the university's parkade and checked her watch. Twelve-fifteen. Corporal Lundy would be expecting Hannah's letters, but she needed to contact Gabrielle first. During class, she'd decided to trap her into seeing Lundy. One way or another, that nasty woman would talk.

Casey slid behind the wheel and retrieved her cell phone. Before class, she'd looked up and memorized Birch's number. All she had to do was punch in the digits. By the twelfth ring, it was obvious Gabrielle either wasn't there or wouldn't answer. Casey called Lundy.

"Shouldn't you be handing me some letters right now?" he asked.

"Yes, but I got an urgent message from Gabrielle O'Reilly this morning. She wants to see me at twelve-thirty to discuss Jasmine. She left the message with my supervisor and didn't go into detail. I'm supposed to meet her at Elliott Birch's trailer."

"I thought I told you not to play detective."

"The meeting wasn't my idea; she called me because she won't talk to the police. I really don't want to *play detective*, as you put it, so could you meet me at the trailer and take over from there?"

"Did you try canceling the meeting?"

"I just called, but she's not answering, and we're supposed to meet in fifteen minutes. If you go in my place, she might not open the door at all, so I thought I'd go in a few seconds ahead of you."

"We can manage to gain entry ourselves, Miss Holland."

She ignored the sarcasm. "She'll be watching for me. If she sees you, she'll probably take off. The chase would be a waste of time and manpower because I doubt you'll ever get anything out of her. Anyway, a friend's already on his way there. See you in fifteen minutes."

Casey disconnected the line. She'd called Roberto as soon as she finished this morning's class and he'd promised to meet her outside the trailer park. She'd left a message on Lou's cell, too, but hadn't heard back from him.

Fifteen minutes later, Casey pulled onto the shoulder of Dewdney Trunk Road and parked across from Cedarbrook Estates' entrance. She looked up and down the winding, narrow street. There was no sign of Roberto or Lundy, unless they'd parked inside the property and were already at the trailer. The absence of Roberto's Corvette in the visitor's stalls didn't surprise her. Punctuality had never been his strong suit. But there weren't any police cruisers or unmarked vehicles either. What to do? Wait for Roberto and Lundy, or face Gabrielle alone? It was twelve-thirty. Gabrielle would be expecting her, and Birch would be home from work soon. On the other hand, he might already be here.

Casey popped a stick of gum in her mouth and entered the trailer park. As she drew closer, she noticed streaks of grime on Birch's trailer and the weeds that filled the tiny plot of dirt in front. Gabrielle's silver Jetta was parked in the covered stall beside the trailer.

When Casey reached the trailer, she stopped and turned around. Where the hell were Roberto and Lundy? She studied the trailer a few moments, then tiptoed up four rickety wooden steps and listened for sounds inside. All was quiet. Across the lane and two trailers down, a man washed his car. A middle-aged lady walking her poodle looked at Casey. Someone had the TV on next door.

Feeling a little safer by all this activity, Casey knocked. Seconds later, she tried again and blew a huge pink bubble which splattered over her mouth and grazed the tip of her nose. She peeled the sticky gum from her face, and knocked a third time.

She zeroed in on the small window to the right of the door. The blinds were open, but no lights were on. She craned her neck toward the window, but it was too far away to get a good look inside. Damn it, what was Gabrielle playing at? Casey scanned the lane as someone headed out of the trailer park on a motorcycle.

Casey rattled the door handle to get Gabrielle's attention, but the door started to open. Casey stepped back. Had Gabrielle purposely left it unlocked? It was probably a good idea to hightail it back to the car, but what about Jeremy? Was he inside? Was he okay? Casey recalled what Paval had said about Gabrielle scarcely giving the boy a second glance when he introduced her to the toddler.

She poked her head inside. "Hello? Gabrielle?"

The silence creeped her out. "Jeremy?"

More silence. Something was wrong, she could feel it. Taking a step inside, the smell of sweat and overripe bananas bombarded her. Dirty plates and mugs littered a table next to a love seat in the cramped living area. A tattered sock monkey and toy cars were scattered on the braided rug.

"Hello, anyone home?"

The mess in the adjacent kitchenette was worse. Casey stepped farther inside and stared down a short, narrow hallway with two doors on the left, one on the right, and a fourth at the end.

"Hello?"

More silence. Chomping her gum to curb the growing unease, she headed for the door on her left. There was a stronger smell at this end of the trailer, something she couldn't identify. Casey turned the handle and found herself peering into a closet. The second door on her left was a cluttered little bathroom in need of a good scrubbing. She stepped across the hall.

"Hello? Anyone here?" She tapped on the third door. No response.

Casey peeked inside at an unmade toddler's bed and three stuffed animals on the grungy carpet. The box of clothes Casey had seen Birch carry out of Jasmine's place was wedged between the wall and Jeremy's bed. Maybe Jeremy was at daycare, and Birch didn't know Gabrielle would be here. Was Gabrielle planning to end a relationship whose main purpose might have been to destroy Jasmine? Did she want to cut Birch loose to keep her inheritance for herself?

The closer Casey came to the door at the end of the hall, the faster her heart beat. She wasn't sure why she dreaded looking in that room. Wasn't even sure she should, yet if Jeremy was in there . . . She gripped the doorknob and tried to ignore the warning signals crashing through her brain.

"Casey?"

She jumped back, bumping her elbow against the wall. "Roberto?"

"Yeah, sorry I'm late. Sweet jesus, this place reeks."

She went back to the front door and found him standing there, his expression pensive. "Come in."

"Where's Gabrielle?"

"I don't know, the door was unlocked. I've looked around, but no one's here." She glanced at the hallway. "There's one more room to check."

Roberto followed her down the hall.

"I have a bad feeling about this," she murmured.

"Let me do it." He stepped in front of her and reached for the handle. "If this is Birch's room, it could be in worse shape than the rest of this dump."

Fear pricked Casey's arms with the force of dozens of tiny needles. "Maybe we should wait."

Roberto pushed the door open. "Holy shit!"

Casey nudged him to the side, looked in, and gasped. Gabrielle was sprawled on the double bed. Her blood-soaked T-shirt clung to her ribs. Dull eyes stared up at the ceiling, her mouth set in a grimace. Sweat broke out on Casey's back and torso. She tried to speak, but her gum slid to the back of her throat, causing her to choke.

Casey yanked the door shut while Roberto pressed digits on his phone. Her stomach convulsed. Dashing to the bathroom, she collapsed in front of the badly stained toilet bowl and heaved. By the time she'd lost everything, her eyes were watery and she was shaking so hard she couldn't stand. Lowering her head, she rested her arms on the bowl's cool porcelain. Bile burned her throat. Tears seeped out from her closed eyes.

"Feeling better?"

Casey flinched and looked up. Corporal Lundy was staring down at her. She wiped her eyes and reached for the toilet paper roll.

"Did you touch anything?" he asked.

"Doorknobs, toilet seat." She tore off two squares of toilet paper, wiped her mouth, and flushed the toilet. As she got to her feet she said, "I only saw Gabrielle. Was Jasmine's little boy in there too?"

"No one else is here." She noticed that he'd already put on latex gloves. "Let's go before you contaminate more of the crime scene. And don't touch anything."

Casey shuffled down the hall on unsteady legs and saw Roberto leave the trailer with another officer. She followed Lundy to an unmarked vehicle.

"Okay, Miss Holland, tell me what happened from the moment you reached the trailer."

After Casey described everything she did and saw, Lundy said, "When was the last time you talked to Miss O'Reilly?"

"In Parksville."

"What did you talk about?"

"Her mother. She didn't want me talking to Hannah again."

"What else?"

After Casey gave him the highlights, Lundy said, "Quite the confrontation."

A cruiser pulled up and blocked the entrance.

"Well, no one threw punches."

He flipped through his notes. "The last conversation you had with your ward's grandmother before her attack was also confrontational, was it not?"

"Yes." He knew it was. They went over this last night.

"And you argued with Jasmine Birch before she died?"

"Your point, Corporal?"

"I'm just wondering why people die, or nearly do, after they argue with you."

"I have alibis, you know."

Lundy closed his notepad and tried not to smirk. "If I value my life, I'd better not argue the point."

Casey rolled her eyes. Cops, death, and dark humor. She'd heard them deal with the bad stuff through sarcasm and lousy jokes before, but she never thought she'd be the joke.

"Corporal?" A third officer, who looked about seventeen years old, appeared behind Lundy and handed him a sheet of paper. "I found something."

Lundy turned his back to Casey, blocking her view.

"Look for a computer or typewriter," Lundy told his colleague.

Casey moved closer. As if aware of her action, he lowered his voice so she could only hear him say something about picking up Birch. The young cop headed toward the cruiser parked near the entrance, while Lundy turned his attention back to Casey.

"So tell me, what do you really think Miss O'Reilly wanted to see you about?"

"Maybe to tell me she saw who shot Jasmine. I'm betting hers was the silver car in the church parking lot that day."

Lundy nodded. "We knew the first three letters on the license plate. They match the plate number you gave us."

She should have known he'd keep that information from her. "I think one of the Gallenskis killed Jasmine, and that Gabrielle recognized the shooter. Given what her mother told me about Gabrielle's greed, it's possible she was blackmailing one or both of them, although I have to say that after my talk with the Gallenskis yesterday, I would have thought that Ursula was the one doing the blackmailing, but it must be the other way around."

"Why can't I go in!" a familiar voice shouted.

Casey turned and saw Marie trying to slip past the police by the entrance. She hoped they'd make her leave.

"You invited another friend?" Lundy asked.

"No, Marie Crenshaw's butting in again."

She followed Lundy as he strolled up to Marie. "What brings you here, Mrs. Crenshaw?"

Marie squinted at Birch's trailer. "What happened? Is Jeremy okay?"

"He's not there. What did you want to help Miss Holland with?"

"Confronting Gabrielle."

Casey shook her head. How had she found out about the meeting?

"Why would you need to confront her?" Lundy asked.

"Because Gabrielle's a horrible bitch, and Roberto told me she's hooked up with Birch who's the real killer, not my brother."

Casey spotted Roberto talking to two officers. His hands were in his pockets and his head lowered.

"What makes you think Mr. Birch is guilty?" Lundy asked Marie.

"I just know, and I believe you're about to arrest my brother, which would be a huge mistake."

"Go home, Mrs. Crenshaw."

"Why won't you tell me what happened?" Her voice rose. "Obviously, Casey knows or she wouldn't look so green."

Funny, her face felt flaming hot.

"Casey, what's going on, damn it?" Marie asked. "I have a right to know."

"Better not argue with Miss Holland," Lundy remarked. "I have all the homicides I can handle."

Casey glared at him so he'd know he wasn't funny.

# THIRTY-ONE

**CASEY SCARCELY NOTICED HOW COLD** it was on the empty M6 bus. The Kevlar vest was keeping her warm enough; so was the adrenaline rush as she anticipated the rockhound's appearance. He was overdue for another strike and conditions were perfect tonight. She wanted more than a rock-throwing nut, though. She wanted Jasmine's killer. Violence had escalated since her return from Parksville, and enough was enough. As Wesley drove toward New Westminster, Casey fidgeted in her seat, eager to reach the rockhound's turf minutes from here. She sat in front for a better view of the sidewalk and intersections.

Before she left the trailer park this afternoon, Corporal Lundy inadvertently confirmed that they'd found a suicide note next to Gabrielle. Judging from Lundy's abrupt manner and monosyllabic replies to her questions, the corporal had decided he'd already said too much. Unfortunately, Roberto and Marie had overheard them.

"That's it then," Marie had said to everyone with earshot. "Gabrielle and Birch stole the guns from Wesley's place, and one of them shot Jasmine so Birch could have Jeremy. Birch then killed Gabrielle and forged the note to save his lying ass."

Lundy's chilly response hadn't surprised Casey. "That note is confidential, Mrs. Crenshaw, and accusing someone without knowing all the facts is begging for trouble." He then asked Marie if she knew where her brother was at that moment. Marie had assured him he was home, at which point she took off.

Lundy wouldn't reveal the type of gun found in Gabrielle's hand, but Casey had a hunch it was Wesley's Glock twenty-seven. She hadn't told Wes about the shooting. Didn't have the stomach for it. Besides, Rude Wesley Axelson looked grumpier than usual. Thanks to Marie and Roberto's love of gossip, he might have heard the news anyway.

Wesley pulled up to the stop where the plainclothes officer was waiting. Casey recognized the guy from last night's shift, but couldn't recall his name. Undercover Man wasn't a big talker and he usually mumbled. The cop climbed on board, nodded to Wesley, and then took his usual seat behind the center door. As he ambled past Casey, he barely gave her a glance. He'd hardly looked at her since they met. Maybe the guy didn't think much of female security officers, or just her. His behavior made her even more determined to catch the rockhound, but it wouldn't be easy.

After discussions between Stan, Eisler, and the police, it was decided that only Undercover Man could sit in seats nearest the sidewalk, which meant he'd probably spot the suspect first. More officers would be patroling the area, especially near Fourth and Clarkson, where Casey had chased the rockhound a few days ago. The other problem was police insistence that the M6's Not in Service sign be left on. To Eisler's chagrin, no fares would be picked up.

While Casey understood the cops' determination to catch the shooter, their presence was a waste of time. No one at Mainland, except Stan, knew she was on duty tonight, and she'd made sure she wasn't followed to work. Still, the cavalry was here; ready to protect, defend, arrest, and annoy.

As Wesley drove under the Pattullo Bridge, Casey shifted forward in her seat. A few pedestrians were walking down the sidewalk, or entering bistros and restaurants on this cold, dry Friday night. As usual, traffic was heavy and slow, not only because of the many traffic lights, but because parking was allowed on the street.

The M6 cruised into the hot zone and passed a man with a loping gait, dark hoodie, and the same scraggly beard she'd seen the night of the shooting.

Casey stood and approached Wesley. "Let me off here. I want to talk to the man we just passed."

"Dumb idea."

"He's not the shooter, Wes. I was watching him walk away when it happened. Anyway, Undercover Man's here; you don't need me."

The hairy bear scowled. The traffic light turned red and he stopped the bus. "What if he's the rockhound?"

"Then the only weapon he'd have is a rock and I can handle that."

Casey watched the guy catch up with the bus and then continue through the intersection, despite the red light. "Open the door, Wes."

"It's still a stupid idea." He did as asked.

"Wait for me at the next stop."

"Hey," Undercover Man shouted at her, "what do you think you're doing?"

"Going to talk to someone I saw the other night."

"You can't do that."

"If you're worried, radio your backup for help, but I'm going after that guy up ahead. He was nearby when I was shot at the other night and could have seen something."

Before he could respond, she stepped onto the sidewalk and started walking while Wesley moved the M6 ahead. Zipping up her jacket, she breathed in the late October air, then exhaled slowly. In front of her, two blondes in short denim skirts, leather jackets, and high heels giggled and clung to each other as they tried to walk a straight line. Beyond them, a group of guys and girls strolled behind the bearded man. Strutting toward Casey and the blondes were three gangly teens who gawked at the girls.

The M6 stopped for a red light at Columbia and Fourth. Casey moved faster. Bearded Guy and the group of five were now beside the bus.

Casey waited for the geeks to pass by before she overtook the girls. She was still waiting when the sound of cracking glass made her flinch. Casey hurried past the girls as a man ran up Fourth Avenue.

"There goes someone's booze," one of the blondes remarked. "What a waste."

Ahead of them, someone yelled, "Whoa! He smashed the window!"

Casey spotted a man running toward her. The blondes were too busy laughing and staggering down the sidewalk to notice the approaching man.

Casey jumped in front of the pair, ID in hand. "Ladies, step out of the way, please. You're in danger."

The runner spotted her and slowed down. He wasn't the bearded man. This one was short, sported a ball cap, and carried a white plastic bag.

She flashed her ID card at him. "MPT security! Stop right there!"

The blondes scurried away; the suspect stopped moving.

Casey edged closer to him. "Put the bag down."

Behind the suspect, a uniformed officer jogged toward them. Farther down, Undercover Man talked to witnesses. Casey edged closer to the suspect until she was only two strides away from the suspect. She'd put in too many hours to let New Westminster police bust her rockhound.

"Get away!" He began pinwheeling his arm, swinging the bag in a circle.

Judging from the way the bag moved, there had to be at least one more rock inside. Curious that he'd brought a spare. Had he planned two strikes to make up for lost time? While the bag was high above his head, Casey rushed the guy and tackled him to ground. The man's cap fell off, exposing a bald head fringed with scraggly gray hair. Casey was about to handcuff him when the uniformed cop caught up to her.

"I'll take over from here, Miss."

She grabbed the bag from the suspect.

"Give me my bag!"

Peering inside, Casey saw a large rock. The suspect lifted his head. Lines creased his brow and bracketed his mouth. The guy had to be at least forty-five, but he was fit enough to run up and down hills.

"I ain't done nothin'!"

"You broke a window on one of our buses." Casey noticed Wesley marching toward her. "Police are interviewing witnesses now."

"Prove it!" he shouted.

"Let's see some ID, sir," the officer said.

"It's at home."

"What's your name?"

"Avery."

"Last or first?"

"I'm Avery Watts."

Wesley caught up to her. "You okay?"

"Yeah, he ran right toward me. Go figure, huh?"

He mumbled something about a lucky break. "We found a good-sized rock on the sidewalk."

Casey knelt down near Watts. "Yours, by any chance, sir?"

"No, I just found that bag a couple minutes ago."

The officer helped him to his feet.

"It's amazing how technology can lift fingerprints off practically anything these days," Casey said. "Seeing as how you aren't wearing gloves, I wonder what the technicians will find?"

She had no idea if prints really could be lifted off a rock, but he didn't need to know that. The officer started to read the rockhound his rights, but Watts cut him off. "Your lousy buses got what they deserved! I'm a good driver, I shoulda got a chance!"

The cop warned him about saying anything, but Watts didn't even look at him.

"Are you talking about working for MPT?" Casey asked.

"Damn straight. I sent in an application, but they didn't even call. It's not fair!"

"Mr. Watts," the officer tried again. "I caution you not to say—"

"I deserve a shot at driving." An approaching police siren caught Watts' attention. He turned to the officer. "Let's make a deal. I got information 'cause I saw the guy who shot the bus the other night."

Wesley and Casey exchanged wary glances.

"He shot the stupid door and took off," Watts went on. "He shouldn't have been on my turf."

"Did you see his face?" Casey asked. "Could you identify him in a police line?"

"That depends on what I get out of it."

When Undercover Man joined them, the uniformed cop filled him in on what was happening.

"I doubt this loser could pick anyone out of a line," Wesley said. "The shooter wore a wide-brimmed hat."

"True." Casey's hopes sank.

"I saw him! The moron nearly knocked me over when he ran into the station. I was standing at the entrance."

"Did you see the weapon?" Undercover Man asked.

"It was a handgun."

The uniformed officer opened a notepad. "What did he look like?"

"About my age. Average height and weight."

Casey stared at Watts. "A middle-aged man?"

Two police cruisers pulled up.

"Yeah, with dark watery eyes, and he had a big nose."

Casey's mouth grew dry and the adrenaline soared. "Oh."

"I ain't saying more till I see a lawyer."

Undercover Man didn't look pleased. "Get him out of here."

The officer escorted Watts into a cruiser.

"I know someone who fits that description," Wesley murmured to Casey. "He was at the funeral, and I've seen him a couple of times when I was at Jasmine's place."

"Me, too."

"The apartment manager, right?"

"Yeah." She shivered in the cool night air. "Paval Gallenski."

# THIRTY-TWO

**DAMN IT, ANOTHER BLOODY COP** had dismissed her. Casey had lost track of the times she'd busted someone, called police to process the suspect, then once they arrived, had been brushed off in countless irritating ways. Tonight, Undercover Man had said, "We'll take over from here, Miss. Go back to your bus, and stay away from Mr. Gallenski." She was almost sorry she'd told the New Westminster police about Paval. Corporal Lundy was the one who needed to know. Although Undercover Man assured her he'd contact Lundy, Casey had left her own message for the corporal.

Traffic was sparse now at ten-thirty, so Casey sped through the intersection, anxious to get home and then go see Summer. After a brief chat with Stan a half hour ago, she'd called Summer to tell her she'd caught the rockhound. She'd left out any reference to Paval.

"That's awesome. You won't have to work nights for a while," Summer had said. "Can we celebrate with some double chocolate fudge ice cream? There's still a full carton in the fridge, and you could pick it up before you came over, right?"

Since it was Friday night and Casey felt like celebrating herself, she'd agreed. When she called Lou to give him a more detailed account of events, his response was less positive.

"For god's sake, Casey, you were in Paval's apartment yesterday. You could have been killed."

"Only if I'd accused him of murder, and I'm not that stupid."

"This freak passes himself off as a gentle guy who loves kids and pets, when he actually killed two women, beat up a senior, and threatened kids' lives. God knows what he's done to the babies he looks after."

After Lou's tirade, he told her that his sister had brought his truck back from Parksville and that he insisted on picking her up. "Pack a bag," he'd added. "We're not staying there until the bastard's caught. I'll be there in twenty minutes."

His call had left her edgy. She thought about phoning Marie to tell her what had happened, but she was furious with her. Marie's friendship with Paval had made it easy for him track her movements. He must have seen the gun rack in Wesley's truck when Wes had visited Jasmine. Paval could have asked Jasmine about Wesley's interest in firearms. When he decided to kill Jasmine, he probably broke into Wesley's apartment.

Now she understood why Jasmine had kept those two photos in her locker. She'd probably found them while searching the Gallenskis' place for her missing jewelry. It would have been like Jasmine to confront Paval about the photos, or accuse Ursula of stealing. No wonder she'd planned to move away and hadn't been that upset when Stan suspended her.

Paval could have seen Jasmine leave to pick Jeremy up from preschool. She might have gone to the church early that day to avoid spending more time at home than necessary. Still, Paval looked after little kids weekdays, so how had he pulled it off? Noel's van was stolen at 3:00 AM. Had Ursula driven him there, or had he gone himself and left his car within walking distance of Noel's house? Noel had been to Jasmine's apartment many times, so maybe he knew what Paval drove. If he did, he could ask his neighbors if they'd seen the vehicle. It was a long shot, but worth a try.

Casey drove past Rhonda's big old house on the corner and made a right turn into the lane behind the house. She pulled into her parking spot and, turning off the engine, studied the house. As expected, the lights on the main floor and in her third-floor suite were out. The two studio suites on the second floor were also in darkness. The tenants' cars weren't parked at their usual spots, but they were rarely home these days. She didn't blame them for wanting to stay away. The students had come home when the police and paramedics were here yesterday, and she had to tell them about Winifred. Both girls were understandably nervous about being here until the assailant was caught.

Casey looked at the dying cedar hedge separating Rhonda's property from the sidewalk on Violet. Scanning the yard, she hurried out of her car, up the steps, and into the kitchen, locking the door behind her. She flipped on the light and listened to the silent house.

She peered into the refrigerator's freezer to make sure the double chocolate fudge was there. Having access to a fridge here on the ground floor and another in her apartment had proven handy when it came to keeping the fattening food out of easy reach.

Casey marched down the dark hallway and upstairs. Normally, the creaking stairs didn't bother her, but with all that had happened lately, the noise unnerved her. When she entered her apartment, the guinea pigs began their usual chorus of whistling.

"How about a treat guys? You might as well celebrate too."

Casey flung her coat onto the sofa, and then fed the animals fresh veggies. When she was done, she retrieved Noel's phone number. Seconds later, she heard his voice and background chatter.

"Have I called at a bad time?" she asked.

"No, we're just playing poker. Hold on a sec."

Casey heard the voices fade. She sat in her rocking chair and waited until Noel said, "I was hoping you'd call. Marie told me about Gabrielle's murder. It's bloody awful."

"I know, and I'm pretty sure Paval Gallenski did it."

"What?" Noel paused. "You're joking, right?"

"He's been identified as the guy who took a shot at me the other night."

"Oh, my god."

"Corporal Lundy confirmed that Gabrielle's silver Jetta was in the church parking lot when Jasmine was shot. I think she might have tried to blackmail him."

Noel let out a whistle.

"Gabrielle met Paval three days earlier when she came to see Jasmine," Casey added. "She must have recognized him at the church, and there's something else." Casey told Noel about the Gallenskis' bathroom; how the photo of Jeremy had likely been taken there.

"Shit, I can't believe this. Paval looked after Jeremy for over a year and the little guy always seemed happy around him. If Jasmine had heard even a whisper about abuse she would have moved out right away."

"Maybe taking a photo was all Paval did. From what I've read about aberrant behavior, people don't just wake up one morning and decide to become sexual predators. The urge develops over a period of time."

"I can't wrap my head around this," Noel said. "I mean, Jasmine really liked him. And why didn't she tell me about Paval and those photos?"

"She was about to give your ring back, so maybe she thought you'd be too angry to take much interest in her problems. I just wish she'd taken the photos to the police."

"Yeah well, given that her abuser got away with his crime, I know how useless she thought cops were."

"That photo would have made her mad enough to threaten Paval with the police and want to move," Casey said. "Do you know what kind of car he drives?"

"An old Honda Civic. White and a bit rusty, I think."

"If Paval had acted alone when he stole your van, he would have had to leave his car near your place, but could he have driven a specialized van?"

"It didn't take Marie long to learn. He could have test driven one."

"Marie said the van was found at a park near your house?"

"Actually, it was on the other side of Como Lake."

The lake wasn't large. Anyone walking from the other side could be at Noel's place in five minutes. "Would he have parked his car in that area, too?"

"Possibly."

"We need to find some neighbors who might remember seeing a rusty white Honda Civic on the morning of September twenty-eighth."

"This whole area had a lot of break-ins last year, so there's a Neighborhood Watch program on both sides of the lake. I'll find out who's in charge."

"What are the odds of someone remembering the car more than three weeks after her death?"

"Who knows? An unfamiliar car would only have been reported if a crime had been committed. I gather some of the volunteers are pretty zealous about writing down models and license plate numbers of cars they don't know."

Casey thought she heard the stairs creak. She held her breath until she remembered that Lou would be joining her. "Did you tell Neighborhood Watch about your van?"

"I was going to, but Jasmine's death pushed it out of my mind, and then there were the police at my door, meetings with the lawyer, and work deadlines."

"Even if people knew about the van, they wouldn't have made the connection with it and the appearance of a white Honda Civic."

"Someone around here might know something. I'll call the Coquitlam detachment to see if Neighborhood Watch reported any suspicious vehicles around the twenty-seventh or eighth of September."

There was a knock on the door. Lou had a key, but he didn't use it if he knew she was here.

Casey rose. "Call me if you find anything."

"I will, and take care, okay?"

"You, too." She shoved her phone in her jeans pocket and headed for the door. "Lou?"

No answer. Fear swept over her. "Lou?"

"It's Paval Gallenski. I need to talk to you."

# THIRTY-THREE

OH GOD, HOW HAD THE murdering maniac gotten in the house? Casey bolted for her bedroom.

"I want to talk now," Paval called through the closed door. "You need to hear the truth."

Casey grabbed her cell phone and called 911. "A man's trying to break into my apartment! I'm in the top floor suite of a house." She rattled off her name and address.

"Come on, Casey, open up!" Paval kicked the door. "I'll use the rifle if you don't co-operate."

Casey's heart tap danced. "The intruder's Paval Gallenski and he's got a rifle!" she blurted. "He's already killed two people." She locked the bedroom door. "Hurry!"

Leaving the line open, Casey shoved the phone in her pocket and dashed to the window. She lifted the wood frame, then flung her leg over the sill. She could hear the dispatcher's raised voice asking her to respond. Casey stepped onto the fire escape. A shot rang out from behind her and then a loud bang. Shit, it sounded like he was in her apartment.

Stepping onto the first rung, she clambered down the ladder. She'd almost reached the bottom when she heard what sounded like a door banging open. Casey leapt to the ground. She landed on damp grass, skidded, and fell on her side. Pain flared through her right hip as she struggled to her feet and started to run. A noise above made her look up.

Paval was on the fire escape. "Stay there, Casey!"

She heard the shot about the same time she felt a whoosh of air pass her right ear.

"I could have hit you, but I want you to hear my side," he called out.

Was he stupid, or crazy? All that noise would lead the cops straight to him. Not a bad idea, though. Casey glanced at her Tercel. Crap, she'd left her keys in the apartment; wouldn't reach it in time anyway. She ran along the back of the house. She was about to turn the corner when pain seared her right upper arm. She slumped against the house while the burning sensation streaked to her wrist. She clamped her hand over the source. Blood warmed her palm.

"That was your last warning," Paval shouted. "You have to hear the truth!"

Across the back lane, a dog's deep bark broke the silence.

Casey turned and looked up at Paval on the fire escape. "What truth, Paval?" She took a small step backward.

"Jasmine got it all wrong."

Casey took another step back. She was at the corner. There was no time to hesitate. She bolted. Paval would have to use the fire escape or go through the house. The willow tree and hedge wouldn't be enough to hide her. Sweat seeped down her forehead. She thought she heard a voice, then remembered her phone and pulled it from her pocket.

"I've been shot!" Her voice trembled. "I'm at the front of the house, trying to hide."

"Stay calm, ma'am. Help's on the way."

Stay calm? Really? She'd never realized how dumb that sounded when she dealt with irate passengers. Casey entered the front yard and looked at the porch. The door was closed. She ran toward the willow, tripped over something and fell, dropping the phone.

"Shit!"

Casey groped cold blades of grass and the tree root she'd tripped over. She tried using her right hand, but deep, blazing pain made her arm quiver. Wincing, Casey got to her feet and raced for the gate. Her hand shook as she lifted the rusty latch and took off.

"Are you too ignorant to hear the truth, too?" Paval shouted from the front porch.

Too? A fourth shot rang out and ricocheted off a vehicle. Casey raced down the sidewalk, her eyes scanning for help, but no one was around. Somewhere nearby, two more dogs started barking. Had Lou arrived? He always pulled up at the back of the house. She prayed he'd heard Paval and was staying clear.

Casey's breathing grew ragged. She looked at cars and darkened windows. Most of the neighborhood had already gone to bed. Paval fired again. He was close—too close. Veering to her left, she cut across someone's yard. Beneath her sweater and long-sleeved shirt, blood trickled down her throbbing arm.

"I'm not a pervert!" Paval yelled.

Adrenaline ricocheted through her body.

"They were only two harmless photos!" he shouted. "That's all."

Casey's ears and chest pounded. The dogs kept barking. Why were there no signs of cops? She swung her leg onto a waist-high, wooden fence separating two front yards. Using only her left arm, she hoisted herself over the fence, lost her balance, and collapsed onto a bed of dirt. Groaning, she scrambled upright and looked at the house. Lights were on and curtains drawn. A couple with four kids lived here. Part of her wanted to rush up the steps and pound on the door, but if Paval was close she'd be dead before she reached it.

Keeping low, she scurried down a weedy path toward the back of the house and headed for the lane. Garages and sheds might keep her hidden. The sound of footsteps behind Casey forced her to dive behind a compost bin at the back of the property. She nestled between the bin and a chain-link fence bordering the lane. Near the house, a garbage can fell over and a man swore.

"Jeremy had messed in his pants," Paval called out. "I had to clean him up. He was having so much fun in the tub that I snapped a picture, and that's it!"

Let him talk. Let the whole world know where he was. Obviously, Paval didn't care. The man had lost his mind. Casey pressed down on her wound. Mercifully, the back lane was unlit. No floodlights in the yard either.

She peeked around the compost. Paval was at the corner of the house, to her right. Three feet from her, a gate opened onto the lane. The latch looked easy enough to release, but what if Paval heard her?

"You saw the photos, didn't you, Casey? Jasmine must have taken them to work. I saw the look on your face when you were in my bathroom last night."

Casey held her breath. Her shirt clung to her damp back.

"Jasmine freaked out and threatened to tell everyone I abused kids! What was I supposed to do?"

The porch light went on. A door started to open. It was all the distraction she needed. Casey bounded to the gate, lifted the latch, and took off. She scanned fences across the lane. The nearest ones were too tall to jump.

"It was just a stupid photo," Paval shouted. "Can't you understand that?"

"Hey!" a man yelled. "Get off my property! I've called the cops."

The asphalt was cracked and dotted with potholes. Head down, Casey stayed to the right until another shot zinged past her. She darted onto a property without a fence and headed back the way she had come. When she reached the side of the house, floodlights blinked on.

"I told you to stop!" Paval shouted from the lane. "This is your last chance. I mean it!"

Casey bolted through the front yard when two police cruisers sped toward her place. Terrified that Paval was too close, she didn't call out.

Paval yelled, "I hate people who won't co-operate!"

He fired another shot. Casey could almost feel the bullet fly past her head. She dove behind a large rhododendron, scrambled to her feet, and dashed behind a parked SUV. Home was five houses back. Street lamps illuminated the police cruiser parked in front of it.

A bullet struck the SUV's window. Casey's stomach somersaulted. The cops must have heard the shot. Casey darted to the next parked vehicle closer to home. Her entire arm and shoulder were burning now; blood dripped off her fingertips. She had to make Paval keep talking; the cops needed to know where they both were.

"Paval, did you or Ursula shoot Jasmine?"

"Ursula had nothing to do with this! Don't you ever spread stories about my wife!"

Casey stole a look through the driver's side window. Paval was on the sidewalk, rifle raised, as he walked toward the vehicle. Why wasn't he running away? Surely he'd seen the cruiser.

"I photographed my favorite tenants all the time." He sounded close to tears. "It didn't mean anything."

"But Jasmine didn't like the pictures you took?" She kept her voice loud.

"She never let me take her picture, and I needed one for my collection. She was so damn stubborn. The other tenants didn't care."

"You collect pictures of your tenants?"

"I told you before, the good ones are like family."

What a freak. Casey spotted movement behind a hedge bordering the sidewalk. "So, you slipped into Jasmine's bedroom and snapped a picture without her knowing?"

"She was always complaining about insomnia, so I gave her something to help her sleep."

Casey heard desperation in his voice. "How did she find the photos, Paval?"

"By snooping through our bedroom. Jasmine had no right to call me a pedophile and Ursula a thief! She said she'd destroy both of us!"

Casey raced for the next vehicle and knelt by a tire. She gulped more air while her stomach swirled. Why weren't the police taking him down? And where was Lou?

"What about Gabrielle?" she yelled. "Why kill her?" No response. "Was she blackmailing you?"

"She was a greedy evil bitch who wanted everything I'd saved for our baby!"

Casey scampered to a Jeep Cherokee. Behind her, a police cruiser roared closer.

"Freeze!" a cop shouted on the other side of the Cherokee.

Another shot rang out. Casey felt a hand on her shoulder and screamed.

# THIRTY-FOUR

**STAN'S OLD CHAIR SQUEAKED AS** he leaned back and grinned at Casey. "So, you nabbed your rockhound and Jasmine's killer on the same night. Impressive, kiddo."

"I didn't actually nab Paval. He came after me."

Casey adjusted the sling supporting her injured arm. Noel sat on her left, nearest Stan's door. Marie was on her right, uncomfortably close to the sling.

"How bad is the damage?" Noel asked, gazing at her arm.

"The bullet took a chunk of flesh, but it's not so bad, thanks to some heavy-duty painkillers."

"Thank god that's all he hit," Noel said.

Casey appreciated his concern, but didn't want to say so in front of Marie. "Paval said he could have killed me if he wanted. I guess I should be grateful he was hell-bent on telling me how misunderstood he was."

"Noel's lawyer found out that he used to belong to a gun club," Marie remarked.

"Shit, Casey, you could have been hit in the crossfire between him and the cops," Stan said.

"There wasn't really any crossfire. A cop shot Paval once in the shoulder, and game over."

Except it wasn't a game. Casey remembered the shot, and Paval falling as a cop approached her from behind. She'd screamed from pain when he'd touched her wounded arm. Casey squirmed in the hard wooden chair. The hip she'd fallen on was sore, and she wished this meeting was over. She hadn't planned to tell Marie what happened, but Marie had barged in to say that Noel insisted on thanking her in person. She'd then had the gall to chastise Casey for not answering her phone all weekend. Casey had neither the energy nor desire to explain that she'd been too tired to talk to anyone but Lou and Summer. She'd also managed a brief chat with Hannah O'Reilly while Lou had taken Summer to see Winifred in the hospital.

"You still look pale," Stan said. "Now that your report's done, take a few days off."

"Thanks." Oh sweet heaven, back to her comfy bed.

"The reason Noel was trying to call you," Marie said, giving her an exasperated look, "was to let you know that a guy who lives on the other side of Como Lake saw a rusty white Honda Civic parked in front of a neighbor's house the morning Jasmine died. The cops confirmed that it was Paval's."

Casey turned to Noel. "How did he remember?"

"It seems he's one of the more fanatical members of Neighborhood Watch. When he was getting ready for work the morning of the twenty-eighth, he noticed the Honda parked in front of a neighbor, who's a senior. Apparently, the neighbor never has visitors at 5:00 AM, so he wrote down the plate number. The car was gone by the time he came home from work later that afternoon."

"He didn't report the vehicle to the police?" Casey asked.

"There was no reason to," Noel answered. "He checked on the neighbor and she was fine. No crimes happened in his area that week, and he didn't know about my van."

"Did Ursula know what Paval had done?" Casey asked.

"She claims she didn't," Marie replied. "The lawyer said Ursula totally lost it when she heard why Paval was arrested, although I wouldn't be surprised if it was an act. And she told the cops that Paval was the one who stole from tenants."

"Paval also confessed to killing Gabrielle," Noel said. "Worse, he admitted having two babies in the van when he shot Jasmine."

Casey flinched. "He brought kids to a murder?"

"Ursula was at work." Noel's face was grim. "He said he couldn't leave them alone."

"I think Gabrielle wanted to tell you about Paval," Marie said to Casey.

"Why wouldn't she have told the cops?" Stan asked.

"She wouldn't want her mother finding out that she saw Jasmine's killer and said nothing." Casey rubbed her forehead. Rehashing events was giving her a headache. "I told Hannah about Paval's arrest."

"She must have been relieved," Noel said.

"And angry, although I'm not sure who she was most angry with. Hannah confronted Gabrielle about her affair the morning Lou and I left Parksville. She actually accused Gabrielle of conspiring to kill Jasmine, and then told her to move out of the house," Casey said. "Since the free ride was over, we figured the confrontation prompted her to come to Vancouver and demand money from Paval."

"Meanwhile, Birch gets what he wanted all along," Noel said. "No alimony and Jeremy."

"Not necessarily. Hannah's lawyers are filing for custody this week."

"So, is the landlord a pervert or not?" Stan asked.

"My lawyer says there's no evidence of child molestation yet," Noel said. "The police are talking to tenants and trying to locate former ones."

"It turns out the freak has quite a collection of photos," Marie said, crossing her arms. "A few were pictures of naked kids. The rest were candid shots of them and their parents. Some people knew they were being photographed and smiled for the camera."

"She must have found the photos of her and Jeremy some time over the weekend," Casey said. "Possibly Sunday evening."

"That makes sense." Marie paused. "I never made the connection until now, but when they called me to come get Jeremy at the church that morning, I was approached by an older lady who was really upset. She said she'd been looking after Jeremy the day before and was worried about what would happen to him."

"Which must mean that Jasmine hadn't wanted Paval near her son on Monday," Casey said.

No one said anything for a few seconds.

"Jeremy seemed so happy all the time," Marie murmured. "If he'd been abused, you'd think there would have been some kind of sign when Jasmine left him with Paval. Still . . ."

"Speaking of unanswered mysteries," Casey said, turning to Marie, "did you tell Paval that I was on the M6 the night he shot at me? And did you give him my cell phone number?"

Marie's freckled cheeks turned bright pink.

"Answer her, Marie." Noel stared at his sullen sister.

The pink turned an unattractive red. "He called me once, sounding all choked up, and asked for your number because he wanted to adopt a couple of Jasmine's pets."

Noel glared at her. "After three husbands, why are you still so gullible about men?"

"Paval fooled a lot of people," she shot back. "You thought he was a good guy too."

"Because Jasmine thought he was. I really didn't know him."

"Anyway," Stan said, "it's over." He turned to Casey. "Summer must be glad."

"She is." And looking forward to the weekend. On Sunday, she'd be visiting Rhonda for the first time. Casey was already nervous about it. Given Summer's last emotional and argumentative phone conversation with her mother, who knew what would happen?

"By the way," Marie said, "I found homes for the rest of Jasmine's pets. Our aunt Delia has a farm in the Okanagan. I'm taking the kids there this weekend."

"I want to keep one of the guinea pigs, if that's okay." She'd grown rather attached to Ralphie.

Marie grinned and was about to say something when there was a knock on the door.

"Come in," Stan said.

Lou opened the door and bumped into Noel's wheelchair.

"Oh, sorry." His puzzled glance at Noel turned to recognition after Casey made the introductions.

"Good to meet you." Lou shook his hand, then turned to Casey. "I thought you might be here. Are you free for coffee?"

"Sure, and then I'll head home. Stan's giving me some time off."

"She deserves it," Noel said. "Casey's one hell of an investigator who helped us out a lot." He turned to his sister. "Didn't she, Marie?"

Marie's lips twitched. "You did a great job for Noel, Casey, and I thank you for that."

But it changed nothing between them. Casey saw the resentment. "You're welcome." She struggled to her feet.

As Noel backed up his wheelchair, Marie followed them.

"Marie, wait a sec," Stan said. "I have an assignment for you."

Bless him. The last thing Casey wanted was more time with her. Seeing Marie's disappointment, she tried not to smile.

"I really don't know how to thank you properly, Casey," Noel said, joining them outside Stan's office. "Not many people would go out of their way to help strangers, like you did for me and Hannah."

"I bailed on you, remember?"

"I think you tried to, but you wanted answers as much as I did."

"Yeah, well, I was born with an inquiring mind."

"And a compassionate heart," Lou added.

"If you two are ever in Coquitlam," Noel said, "drop by, okay?"

"Absolutely." Casey put her arm around Lou, knowing it wouldn't happen.

"Want to join us for coffee?" Lou asked Noel a little too politely.

"Thanks, but Marie's giving me a ride to the dealership so I can lease another van. The police will have mine tied up a while."

"Good luck," Casey said.

"Same to you."

Lou and Casey didn't speak until they were in the stairwell.

"It looks like things can finally get back to normal around here," he said.

"Yeah, maybe, but with Jasmine gone, they'll never be the same."

Lou stopped on the steps and squeezed her hand. "They could be better, right? At work and at home."

Casey kissed his cheek. "Better would be good." In fact, better would be great. "A lot will depend on how Sunday's visit with Rhonda goes, and who replaces Jasmine."

"Then we'll have to wait and see, won't we?" He wrapped his arms around her.

"Yeah." Casey sighed. "Wait and see."

# Acknowledgments

Thanks and gratitude to members of Port Moody's Kyle Centre Writers' Group for their insightful comments and for patiently reading every chapter over many months. I always came away with new ideas for improving my manuscript. It was, and still is, a wonderful experience. I'm indebted to every writer and editor at the table.

Thank you to Ruth Linka for believing in my work and for her collaborative approach to publishing. Also, huge thanks to Frances Thorsen and Lenore Hietkamp for their amazing editing skills. I've learned a great deal from them.

Endless thanks and much love to Bark, Elida, and Alex for their continued support while I plunged into the world of fiction and forgot about everything else.

Although I use real cities and street names (with one or two exceptions) in this novel, structures and businesses within the cities are often fictional. Mainland Public Transport is a product of my imagination, as is the Silver Groove night club, Cedarbrook Estates trailer park, Barley's Gym, and Grantwood Manor.

DEBRA PURDY KONG was born in Toronto but has spent most of her life in British Columbia. She has a diploma in criminology from Douglas College and has worked in the security field as a patrol and communications officer. She is the author of three previous mysteries: *Taxed to Death*, *Fatal Encryption*, and *The Opposite of Dark*, the first book in the Casey Holland mystery series.

Debra has also written more than one hundred short stories, essays, and articles for publications that include *Chicken Soup for the Bride's Soul*, *BC Parent Magazine*, and the *Vancouver Sun*. Her short stories have won first place in competitions sponsored by *NeWest Review* and other publications, as well as honorable and finalist mentions at the Surrey International Writers' Conference.

For the past twenty-five years, Debra has lived in Port Moody with her husband, children, and more pets than she can count. More information about Debra and her work can be found at debrapurdykong.com and on her blog at writetype.blogspot.com. You can also follow Debra on Twitter at @DebraPurdyKong.